HELL

HELL

HENRI BARBUSSE

Translated from the French by

ROBERT BALDICK

TURTLE POINT PRESS

First published in France in 1908

English translation first published in Great Britain in 1966
by Chapman and Hall, Ltd.

© 1995 Turtle Point Press

Library of Congress Catalogue Card Number: 94-061776
ISBN: 1-885983-01-8

Translation rights reserved

Design and composition by Wilsted & Taylor

Printed in the U.S.A.

Translator's Preface

Observation of humanity in its most private moments and secret activities has been a popular theme with writers and artists for thousands of years, but it has rarely been carried to such lengths as in Henri Barbusse's novel *Hell*.

A young man staying in a French hotel finds a hole in the wall above his bed, through which he can see and hear the occupants of the next room. Before long he has become obsessed with the study of the hidden lives of his neighbours, and he spends long hours and days at his spy-hole, not as a *voyeur* but rather as a seer. He sees in their naked reality childbirth, first love, marriage, adultery, lesbianism, illness, religion and death; and he hears the voices of his fellow humans whispering, screaming, pleading, arguing, exulting and dying. Only when he has explored every circle of the hell of human life does he pack his bags and return to the everyday world of pretence.

O N E

The proprietress, Madame Lemercier, leaves me alone in my room, after reminding me in a few words of all the material and moral advantages of the Pension Lemercier.

I stop in front of the mirror, in the middle of this room in which I am going to live for some time. I look at the room and I look at myself.

The room is grey and smells of dust. I see two chairs, one of which has my suitcase on it, two armchairs with narrow wings and greasy upholstery, a table with a green woollen cover, and an Oriental carpet with an eye-catching pattern repeated over and over again. But, at this time of the evening, this carpet is the colour of earth.

All this is new to me, and yet how well I know it all: this fake mahogany bed, this cold dressing-table, this inevitable arrangement of the furniture, and this emptiness between these four walls . . .

The room is worn out; it is as if people have been coming here since the beginning of time. From the door to the window, the carpet is threadbare; a crowd of people have trodden it day after day. The ornamental mouldings, at hand level, are twisted, worn away, shaky, and the marble of the mantelpiece has been rounded at the corners. At the touch of mankind, things wear away with heartbreaking slowness.

They grow darker too. Little by little, the ceiling has become overcast like a stormy sky. On the white panels and the pink paper, the places touched most often have turned black: the door, the painted latch of the cupboard, and the wall to the right of the window, at the place where you pull the curtain cords. A whole horde of human beings have passed this way like smoke. The window is the only thing which is white.

And I? I am a man like all the rest, just as this evening is an evening like all the rest.

●

I have been travelling since this morning; hustle, formalities, luggage, the train, the breath of the various towns.

There is an armchair here; I drop into it; everything becomes calmer and gentler.

My permanent move from the provinces to Paris marks an important phase in my life. I have found a job in a bank. My life is going to change. It is because of this change that, this evening, I am tearing myself away from my usual thoughts and thinking of myself.

I am thirty years old, or will be on the first day of next month. I lost my father and mother eighteen or twenty years ago. The event is so far distant that it is insignificant. I am not married; I have no children and shall have none. There are times when that disturbs me: when I think that a line which has lasted since the beginning of mankind will end with me.

Am I happy? Yes; I have nobody to mourn, no regrets, no complicated desires; so I am happy. I remember that when I was a child I used to have emotional experiences, mystical crises, a sickly love of shutting myself up with my past. I attributed an

exceptional importance to myself, even going so far as to think
that I counted more than other people. But all that has gradually
disappeared in the positive nothingness of day-to-day existence.

◐

And now here I am.

I bend forward in my armchair to be closer to the mirror, and
I take a good look at myself.

Rather short, quiet-looking (though I can be quite boisterous
at times), and very neatly dressed; there is nothing in my exterior
personality to find fault with, nothing to notice.

I gaze hard at my eyes, which are green, and which people
generally describe as black, by some inexplicable aberration.

I vaguely believe in a great many things, above all in the existence of God, if not in the dogmas of Christianity; all the
same, religion offers certain advantages for humble folk and for
women, who have a smaller brain than men.

As for philosophical discussions, I consider them to be absolutely futile. Nothing can be checked, nothing can be proved
to be true. After all, what is the meaning of truth?

I have a sense of good and evil; I would never commit a base
deed, even if I were certain of impunity. Nor could I ever accept
the slightest exaggeration in anything at all.

If everybody were like me, all would be well with the world.

◐

It is already late. I shan't do anything more today. I remain sitting
here, in the fading light, opposite the corner of the mirror. In
this setting which the shadows are beginning to invade, I catch
sight of the shape of my forehead, the oval of my face, and, under
my flickering eyelids, my gaze through which I enter into myself
as into a tomb.

Tiredness, the dismal weather (I can hear rain in the evening air), the darkness which increases my solitude and magnifies me in spite of all my efforts, and then something else, I don't know what, makes me feel sad. It annoys me to feel sad. I try to shake myself out of it. What's the matter? Nothing's the matter. It's just me.

◐

I am not alone in life as I am alone this evening. Love has assumed for me the face and gestures of my little Jeannette. We have been together for a long time; it is a long time since the day when, in the back room of the milliner's shop where she worked at Tours, seeing that she kept smiling at me with a strange persistence, I took her head between my hands and kissed her on the mouth—and suddenly discovered that I loved her.

I can no longer remember very well now the strange pleasure that we derived from undressing. True, there are moments when I long for her as madly as the first time; they come most of all when she isn't there. When she is there, there are moments when she disgusts me.

We shall meet again over there, in the holidays. We could count the number of days on which we shall see each other again before dying . . . if we dared.

Dying! The idea of death is undoubtedly the most important of all ideas.

I shall die one day. Have I ever thought about it? I try to remember. No, I have never thought about it. I can't. One can no more look destiny in the face than one can look straight at the sun, and yet destiny is grey.

And dusk falls as every dusk will fall, until the one which will be too dark.

◐

But now, all of a sudden, I have jumped to my feet, staggering, with a great pounding of my heart like a great beating of wings . . .

What is it? In the street, a horn is sounding a hunting call . . . Presumably some high-born huntsman, standing near the bar of a fashionable restaurant, with a fierce look in his eyes, his cheeks puffed out, his lips pursed, is fascinating an audience he has reduced to silence.

But it isn't only that, this fanfare echoing round the stones of the city . . . When I was a boy, in the country district where I was brought up, I used to hear this sound of a hunting-horn in the distance, on the roads leading to the woods and the château. The same hunting-call, exactly the same thing; how can it be so absolutely similar?

And in spite of myself, my hand has moved to my heart in a slow, trembling gesture.

In the past . . . today . . . my life . . . my heart . . . me? I think of all that, all of a sudden, for no particular reason, as if I had gone mad.

◖

. . . Since the old days, since the beginning, what have I done with myself? Nothing, I am already on the downhill slope. Because that hunting-call reminded me of the past, it seems to me that I am done for, that I haven't lived, and I feel a longing for a sort of lost paradise.

But it is no use my imploring, it is no use my rebelling, there will never be anything more for me; henceforth I shall never be either happy or unhappy. I can't return to life. I shall grow old as peacefully as I am sitting today in this room where so many human beings have left their trace, where no single human being has left his own.

This room can be found anywhere. It is everybody's room. You think that it is closed, but no: it is open to the four winds. It is lost in the midst of similar rooms, like light in the sky, like one day among other days, like myself everywhere.

Myself, myself! Now I can no longer see anything but the pallor of my face, with its deep eye-sockets, buried in the dusk, and my mouth full of a silence which is gently but surely stifling and destroying me.

I raise myself on one shoulder as on the stump of a wing. I would like something of an infinite character to happen to me.

◐

I have no genius, no mission to carry out, no great devotion to give. I have nothing and I deserve nothing. But in spite of everything, I would like a sort of reward . . .

Love; I dream of an incomparable, unique idyll, with a woman far from whom I have hitherto wasted all my time, whose features I cannot see, but whose shadow I imagine next to mine on the road.

Something infinite, something new! A journey, an extraordinary journey into which I can throw myself, in which I can multiply myself. Bustling, luxurious departures in the midst of the servile attentions of humble folk, and languid poses in carriages thundering along at full speed through wild landscapes and cities looming up suddenly like the wind.

Boats, masts, orders given in barbaric tongues, landings on golden quays, and then strange, exotic faces in the sun, and, dizzily similar, monuments familiar from pictures and which, with a traveller's pride, you would imagine had come close to you.

My brain is empty; my heart is dried up; I have nobody around me; I have never had anybody, not even a friend; I am a poor man who has been washed up for a day in a hotel room where everybody comes, and which everybody leaves—and yet I long for glory! Glory mingled with me like a wonderful, astonishing wound which I would feel and everybody would talk about; I long for a crowd in which I would be the principal figure, acclaimed by name as by a new cry under the face of heaven.

But I can feel my grandeur diminishing. My childish imagination plays in vain with these exaggerated pictures. There is nothing for me; there is only myself, stripped by the evening, and rising like a cry.

The time of day has made me almost blind. I guess at myself in the mirror more than I see myself. I see my weakness and my captivity. I hold my hands out towards the window with the fingers outstretched, my hands with their appearance of torn objects. From my shadowy corner I raise my face towards the sky. I lean backwards and support myself on the bed, that big object which looks vaguely human, like a dead body. Lord, I am lost! Have pity on me! I believed myself to be wise and happy with my lot; I said that I was free from the thieving instinct; alas, that isn't true, since I would like to take everything that isn't mine.

T W O

The sound of the horn stopped a long time ago. The street, the houses have grown quiet. Silence. I pass my hand over my forehead. That attack of emotionalism is over. So much the better. I regain my composure by an effort of will-power.

I sit down at my table and take some papers out of my briefcase, which has been left there. I have to read them and sort them out.

Something spurs me on: the idea that I am going to earn a little money. I will be able to send some to my aunt who has brought me up and who waits for me all the time in the low-ceilinged room where, in the afternoon, the sound of her sewing-machine is as wearisome and monotonous as that of a clock, and where, in the evening, there is a lamp beside her which, I don't know why, looks like her.

The papers . . . The material for the report which is to give an idea of my ability and confirm my entry into Monsieur Berton's bank . . . Monsieur Berton, the man who can do everything for me, who has only to say the word, Monsieur Berton, the god of my present life . . .

I get ready to light the lamp. I strike a match. It doesn't catch fire, the phosphorus flakes off, it breaks. I throw it away and, feeling a little tired, I wait . . .

Then I hear a song being murmured close to my ear.

It seems to me as if somebody leaning over my shoulder were singing for me, for me alone, confidentially.

It must be an hallucination . . . Now I am suffering from brain-fever . . . This is my punishment for thinking too much just now.

I am standing up with my clenched hand on the edge of the table, gripped by a sense of something supernatural; I look around at random, my eyelids fluttering, watchful and suspicious.

The humming is still there; I can't get rid of it. My head is spinning . . . It's coming from the next room . . . Why is it so clear, so curiously close, and why does it move me like this? I look at the wall which separates me from the next room, and I choke back a cry of surprise.

Up near the ceiling, above the blocked-up doorway, there is a twinkling light. The song is falling from that star.

There is a hole in the partition there, and through that hole, the light in the next room is entering the darkness of mine.

I climb onto my bed. I stand up on it with my hands against the wall, and I bring my face up to the level of the hole. A rotten plank, a couple of bricks out of place; some plaster has come away; an opening is revealed to my gaze, as big as a hand, but invisible from below, on account of the ornamental mouldings.

I look . . . I see . . . The next room offers itself to me, completely naked.

It stretches out before me, this room which isn't mine . . . The voice which was singing has left it; this departure has left the door open, almost still moving. The only light in the room comes from a candle which is flickering on the mantelpiece.

In the distance, the table looks like an island. The bluish, reddish pieces of furniture appear to me in the guise of vague organs, dimly alive, set out before me.

I gaze at the wardrobe, a medley of bright, upright lines, its feet in the shadows; at the ceiling, the reflection of the ceiling in the mirror, and the pale window which is like a face on the sky.

I have come back into my room—as if I had really left it—astonished at first, all my ideas so muddled up that I forget who I am.

I sit down on my bed. I think hurriedly, trembling a little, depressed by the idea of the future . . .

I dominate and possess that room . . . My gaze enters it. I am present in it. All those who will be in it will, unknown to themselves, be in it with me. I shall see them, I shall hear them, I shall be as fully present at them as if the door were open . . .

●

A moment later, in a long shudder, I raise my face to the hole, and I look once more.

The candle is out, but somebody is there.

It's the maid. She had probably come in to do the room, then she has stopped.

She is alone. She is quite close to me. Yet I can't see very well the living creature which is moving, possibly because I am dazzled at seeing it so real: a sky-blue apron, of an almost nocturnal colour, which falls in front of her like the rays of the evening sun; white wrists; hands which are darker because of her work. The face is shadowy, dim, yet striking. The eyes are hidden in it, yet glow; the cheekbones stand out and gleam; a curve of the chignon shines above the head like a crown.

Just now, on the landing, I caught a glimpse of this girl who was bent double, polishing the banisters, her flushed face close to her big hands. I found her repulsive, on account of her black hands and the dusty tasks in which she bends over and squats down . . . I have seen her in one of the corridors too. She was walking clumsily in front of me, her hair hanging down, trailing behind her the insipid smell of her body which you could tell was grey and wrapped up in dirty underwear.

◖

And now I am looking at her. The evening gently removes the ugliness, wipes away the poverty and the horror, and, in spite of me, changes the dust into a shadow, like a curse into a blessing. Nothing is left of her but a colour, a mist, a shape; not even that; a shiver and the beating of her heart. Of her, there is nothing left but herself.

It is because she is alone. By some astonishing, almost divine chance, she is really alone. She is in that innocence, that perfect purity: solitude.

I am violating her solitude with my eyes, but she knows nothing about it, and she isn't violated.

She goes towards the window, her eyes brightening, her hands dangling, her apron heavenly. Her face and the upper part of her body are lit up: she looks as if she were in heaven.

She sits down on the big, low, dark red sofa which occupies the end of the room near the window. Her broom is propped up beside her.

She takes a letter out of her pocket, reads it. In the dusk, this letter is the whitest of all the things in existence. The folded sheet of paper stirs between the fingers which are holding it carefully—like a dove in space.

She has pressed the trembling letter to her mouth, has kissed it.

Whom is this letter from? Not from her family; a daughter, when she is a woman, does not retain sufficient filial piety to kiss a letter from her parents. A lover, a fiancé, yes . . . I don't know the name of the beloved who may be known to a great many people; but I witness the love as no living person has ever done. And this simple gesture of kissing this piece of paper, this gesture buried in a bedroom, this gesture stripped and flayed alive by the darkness, has something august and terrifying about it.

She has risen and gone right up to the window, with the white letter folded in her grey hand.

The dusk is deepening everywhere, and it seems to me that I no longer know either her age or her name, or the occupation she happens to pursue here on earth, or anything about her, or anything at all . . . She is looking at the pale immensity which touches her. Her eyes are shining; you might think that they were weeping, but no, they are overflowing only with light. Her eyes are not light by themselves; they are simply all the light there is. What would this woman be if reality flourished on earth?

She has sighed and walked slowly to the door. The door has closed behind her like something falling.

She has gone without having done anything but read her letter and kiss it.

◐

I have returned to my corner, alone, more superbly alone than before. The simplicity of this encounter has moved me tremendously. Yet she was nothing but a living creature, a living creature like myself. Am I to suppose, then, that there is no sweeter or more disturbing experience than approaching a living creature, whatever it may be?

This woman concerns my inner life, she has a place in my heart. How, why? I don't know . . . But how important she has become! . . . Not by herself—I don't know her and have no desire to know her—but by the simple value of her existence revealed for a moment, by her example, by the wake of her real presence, by the true sound of her footsteps.

It seems to me that the supernatural dream I had just now has come true, and that what I called something infinite has happened. What this woman who has just passed so profoundly beneath my gaze has given me, by showing me her naked kiss—isn't it the kind of beauty which reigns triumphant, and whose light covers you with glory?

◐

The dinner gong has sounded throughout the hotel.

This reminder of everyday reality and commonplace activities temporarily changes the course of my thoughts. I get ready to go down to dinner. I put on a fancy waistcoat, a dark suit. I stick a pearl tie-pin into my tie. But soon I stop and prick up my ears, hoping to hear—next door or in the distance—another sound of footsteps or of a human voice.

While performing the necessary movements, I remain obsessed by the great event which has just occurred: this apparition.

I have come downstairs to join the others who live in this house with me. In the dining-room, all brown and gold and full of lights, I have taken my seat at the residents' table. There is a general sparkling, a hubbub, the great meaningless bustle of the beginning of a meal. A great many people are here, who are taking their seats with well-bred circumspection. Smiles everywhere, the noise of chairs being pulled up to the table, voices seeking each other out and linking up again, conversations starting . . . Then the concert of cutlery and plates begins, regular in rhythm and growing in volume.

My two neighbours are both chatting away. I hear their murmur which isolates me. I raise my eyes. In front of me is a row of gleaming foreheads, shining eyes, ties, bodices, hands busily occupied on the brilliantly white table. All these things attract my attention and repel it at the same time.

I don't know what these people are thinking; I don't know what they are; they conceal themselves from one another and remain on their guard. I come up against their light, against their foreheads, as if against cornerstones.

Bracelets, necklaces, rings . . . The sparkling gestures of jewels repel me as far as would stars. A girl looks at me with her vague blue eyes. What can I do against that sort of sapphire?

Everybody is talking, but this noise leaves each person to himself and deafens me, just as the light blinded me.

Yet these people, because, by some chance turn of the conversation, they think of things which mean a great deal to them, reveal themselves at certain moments as if they were alone. I recognize that truth and turn pale at a memory.

Somebody has mentioned money; the conversation becomes general on this subject and the company is stirred by a feeling of idealism. A longing to seize and touch appears in every eye, just below the surface, as a little adored adoration appeared in the maid's eyes as soon as she felt alone: infinitely calm and free.

They talk proudly about military heroes; some of the men think: 'Like me!' and become excited, showing what they are thinking, in spite of its ridiculous incongruity and the servitude of their social position. One girl's face seems to me to light up with a dazzling glow. She is unable to restrain a sigh of ecstasy. Some thought which it is impossible to guess makes her blush. I see the flush spreading over her face; I see her heart shining out.

They talk about occult phenomena and the hereafter. 'Who knows?' says somebody; then they talk about death. While they are talking, two people at opposite ends of the table, a man and a woman who have not spoken to each other and seemed to be ignoring each other, exchange a glance which I intercept. And seeing this glance spring from each of them at the same time at the thought of death, I realize that these two beings love each other and belong to each other in the depths of the nights of life.

●

. . . The meal is over. The young people have moved into the drawing-room.

A lawyer starts telling his neighbours about a case which has been tried during the day. He expresses himself in guarded, almost cryptic terms, on account of the subject. It was a case of a man who had slit the throat of a little girl at the same time as he was raping her, and who, to drown the little victim's screams, had sung at the top of his voice. In court, the brute had declared: 'She screamed so loud that people might have heard her all the same, but luckily she was very young.'

One by one, the mouths have fallen silent; all the faces, without appearing to do so, are listening, and those which are a long way off would like to draw closer and crawl up to the speaker. Around the picture which has been conjured up, around this frightening paroxysm of our timid instincts, silence has spread out in widening circles, like a terrible noise in our souls.

Then I hear a woman, a respectable woman, laugh: a dry, broken laugh, which she may believe to be innocent, but which caresses the whole of her body as it bursts out: a laugh which, made up of shapeless, instinctive cries, is almost a carnal act . . . She falls silent and closes up. And in a calm voice, sure of the impression he is producing, the speaker goes on tossing the monster's confession at his audience: 'She was hard to kill, and she screamed and screamed! I was forced to rip her open with a kitchen knife.'

A young mother, who has her little girl beside her, has half risen to her feet, but she can't tear herself away. She sits down again and leans forward to conceal the child; she longs to hear more but is ashamed of listening.

Another woman remains motionless, her head bowed; but her mouth has tightened as if she were defending herself tragically, and beneath the polite mask of her face I can almost see, like writing, the mad smile of a martyr.

And the men! . . . This one, who is a simple, placid fellow, I distinctly heard panting. That one, who has the noncommital face of a bourgeois, is strenuously talking of trivialities to the young woman beside him. But he is looking at her with a gaze which would like to penetrate to her flesh, and even further, a gaze stronger than himself, of which he himself is ashamed, whose brightness makes him blink his eyes, and whose weight crushes him.

And I see a crude gaze in the eyes of that other man too, I see his mouth quiver and try to open; I have caught a glimpse of the triggering-off of that process of the human machine, the convulsive snap of the teeth in the direction of the young flesh and blood of the opposite sex.

And everybody gives vent to a chorus of extravagant abuse of the satyr.

. . . Thus, for a brief moment, they have not lied. They have almost confessed, perhaps without knowing, and even without knowing what they were confessing. They have almost been themselves. Envy and desire have burst forth, and their reflection has passed—and I have seen what was there in the silence, sealed by human lips.

It is that, it is that thought, that living spectre, which I want to contemplate. I get up, raised up, driven along by an impatient desire to see the true nature of men and women laid bare before my eyes, despite its ugliness, like a masterpiece; and once again, upstairs, leaning with my arms outstretched against the wall as if in an embrace, I look at the room.

It is lying there at my feet. Even empty, it is more alive than the people you meet and among whom you live, the people who have the vastness of their numbers to help them disappear, who have a voice to help them lie and a face to help them hide.

T H R E E

Night, complete night. Darkness as thick as velvet bears down upon me from all sides.

Everything around me has crumbled into darkness. In the midst of this blackness, I am sitting at my round table lit up by the sunshine of the lamp. I have settled down here to work, but in fact I have nothing to do but listen.

Just now, I looked into the room. There is nobody there, but no doubt somebody is going to come.

Somebody is going to come, this evening perhaps, tomorrow, another day; somebody is bound to come, then other living creatures will follow one after another. I wait, and it seems to me that I no longer have any other purpose in life.

I wait for a long time, not daring to rest. Then, very late at night, when silence has been reigning for so long that it paralyzes me, I make an effort. I cling to the wall again. I raise my eyes in prayer. The room is dark, mingled with everything, full of all the night, of all the unknown, of every imaginable thing. I fall back into my room.

The next morning, I see the room in the simplicity of daylight. I see the dawn spread out in it. Little by little it begins to blossom out from its ruins to rise up.

It is arranged and furnished on the same pattern as mine: at the far side, facing me, the fireplace with the mirror over it; on the right, the bed; on the left, by the window, a sofa . . . The two rooms are identical, but mine has finished and the other is going to begin . . .

After the vagueness of lunch, I return to the precise point which attracts me, the crack in the wall. Nothing. I get down.

The air is close. A slight smell of cooking remains, even here. I stop in the boundless expanse of my empty room.

I open my door a little way, I open it wide. In the corridors, the doors of the rooms are painted brown, with the numbers engraved on brass plates. Everything is closed. I take a few steps which I can hear all alone, which I can hear all too well, in the house which is as vast as immobility.

The landing is long and narrow, the wall covered with imitation tapestry with a dark green floral design in which there shines the brass of a gas bracket-lamp. I lean my elbows on the banisters. A servant (the one who waits at table and who, at the moment, is wearing a blue apron and is scarcely recognizable with his hair all tousled), comes skipping downstairs from the next floor, with some newspapers under his arm. Madame Lemercier's little girl comes upstairs, her hand cautious on the banisters, her neck poking forward like a bird's, and I compare her little footsteps to split-seconds passing by. A lady and a gentleman go past me, breaking off their conversation so that I can't hear them, as if they were refusing to give me the alms of their thoughts.

These trivial events vanish like scenes in a play on which the curtain has fallen.

I walk through the sickening afternoon. I have the impression of being alone against the world, while I prowl inside this house and yet outside it.

As I pass along the corridor, a door shuts quickly, cutting off the laugh of a woman taken by surprise. People run away, put up their defences. A meaningless noise oozes from the shadowy walls, worse than silence. Under the doors there crawls, crushed and killed, a ray of light, worse than darkness.

I go downstairs. I go into the drawing-room, drawn by the sound of conversation.

A few men, in a group, are pronouncing phrases which I can't remember. They go out; left alone, I can hear them arguing in the corridor. Finally their voices die away.

Now an elegant lady comes in, with a sound of silk and a scent of flowers and incense. She occupies a great deal of room on account of her perfume and her elegance.

This lady, whose head is bent forward slightly, has a beautiful long face distinguished by a gaze of great gentleness. But I can't see it very well for she doesn't look at me.

She sits down, picks up a book, leafs through it, and the pages cast a glow of whiteness and thought over her face.

I surreptitiously examine her bosom rising and falling, and her motionless face, and the living book which is joined to her. Her complexion is so luminous that her mouth looks almost black. Her beauty saddens me. I inspect this unknown woman from head to foot, with sublime regret. She caresses me with her presence. A woman always caresses a man when she approaches him and she is alone; in spite of so many sorts of separation, there is always a frightful incipient happiness between them.

But she goes away. It's all over with her. Nothing has happened, and yet it's all over. All that is too simple, too strong, too true.

This sweet despair, which I would not have had *before*, worries me. Since yesterday I have changed; I used to know human life, the living truth, as we all know it; I had experienced it since birth. I believe in it with a sort of fear now that it has appeared to me in a divine fashion.

◐

In my room, to which I have returned, the afternoon drags on endlessly, and yet evening comes.

From my window, I watch the evening rising in the sky, an ascent so gentle that you can see it and yet not see it; and the crowds spilling out over the pavements.

The passers-by are returning to the houses of which they have been thinking. Through the walls, I can hear the one in which I am, filling up, far away, with light-footed occupants, with faint murmurs.

A noise has made itself heard on the other side of the wall . . . I stand up against the wall and look into the next room, which is already all grey. A woman is there, dimly visible.

◐

She has gone over to the window as I went over to mine just now. That is no doubt the eternal gesture of all those who are alone in a room.

I see her more and more clearly; as my eyes become accustomed to the light, she becomes more distinct; it seems to me that, out of charity, she is coming to me.

On this early autumn day, she is wearing one of those pale dresses with which women light themselves up as long as there is still some sunshine. The faded rays from the window cover her with an almost dim glow. Her dress is the colour of the vast twilight, the colour of the time as in fairy stories.

A whiff of the perfume she is wearing, a smell of incense and flowers, comes to me, and by this perfume which marks her out like a real name, I recognize her: it is the young woman who settled near me earlier today, then flew away. Now she is there, behind her closed door, a prey to my gaze.

Her lips have moved; I don't know if she is talking to herself in a whisper or if she is humming . . . She is there, near the sad whiteness of the window, near the image of the window in the mirror, inside that vague room which is in the process of losing its colour; she is there, with her dark eyes and her dark flesh, with the brightness of her face, which so many gazes have caressed during its existence.

Her white neck, terrifying in its rarity, bends forward; the profile, close to the window, with the forehead resting against it, is bathed in a bluish half-light as if thought were blue; and floating over the dark mass of the hair, a faint halo shows that it is fair.

Her mouth is dark as if the lips were parted. Her hand is resting on the heavenly pane, like a bird. Her bodice is a pale yet intense colour, green or blue.

I know nothing about her, and she is as far from me as if worlds or centuries separated us, as if she were dead.

Yet there is nothing between us: I am near her, I am with her; trembling, I open out over her.

. . . My hands stretch out to embrace her. I am a man like the rest, always pitifully ready to be dazzled by the first woman who comes along. She is the purest image of the woman one loves: the woman one doesn't know yet completely, the woman who will reveal herself, the woman who contains the only living miracle on earth.

◐

She turns round and glides across the room, already invaded by the night, like a cloud with her soft round lines. I hear the deep murmur of her dress. I look for her face as for a star; but I can no more see her face than her thoughts.

I try to discover the purpose of her gestures, but they escape me. I am so close to her, and I don't know what she is doing! Creatures whom one sees without their realizing it look as if they don't know what they are doing.

She locks her door, which makes her a little more divine. She wants to be alone. No doubt she came into this room to undress.

I don't try to imagine the reasons for her presence, any more than I think of calling myself to account for the crime I am committing by possessing this woman with my eyes. I know that we are together, and with my whole heart, with my whole soul, with my whole life, I beg her to show herself to me.

She seems to be meditating, hesitating. I imagine, from some indefinable, innocent grace of her whole person, that she has been waiting for a long time to be alone in order to unveil herself. Yes, she still feels all beaten by the air outside, brushed against by the passers-by, touched by the taut faces of the men; and, having taken refuge between these walls, she is waiting for that contact to be more remote before taking off her dress.

I take pleasure in reading the virginal, carnal thought in her; I have a feeling that, in spite of the wall, my body is leaning towards her.

●

She goes towards the window, raises her arms, and, a luminous figure, draws the curtains. Complete darkness falls between us.

I have lost her! . . . A sharp pain fills my whole being, as if the light had been torn away from me . . . And I stay here, gaping, holding back a groan, peering into the darkness which is one with her breathing.

She gropes about, picks up some objects. I guess at, I see a match which flares up at her finger-tips. Slowly her picture bursts out of the darkness. The faint white patches of her hands, her forehead and her neck light up, and her face appears before me, like a faery vision.

I can't make out the pattern of the features in this woman's face during the few seconds in which the thin glow she is holding grants me a glimpse of her. She kneels down in front of the fire-place, with the flame between her fingers. I hear and see the crisp crackling of dry wood in the cold, damp darkness. She throws away the match without lighting the lamp, and there is no light in the room except from that glow coming from below.

The hearth turns red, while she walks to and fro in front if it, with a sound like a breeze, as if in front of a sunset. I see the moving silhouette of her tall slim body, her dark arms, and her hands all pink and gold. Her shadow crawls at her feet, leaps up the wall, and flies above her on the burning ceiling.

She is attacked by the brightness of the fire, which rolls to-wards her like a wall of flame. But she takes refuge in her shadow; she is still hidden, still covered and grey; her dress hangs sadly around her.

She sits down on the divan opposite me. Her gaze flutters gently round the room.

For one moment, it meets mine. Without realizing, we look at each other.

Then, in a sort of sharper gaze, a sort of warmer offering, her mouth which is thinking of something or somebody relaxes; she smiles.

The mouth is something naked in the naked face. The mouth, which is red with blood, which is forever bleeding, is comparable to the heart: it is a wound, and it is almost a wound to see a woman's mouth.

And I begin trembling before this woman who is opening a little and bleeding from a smile. The divan yields warmly to the embrace of her broad hips; her finely-made knees are close to-gether, and the whole of the centre of her body is in the shape of a heart.

. . . Half-lying on the divan, she stretches out her feet towards

the fire, lifting her skirt slightly with both hands, and this movement uncovers her black-stockinged legs.

And my flesh cries out, branded as if with a red-hot iron by
the voluptuous line which, growing wider, disappears into the
darkness, vanishes into extraordinary depths.

I clench my hands, anguish in my eyes, she is so utterly open,
agape, almost completely offered—her forehead plunged in
darkness, while the bloody light trailing about below climbs desperately onto her, into her, like a human effort.

The veil of her skirt has fallen back into place. The woman
has become again what she was before. No, she is different. Because I have glimpsed a little of her forbidden flesh, I am on the
watch for that flesh, in the mingled shadows of our two rooms.
She has lifted up her dress, she has performed that great simple
gesture which men worship as a positive religion, which they
pray for, even against all hope, even against all reason, the dazzling and sometimes dazzled gesture.

Once again she is walking, and now the sound of her skirt is
a sound of wings inside me.

My gaze, rejecting her childish face, in which her smile stag-
nates absentmindedly, rejecting and deliberately forgetting her
soul and her thought, seizes her physical form and craves her
blood, like the fire which is laying siege to her and not letting
her go: but my glances can only fall at her feet and brush lightly
against her dress, like the flames in the hearth, the magnificent
imploring flames, the flayed, ragged flames streaming towards
the sky.

At last she shows herself profoundly.

To take her shoes off, she crosses her legs high up, offering
me the gulf of her body.

She shows me her dainty feet, imprisoned in the shining
boots, and in the duller silk stockings, her finely-made knees
and her calves widening out like delicate amphoras over the del-

icate ankles. Above the knees, at the place where the stockings finish in a cloudy white calyx, there may be a little pure flesh: I can't tell underwear from skin in the frantic shadows and the panting brightness of the flames attacking her. Is that the delicate material of her underclothes, or is it her flesh? Is it nothing, or is it everything? My gaze fights with the darkness and the flames for possession of that nudity. With my forehead against the wall, my chest against the wall, and the palms of my hands pressing fiercely against the wall, to break it down and go through it, I torture my eyes over this uncertainty, trying, by cunning or force, to see better, to see more.

And I plunge into the great darkness of her being, beneath the soft, warm, awe-inspiring wing of her raised dress. The embroidered drawers gape open in a wide, dark slit, full of shadow, and my gaze leaps into it and goes mad. And it nearly obtains what it wants, in that open shadow, in that naked shadow, in the centre of her, in the centre of the thin garment which, light as mist and impregnated with the scent of her, is little more than a cloud of incense around the middle of her body—in that shadow which is really a fruit.

This lasts for a moment. I am stretched out against the wall before this woman who just now—I remember a certain gesture—was frightened of her own reflection, and who now, in the perfect chastity of her solitude, has adopted the attitude of a prostitute rubbing up against the gaze of the man drawn into her presence . . . Utterly pure, she offers herself and opens herself.

The blaze in the fireplace dies down, and I can scarcely see her any more when she begins undressing: it is in the dark that this immense festival of the two of us is going to take place.

I see the tall, diffuse, pitiless figure, in its almost invisible beauty, moving gently, surrounded by delicate, warm, caressing sounds. I catch a glimpse of her arms solemnly bending, and

from the exquisite glow of a gesture which softly rounds them,
I can tell that they are bare.

What has just fallen on to the bed, in a thin silky scrap, light
and slow, is the bodice which fitted loosely round her neck and
tightly round her waist . . . The cloudy skirt opens a little way
and, slipping down to her feet, lights up the whole of her body,
very pale in the midst of the shadows. I have the impression that
I can see her disengage herself from that withered dress which
is nothing apart from her, and I can make out the shape of her
legs.

Perhaps I only think so, for my eyes are scarcely serving me
any longer, not only because of the lack of light, but because I
am blinded by the sombre effort of my heart, by the throbbing
of my heart, by all the darkness of my blood . . . It is not my
eyes which are pursuing the sublime figure, but rather my
shadow which is coupling with hers.

A single cry fills me completely: Her belly!

Her belly! What do her breasts, her legs, matter to me?—I
care as little about them as about her thoughts and her face,
which I have already abandoned. It is her belly that I want and
that I am straining after as if it were my salvation.

My gaze, to which my convulsive hands lend their strength,
my gaze as heavy as flesh, needs her belly. In spite of laws and
dresses, the male gaze always thrusts and crawls towards a woman's sex like a reptile towards its hole.

For me she is no longer anything but her sex. She is no longer
anything but the mysterious wound which opens like a mouth,
bleeds like a heart, and vibrates like a lyre. And from her comes
a perfume which fills my nostrils, no longer the artificial perfume with which her dress is impregnated, the perfume with
which she clothes herself, but her essential odour, wild, vast,
comparable to that of the sea—the odour of her solitude, of her
warmth, of her love, and the secret of her body.

With my eyes bloodshot and red like two pale mouths, I strain towards that apparition, awe-inspiring in its magnetism. I become ferocious in my triumph. And her mouth is a long lingering kiss, and I purse my lips in a long sterile kiss.

Now she remains motionless—inexplicable, invisible . . .

A violent impulse seizes me to touch her in reality . . . To destroy this wall, or to leave my room, break down her door, throw myself onto her.

No, no, no! An intuition brings me sharply and firmly back to my senses . . . I would scarcely have time to touch her. I would be seized and rendered harmless—with my reputation tainted, imprisonment, shame, utter poverty, and everything else. I feel terribly frightened, all that is so close to me; a shudder of horror roots me to the spot.

But another idea quickly occurs to me, a dream torments my flesh; once the first shock was over, perhaps she would surrender; perhaps she would be infected by my passion and take fire like an object at my touch, in a delirium of gratitude . . .

No, again no! For then she would be a whore, and you can find as many whores as you could possibly wish for. It is easy to have a woman in your hands and to do what you like with her: that is a sacrilege with a fixed scale of charges. There are even establishments where, at a price, you can watch women making love. If she were a whore, she would no longer be herself—for she is angelically alone.

I must get this into my head and my body: if I can appreciate her in such a perfect manner, it is because she is apart from me and there is a barrier between us. Her solitude enhances her beauty, but triumphantly defends her. Her revelation is made up of her virgin truth, of the universal isolation over which she reigns, and of the certainty in which she lives of that isolation. She shows herself, from a distance, through her virtue, and does not give herself: she is like a masterpiece; she remains as distant and unchangeable, separated by space and silence, as sculpture and music.

And everything which attracts me prevents me from approaching. I have to be unhappy, I have to be at one and the same time a robber and a victim . . . There is no other course open to me but to desire, to surpass myself by dint of desiring, dreaming and hoping, to desire and to possess my desire.

For a moment I turn my head away, so cruel and terrible is the dilemma in which I am struggling, and in the bottomless pit which opens before my eyes, I let the soft sounds she was making die away . . . Am I going mad? No, it is truth which is mad.

With my whole body and my whole mind, I overcome my carnal weakness, my flesh falls silent and ceases to dream, and across my heavy ruins I begin to look.

As if she felt sorry for me, she gets dressed again, covers everything up again.

Now she has lighted the lamp. She has put on a dress again; she is hiding from me the beautiful secrets which she hides from everyone; she has gone back into the mourning of her modesty.

She still gives me a few scattered movements. Now she is measuring her waist; she puts a little rouge on the edge of her ear, then takes it off; she smiles at herself in the mirror, in two different ways, and even adopts a disappointed pose for a moment. She invents a host of little movements, both useless and useful . . . She discovers coquettish gestures which, like the modest gestures, take on a sort of austere beauty from being performed in solitude.

. . . Then, at the moment when, ready and wonderfully enclosed, she has just considered herself with a supreme, sublime glance, our gazes meet once again.

She is leaning with one hand on the table on which the unshaded lamp is shining . . . Her face and her hands are resplendent and the unchecked radiance of the lamp bathes her chin, the outline of her face, and her cheekbones with a brighter glow.

I can no longer recognize her as she emerges from the darkness wearing this mask of sunshine; but I have never seen a mystery at such close quarters . . . I stay where I am, enveloped by her light, quivering with her, overwhelmed by her naked presence, as if I had never known until now what a woman is.

Just as she did a little earlier, she smiles before her eyes leave me, and I feel conscious of the extraordinary value of that smile and the richness of that face . . .

She goes away . . . I admire her, I respect her, I worship her; I have a sort of love for her which nothing real will ever destroy and which has no reason either for hoping or for coming to an end. No, it is true that I did not know what a woman was.

●

She was not present at dinner. She left the house the next day.

I saw her again when she was leaving. I was right at the foot of the stairs, in the half-light of the entrance-hall, while people were bustling forward to meet her. As she came downstairs, her dainty hand, gloved in white, fluttered down the gleaming black banisters like a butterfly. Her feet pointed forward, small and shining. She struck me as shorter than the day before, but she was the same in every respect as she had been the first time I saw her. Her mouth was so small that it looked as if she were pursuing her lips. She was wearing pearl-grey, the twittering dress . . . She was passing by, she was going away, she was evaporating in a cloud of scent . . .

She had brushed past me; she might have seen me at that moment, but of course she didn't—and yet, in the darkness of our rooms, the two of us had smiled a single smile. She had become once more the enclosed, pitiless light which people are when you meet them in the midst of others. There was no wall between us; there was infinite space and everlasting time; there were all the forces of society.

That was how I glimpsed her in my last glance—without really understanding, for nobody ever really understands a departure. I shall never see her again. So much grace was going to wither and fade away; so much beauty, sweet weakness and happiness was lost. She was fleeing slowly towards uncertain life, and then towards certain death. Whatever her days might be, she was going towards her last.

That was all I could say about her.

◑

. . . This morning, while the daylight gathers around me, giving each detail an empty precision, my heart struggles and complains. The entire vista of my life is deserted. When something is really finished, doesn't it seem that everything is finished?

I don't know her name . . . She will go forward into her destiny as I go forward into mine. If our two existences had become linked, they would scarcely have known one another; as it is, what darkness surrounds them! But I shall never forget the incomparable evening when we were together.

FOUR

This morning, I have been thinking about the grandiose vision of the day before yesterday. But already I recall it with less emotion; already it has withdrawn a little way from my heart, because a day has gone by. Is it going to die without my doing anything for it?

A desire takes hold of me: to write it down, to fix in a lasting form every detail of what I have felt, so that the days are not scattered as they pass by, like dust.

But, straight away, the whiteness of the paper brings me oblivion of what I was going to say, a sweet dazzlement in which all the precision of my memories melts.

Thanks to close attention, repeatedly brought back to the point, in spite of growing tiredness behind the eyes, I write, I write everything down. I grow excited. I believe that I am reproducing exactly the reality of things. Then I read over what I have written, and it is nothing—nothing but words lying dead before me.

The extraordinary tension, the tragic simplicity, the intense and anguished harmony—where has all that gone? This writing doesn't live. It is a lattice-work of words on reality; the phrases are there, black and regular, running across the paper like chains.

What must I do for truth to rise from these dead signs?

I try to get round the difficulty. I hunt for the typical, evocative

detail . . . Remembering an impression I had had when I had
first caught sight of her in the glow from the window, I decide
to stress it: *'There was some blue, green and yellow on her.'* This
was never the case; this childish daub isn't the truth; I destroy it
. . . The important thing is to describe her body. I devote minute
care to the process, I make comparisons with a statue of antiq-
uity. Reading what I have written, I angrily drive a line through
this botched-up piece of work.

I try some cruder words which strike me as stronger, and, little
by little, I let myself go to the extent of inventing details in order
to capture the sharpness of the memory. *'She adopted lascivious
postures . . .'*

No! No! That isn't true!

All these are inert words which leave in existence the grandeur
of what was, without being able to touch it; they are vain, futile
noises; they are like the barking of a dog, the sound of branches
moving in the wind.

I open my hand, let my pen roll onto the table, overwhelmed
by a feeling of impotence, defeat, gloomy madness.

How is it that you can't say what you have seen? How is it that
the truth flees from you as if it were not the truth and as if,
however sincere you are, you could not be sincere? You haven't
conjured up a thing when you have called it by its name. It's no
use having known words since your childhood, you still don't
know what they mean.

My trembling, my melancholy, my distress have been lost. I
am condemned to be forgotten. People will pass in front of me
without looking at me or without seeing me. People won't care
what I may contain. I can't be anything on earth but a believer.

●

I stayed for several days without seeing anything. Those days
were torrid. To begin with, the sky had been grey and rainy; now

September was flaming in its decline. Friday . . . So I had already been a whole week in this house! . . .

One sultry afternoon, sitting on a chair, I dreamily abandoned myself to a sort of fairy-tale reverie.

. . . The edge of a forest; in the undergrowth, on the dark emerald carpet, rings of sunshine; in the distance, at the far end of the plain, a hill, and over the waving foliage, all yellow and dark green, a piece of wall and a turret, squared as if they were in a tapestry . . . A page came forward, dressed as a bird. A buzzing of flies. It was the distant sound of the King's Hunt. Things of extraordinary sweetness were going to happen.

◐

The next day, the afternoon was hot and sunny again. I remembered similar afternoons many years before, and it seemed to me that I was living in that vanished period—as if the stifling heat had abolished time, suffocated everything else under its bell-glass.

The room next door was almost pitch-dark . . . The shutters had been closed. Through the double curtains made of some thin material, I could see the window striped with dazzling bars, like the grill of a brazier.

In the torrid silence of the house, in its vast enclosed slumber, trills of laughter rose vainly into the air; voices trailed away, as they had done the day before, as they had always done.

From that distant tumult there emerged the precious sound of footsteps. They were coming towards me. I strained towards that growing sound . . . The door opened, dazzling, pushed open, so it seemed, by the light itself, and two puny shadows, eaten into by the brightness, appeared.

They looked as if they were being pursued. They hesitated on the threshold, a pair of tiny figures framed together in the doorway, and then came in.

I heard the door close again; the room was alive. I gazed intently at the new arrivals; I could just make them out through the red and dark green haloes with which the sudden burst of light of their entry had filled my eyes: a little girl and a young boy, twelve or thirteen years old.

They had sat down on the sofa, and were looking at each other without saying anything, their faces almost identical.

◗

One of them murmured:

'You see, there's nobody here.'

And a hand pointed to the bed with no sheets on it, the coat-stand bare of clothes, the empty table: the careful devastation of unoccupied rooms.

Then, before my eyes, this hand began shaking like a leaf. I could hear my heart beating. The voices whispered.

'We are alone . . . Nobody has seen us.'

'It's as if we were alone for the very first time.'

'And yet we've always known each other . . .'

There was a little quavering laugh.

It seemed to me that they had felt a need for their solitude, the first stage of a mystery into which they were entering together. They had escaped from other people; they had rid themselves of the other people around them. They had created the forbidden solitude. But it was obvious that now they had found that solitude, they no longer knew what to look for.

◗

Then I heard a voice stammer with a tremor which was almost a sob of misery:

'We are very fond of each other . . .'

Then a tender remark rose into the air, panting, trying out the words, as hesitant as a fledgling:

'I would like to love you more . . .'

Seeing them bending towards each other like that, in the warm darkness which surrounded them and which concealed the ages on their faces, you might have taken them for a pair of lovers drawing close together.

A pair of lovers! That was what they dreamed of being, without knowing what it was.

One of them had spoken these words: *the first time*. It was the first time that they had had the impression of being alone, although they had always lived side by side.

Possibly, indeed no doubt, it was the first time that the two childhood friends had ever wanted to leave friendship and childhood behind, it was the first time that a desire for desire had ever come to astonish and disturb two hearts which had hitherto been asleep together . . .

◐

At one moment they stood up and the slender ray of sunlight which passed above them and fell at their feet showed their figures and lit up their faces and their hair, so that their presence illuminated the room.

Were they going to go away, desert me? No, they sat down again; everything fell back into darkness, into mystery, into truth.

. . . Looking at them, I was conscious of a vague mixture of my past and the past of the world. Where were they? Everywhere, seeing that they were . . . They were on the banks of the Nile, the Ganges or the Cydnus, on the banks of the everlasting river of time. They were Daphnis and Chloë, near a myrtle bush, in the sunlight of Greece, all lit up by a green glow of foliage, with their faces reflecting one another. Their vague little dialogue buzzed like the two wings of a bee near the cool fountains and the overwhelming heat of the fields, while in the distance a waggon went by loaded with sheaves of corn and blue sky.

The new world was opening up; the panting truth was there. They were at a loss, they were afraid of the sudden appearance of some divinity, they were unhappy and happy at the same time; they were as close as possible, having brought as much of each other to each other as they could. But they had no idea of what they were bringing. They were too small, they were too young, they didn't exist enough; each was a stifling secret for himself.

Like all human beings, like myself, like all of us, they wanted what they hadn't got, they were begging. But they were asking themselves for alms, they were asking their presences and their persons for help.

He, already a man, already impoverished by this feminine companion of his, drawn and dragged towards her, held out towards her his dim, clumsy arms, without daring to look at her properly.

She, already a woman, laid her head back on the sofa, her eyes shining, her face rather plump and all pink, flushed and warmed by her heart; the skin of her neck, tight and silky, was palpitating; this point, between her face and her breasts, was the precious, delicate centre of her throbbing life. Half-closed, watchful, already revealing a little voluptuous charm, she seemed like a rose breathing in its own perfume. I could see her slender legs in their yellow cotton stockings up to her knees, under her dress which covered her body at the same time as it offered it, like a bouquet.

I could not tear my eyes away from their gestures, and I drank in this sight, pressing my face against it like a vampire.

●

After a long silence he murmured:

'Do you want us to say *vous* to each other?'

'What for?'

He seemed to make an effort to concentrate.

'To begin again,' he said at last.

He repeated his question, this time using the word *vous*.

'Do you want us to?'

She gave a visible start at the touch of this new form of his speech, at the word *vous*, as at a sort of first kiss.

She said hesitantly:

'It's like something that was covering us being taken away . . .'

Now he didn't dare any more:

'Do you want me to kiss you on the mouth?'

Tense as she was, she could not smile completely.

'Yes,' she said.

They took each other by the arms, the shoulders, and stretched out their lips to each other, calling each other softly by name, as if their mouths were birds.

'Jean . . .'

'Hélène . . .'

This was the first thing that occurred to them. Kissing and being kissed in return—isn't that the most tender little caress there is, and the closest bond? Besides, it is so strictly forbidden!

For the second time it seemed to me that the couple they formed no longer had any age. They resembled all lovers while they were holding hands, their faces pressed together, blind and trembling, in the shadow of their kiss.

However, they drew apart, freeing themselves from the caress which they did not know yet how to use.

They spoke, with their mouths which were as innocent as ever. About what? About the past, that past which was so close, so brief.

They were emerging from the paradise of childhood and ignorance. They spoke about a house and garden where the two of them had lived.

This house preoccupied them. It was surrounded by a garden wall, so that from the road only the top of its roof was visible, and it was impossible to see what the house was up to.

They stammered:

'When we were small and the rooms were big . . .'

'It was less tiring walking there than anywhere else.'

Judging by what they said, there was something helpful and invisible between those walls, spread everywhere; something like the kindly God of the past . . . She hummed a tune she had heard there, and she remarked that music remembered better than people.

They had tumbled back into the past by the gentle force of their weight; they were wrapping themselves up warmly in their memories.

'The other day, the night before we left, I went all by myself, with a candle in one hand, through the rooms, and they scarcely woke up to watch me go by . . .'

In the carefully tended, well-behaved garden, they had thought of nothing but the flowers, and not much more than the flowers. They had looked around and seen the pool, the covered alleyway, and the cherry-tree which, in winter, when the lawn was white, had too many flowers.

Only a few days before, they had been in that garden, as brother and sister. Now it seemed that life had suddenly become serious, and that they had forgotten how to play. You could see that they wanted to kill the past. When you are old, you let it die; when you are young and strong, you kill it . . .

She straightened up.

'I don't want to remember any more,' she said.

And he said:

'I don't want us to be like each other any more. I don't want us to be brothers any more.'

Little by little their eyes opened:

'Touching each other with just our hands!' he murmured, trembling.

'Being brothers is nothing.'

It had come, the hour of fine, disturbing decisions and forbidden fruit. Before, neither of them had belonged to himself; now the hour had come for them to take possession of themselves so that they could do what they wished with themselves.

Already they were a little ashamed and a little aware of themselves.

A few days earlier, towards evening, they had taken solemn pleasure in disobeying by leaving the garden against their parents' orders.

'Grandmother came to the top of the steps, which were all grey, to call us back . . .'

'But we both went off; we went through the hedge at the place where a bird usually calls and there is a gap. The bird had flown away and its call too. There was no wind and hardly any light left. The branches of the trees were silent, even though they are very sensitive. The dust on the ground was dead. The darkness enveloped us so gently that we could almost have spoken to it. We felt frightened as we saw night falling. There was no colour in anything any more, only a little light in the darkness; the flowers, the road, the cornfields, themselves were silver . . . And that was when I brought my lips closest to yours.'

'Night,' she said, carried away by a feeling of beauty, 'night caresses caresses . . .'

'I took your hand, and I realized that you were all alive. Before, I used to say *my cousin Hélène*, but when I said that, I didn't know what I know now. From now on, when I say *she*, that will be all . . .'

Once again their lips met. Their mouths and their eyes were those of Adam and Eve. I recalled the original ancestral example from which sacred history and human history flow as from—

spring. They wandered in the piercing light of paradise, without knowing anything; they were as if they were not. When—as a result of the victory of curiosity, although God in person had forbidden that curiosity—they learned the secret, discovered the pleasurable division and understood the grandiose will of the flesh, the sky darkened. The certainty of a future of suffering fell upon them; angels like vultures drove them out of paradise; they travelled the earth from day to day, but they had created love, exchanged divine wealth for the poverty of belonging to each other.

The two little children had taken their places in the eternal drama. They spoke to each other and restored to their *tutoiement* all its old importance:

'I would like to love you more . . . Above all I would like to love you more passionately, but I don't know how . . . I would like to hurt you, but I don't know how.'

◐

They fell silent, as if there were no words left for them. They were on the edge of themselves, and I could see their hands trembling between them.

They obeyed this inspiration of their hands; they groped their way towards the strange, tragic joy, towards the happy sin you commit together, towards the embrace which makes two human beings begin life again, intimately mingled, as a single shapeless creature.

I could not see him clearly . . . It seemed to me that he laid hands on her while she waited with shining eyes. It seemed to me that, in the burning darkness which contained them, he was half-undressed, and that, from his disarranged, opened clothing, his sex had risen erect . . . Strange, sacred flower, which was one with his feelings, with his flesh, with his heart, and which was as it were a living miracle between them, like a miracle, like a child.

. . . No doubt he had raised her dress, for I caught these words breathed out in a whisper, confused, stifled, sacrificed, in the awesome silence:

'This is your real mouth.'

◖

And I trembled before them, while a terrible, frantic love of truth quartered my body on the wall . . . As if this breath of mine were burning them, terrifying them, they took fright and stood up. It was all over. The poignant adventure which, by chance, had begun before my eyes would continue elsewhere and come to an end elsewhere.

They had scarcely got to their feet before the door opened. Their old grandmother was there, leaning forward. She came from the grey world of ghosts; she came from the past. She was looking for them as if they had got lost. She called to them in a low voice. By an extraordinary coincidence which was in harmony with their presence, her tone had a quality of infinite gentleness, almost—amazing though it might seem—of sadness.

'Are you there, children?'

Without thinking, she said with an innocent little laugh:

'Why, what are you doing here? . . . Come along, everybody's looking for you . . .'

She was old and withered, but she looked angelic with her high-necked dress. Beside the two of them, who were preparing for the immensity of life, she had henceforth become like a child: inactive, useless . . .

They threw themselves into her arms, and offered their foreheads to her sacred, deserted lips. It was as if they were bidding her farewell for ever.

◖

She went away. And a moment later they left too, as hurriedly as they had come: united by the invisible, sublime bond of evil;

so united that they no longer held hands as they did when they came in. But, in the doorway, they looked at each other.

And now that room is as empty as a sanctuary, I think of that glance of theirs, their first glance of love which I saw them exchange.

Nobody, before me, has ever been able to see a first glance. I was beside them, but far away from them. I understood and contemplated, without being involved in the excitement of the action or lost in the emotions. That is why I saw that glance. They, for their part, don't know when it began, don't know that it was the first; afterwards, they will forget; the urgent progress of their hearts will destroy those preliminaries. Nobody can know his first glance any more than he can know his last.

I shall remember, when they no longer remember.

I myself cannot recall my first glance, my first gift of love. It existed for all that. Those divinely simple things have vanished from me. Yet what in heaven's name have I kept which can equal them? The little creature that I was has died completely before my eyes. I have outlived him, but forgetfulness has tortured and then defeated me, the sadness of life has ruined me, and I know scarcely anything that he knew. I recall all sorts of things, at random, but the finest and the sweetest have disappeared into oblivion.

Well, this tender hymn to which I have just been listening, full of infinity and overflowing with youthful smiles, this precious song I take, I have, I keep. It trembles over my heart. I have stolen, but I have saved a little truth.

F I V E

For a whole day the room remained empty. Twice I had a great hope, then a disappointment.

Waiting had become my habit, my profession. I postponed appointments, I put off engagements, I saved time, at the risk of losing my job; I organized my life as if for a new love. I never left my room except to go down to the dining-room, where nothing interested me any more.

On the second day I saw that the room had been prepared to receive a new occupant; it was waiting. I indulged in countless speculations as to the identity of this occupant while the room kept its secret like a thinking creature.

Twilight came, then evening, which made the room bigger without changing it, and already I was in despair when the door suddenly swung open in the darkness and, on the threshold, I saw the spectre of a man.

He was hard to distinguish from the evening.

Clothes that were black or verging on black; cuffs of a milky pallor from which hung tapering grey hands; a collar of white a little brighter than the rest. The dark holes of his eyes and mouth were hollowed out in his round, greyish face; under the chin, a shadowy cavity; the gold of the forehead gleamed dully; the cheekbones were underlined by a dark bar. He looked like a skeleton. What was this creature whose face was of such monstrous simplicity?

He drew nearer, came to life. I saw that he was good-looking.

He had a charming, serious face, fringed with a delicate black beard, shining eyes, and a high forehead. His gestures were guided and distinguished by a haughty grace.

He had taken two steps forward, and had then turned round to face the door which had remained half-open. The shadow of that door trembled; a silhouette approached, took shape; a little hand in a black glove clutched the edge of the door, and a woman leant inquiringly into the room.

She must have been a few steps behind him in the street. They had not wanted to go together into the room where the two of them were taking refuge to escape from some pursuit.

She pushed the door to; once it was shut, she leant against it with her whole body, to close it even further, with her life. And it was only slowly that she turned her head towards him, paralysed for a moment, it seemed to me, by the fear that it might not be *he* . . . They gazed at each other, and between them there was a passionate, stifled, almost silent cry which echoed from one to the other, and through which their common wound appeared to re-open.

'You!'

'You!'

She was almost fainting. She fell upon his breast, flung on him by a tempest.

She had had just enough strength to come and fall into his arms. I saw the man's two great pale hands, open, the fingers scarcely clenched, pressed against the woman's back. A sort of desperate trembling took hold of them; it was as if a huge angel were struggling in the room and trying in vain to escape into infinity; and it seemed to me that the room was too small for this couple, even though it was full of the evening.

'Nobody has seen us!'

They were the same words the two children had breathed the other day.

He said: 'Come.' He led her to the divan, by the window. They sat down on the red velvet. I saw their arms join them together like bonds. They stayed there, motionless, gathering around them all the shadows in the world, drawing new life from them, beginning to exist again, rediscovering each other in their element of darkness and solitude.

What an entrance they had made! What an ill-starred irruption!

When the idea of adultery had imposed itself on my eyes, when the woman had appeared in the doorway, driven irresistibly towards the man, I had thought that I was witnessing a blissful joy not without beauty in its fullness, a savage, animal joy, as vital as Nature itself. On the contrary, this meeting was like a heartbreaking farewell.

'Shall we always be afraid, then?'

She had scarcely calmed down at all, and she had said this looking at him anxiously, as if he were really going to reply.

She shivered, huddled in the dark, feverishly squeezing and kneading the man's hand with hers, her head and shoulders erect, both arms stiff. I could see her bosom rising and falling like the sea. They were holding each other, touching each other; but a lingering fear prevented them from exchanging any caresses.

'Always afraid . . . always afraid . . . always . . . Away from the street, away from the sunshine, away from everything . . . I who would have loved a destiny in the broad daylight!' she said, looking at the sky; and her profile was half-tinged with blue, while these words of hers took wing.

They were afraid. Fear moulded them, penetrated them. Their eyes, their bodies, their hearts were afraid. Above all, their love was afraid.

. . . A sad smile appeared on the man's face; he looked at his companion and stammered:

'You are thinking of him . . .'

With her elbows on her knees now, her head leaning forward, her fists against her cheeks, she made no reply.

Ardent, bowed, as small as a child, she was gazing into the distance, towards him who was not there.

She had bent her shoulders before that image, as if she were imploring it with her eyes cast down, and receiving a divine illumination from it. He who was not there, he who existed and was being deceived. The lord and master whom they were wounding and offending. He who was everywhere save where they were, who occupied the immensity outside and whose name made them bow their heads; he to whom they had fallen prey.

As if shame and horror belonged to the dark, night began to fall upon this man and this woman who had come to hide their embrace in this room as in a tomb inhabited by infinity.

◖

He said: 'I love you!'

I heard this great utterance clearly. I love you! I shuddered to the depths of my being as I caught the profound declaration which came from the lips of these two creatures already almost mingled together. I love you! The declaration which offers heart and flesh, the wide-open cry of creature and creation. I love you! I was face to face with love.

Then it seemed to me that sincerity vanished in the hasty, incoherent words which he uttered next, approaching her, drawing close to her. It was as if he wanted to be done with the necessary phrases, and as if he were hurrying as fast as he could to get to the caresses:

'We were born for each other, you know . . . There is a kin-

ship between our souls which was bound to triumph. Nobody
could prevent us from recognizing each other and belonging to
each other any more than they could prevent our lips from joining as soon as they draw together. What do we care about moral
codes or social barriers? . . . Our love is made of the infinite
and the eternal.'

She said: 'Yes,' lulled by his voice.

But I who was listening intently to them could tell that he was
lying or that he was losing himself in his words . . . Love was
becoming an idol, an object. He was blaspheming, vainly invoking the infinite and the eternal, to which he was paying lip
service with the worn-out, everyday prayer.

They dropped the spoken commonplace . . . After remaining
pensive for a while, the woman shook her head, and she for her
part uttered the words of justification, of glorification; more than
that—the words of truth:

'I was so unhappy . . .'

◉

'What a long time ago it seems . . .' she began.

It was her work of art, it was her poem and her prayer, the
repetition of this story, in a low, hurried voice, as if she were in
a confessional . . . You could tell that she launched out on it
quite naturally, without any introduction, it preoccupied her so
completely whenever they were alone together.

. . . She was very simply dressed. She had taken off her black
gloves, her jacket and her hat. She was wearing a dark skirt, and
a red blouse on which a little gilt chain was shining.

She was a woman of about thirty, with regular features and
carefully groomed, silky hair; it seemed to me that I knew her
already or that I wouldn't recognize her again.

She started talking aloud about herself, recalling an infinitely
oppressive past.

'What a life I led! How empty and monotonous it was! The small town, the house, the drawing-room, with the pieces of furniture arranged here and there, and never moving, like tombstones . . . One day I tried to change the position of the table in the middle. I wasn't allowed to.'

Her face turned pale, became more luminous.

He was listening to her. A smile of patient resignation, which quickly resembled a slightly bored weariness, passed over his delicate face. He was really handsome, although a little disconcerting, with his big eyes which you could tell were worshipped, his drooping moustache, his tender, distant air. He looked like one of those gentle creatures who think too much and who do evil. He looked as though he were above everything and capable of anything . . . A little detached from what she was saying, yet stirred by desire for her, he seemed to be waiting.

. . . And suddenly the scales dropped from my eyes, the truth was laid bare before me; I saw that between these two human beings there was an immense difference, an infinite discord as it were, wonderful to see, it was so deep, but so poignant it almost broke my heart.

He was moved only by desire for her; she only by the need to escape from the life she was living. Their hopes were not the same; they seemed to be a united couple, but they were not.

They did not speak the same language; when they said the same things, they scarcely understood each other, and, to my eyes, right from the start, their union seemed more broken than if they had never met.

But he didn't say what he thought; you could tell that from the sound of his voice, from the very charm of his intonation, from the lilting choice of his words: he wanted to please her, and he lied. He was obviously superior to her, but she dominated him by a sort of inspired sincerity. While he was in command of his words, she offered herself in hers.

. . . She was describing the setting of her former life.

'From the bedroom window and the dining-room window I could see the close. The fountain in the middle, with its shadow at its feet. I used to watch the day circling round there, on that little round white close, like a sun-dial.

'. . . The postman used to cross it regularly, without thinking; outside the door of the arsenal, a soldier stood doing nothing . . . And there was nobody left at all when midday struck, like a knell. I remember the knell of midday above all: the middle of the day, the epitome of boredom.

'Nothing happened to me, nothing happened to me. Nothing belonged to me. The future no longer existed for me. If I had had to go on living like that, nothing would have separated me from my death—nothing, nothing! . . . To suffer boredom is to die. My life was dead, and yet I had to live it. It was a suicide. Others kill themselves with poison or a gun; I was killing myself with the minutes and the hours.'

'Aimée!' said the man.

'Then, as a result of seeing the days born in the morning and aborted in the evening, I became afraid of dying, and that fear was my first passion . . . Often, in the middle of calls I was paying, or in the middle of the night, or while I was walking home along-side the convent wall, I would shudder with hope on account of that passion . . .

'But who would rescue me? Who would save me from that invisible shipwreck, of which I myself was aware only now and then? Around me there was a sort of conspiracy, born of envy, spite and stupidity . . . Everything I saw, everything I heard tried to bring me back to the straight and narrow path, to my wretched straight and narrow path.

'. . . Madame Martet—you know, my only fairly close friend—who is only two years older than I, told me that one has to be content with what one has. I replied: "If one has to be content with what one has, then everything is over. Death has nothing left to do. Don't you see that that statement puts an end to life? . . . Do you really believe what you are saying?" She replied that she did. Oh, that horrible woman!

'But it wasn't enough to be frightened of boredom, I had to hate it. How did I come to feel that hatred? I don't know.

'I couldn't recognize myself, I wasn't myself any more, I longed so much for something else. I didn't even know my own name any more.

'There was one day, I remember, when—although I haven't an evil nature—I had a wonderful dream that my husband was dead, my poor husband who had never done anything to me, and that I was free, free, up to anything!

'Things couldn't go on like that. I couldn't hate monotony, solitude, habit to such an extent for long. Oh, habit is the darkest of all shadows, and night isn't night in comparison . . .

'Religion? It isn't with religion that you can fill the emptiness of your days, but with your own life. It wasn't with beliefs or ideas that I had to fight, but with myself.

'And then I found the remedy!'

Hoarse-voiced, admirable, she almost screamed:

'Evil! Evil! Crime to fight boredom, treachery to counteract habit. Evil to be new, to be different, to hate life more than life hated me, evil so as not to die!

'I met you; you wrote poetry and books; you were different from the others; you had a trembling voice which gave an impression of beauty; and above all you were there in my existence, in front of me; I only had to hold out my arms. So I loved you with all my might, and that's really loving, my dear.'

She was speaking now in a low, hurried voice, hoarse with enthusiasm, and she was playing with her companion's hand as with a little toy.

'And you too, you loved me, of course . . . And when, one

evening, we slipped into the hotel—the first time—it seemed to me that the door opened by itself, and I felt thankful that I had rebelled and torn up my destiny as if it were a dress.

'And since then! The lies—which make us suffer sometimes, but which we no longer hate when we think about them—the risks, the dangers which give a flavour to the passing hours, the complications which make life fuller; these rooms, these hiding-places, these dark prisons, which have given inspiration to the sunshine within me.

'Ah!' she said.

It seemed to me that she sighed as if, having fulfilled her dream, there was nothing so beautiful left before her.

◐

She reflected for a moment and said:

'That is how things stand . . . Oh, yes, I too may have thought at the time that it was love at first sight, a supernatural, inevitable attraction, on account of your poetry. But in fact I came to you— I can see that now—with my fists clenched and my eyes shut.'

She added:

'People lie a great deal about love. It is hardly ever what they say it is.

'There may be magnificent attractions between men and women. I don't say that a love like that can't exist between two human beings. But we aren't those two human beings. We have never thought of anybody but ourselves. I know perfectly well that I loved myself with you. The same is true on your side. There is an attraction for you which doesn't exist for me, seeing that I don't feel any pleasure. You see, we strike a bargain: one of us gives a dream to the other, and the other gives pleasure in return. And that isn't love.'

He made a gesture of doubt or protest; he didn't want to speak. However, he murmured in a faint voice:

'It has always been like that; even in the purest of loves, a person can't get out of himself.'

'Oh!' she exclaimed in a burst of pious indignation which surprised me by its vehemence. 'That isn't the same thing! You mustn't say that! You mustn't say that!'

It seemed to me that there was a note of regret in her voice, and in her eyes the dream of a new dream.

She banished all that by shaking her head.

'How happy I was! I felt young again, reborn. I experienced a reawakening of innocence. I remember that I no longer dared to show the tip of my foot outside my dress; I even blushed for my face, for my hands, for my name . . .'

●

Then the man took up the confession where she left it and spoke of the early period of their liaison. He wanted to caress her with words, to take her gradually with phrases, to ensnare her with memories.

'The first time we were alone together . . .'

She looked at him.

'It was in the street one evening,' he said. 'I took your arm. You leaned on me more and more. I gradually felt the whole weight of your body, I felt your growing flesh. The world was swarming with people, but our solitude seemed to be spreading. Everything around us was changing into a wondrously simple wilderness . . . It seemed to me that the two of us had begun walking on the sea.'

'Ah!' she said. 'How kind you were! That first evening of ours, you didn't have the same expression you had later, even at the best moments . . .'

'We chatted about this and that, and while I held you close to me, like flowers, you said things to me about the people we knew, you spoke to me about the sunshine of the day and the cool of the evening. But in fact you were telling me that you were coming to me . . . I could sense the words of admission through your words, and if you didn't say them to me, you gave them to me.

'Oh, how great things are at the beginning! There is never anything petty about a beginning . . .

'Once when we had met in the park, and I was walking you home through the suburbs in the late afternoon, the road was so silent and peaceful that it was as if our footsteps were disturbing the whole of Nature. The gentle calm slowed down our pace. I bent down and kissed you.'

'There,' she said.

She placed her forefinger on her neck. This gesture lit up her neck like a ray of sunshine.

'Little by little, the kiss became more passionate. It circled around your lips and settled on them: the first time by mistake, the second time pretending that it was by mistake . . . Gradually, under my lips I felt . . .'

He spoke in a whisper:

'Your lips parting, and opening . . .'

She bowed her head, and I could see her mouth, a dewy rosebud.

'All that,' she sighed, returning once again to her sweet, pathetic preoccupation, 'was so beautiful, in the midst of the prison watch that was being kept on me!'

How badly she needed the excitement of memory, unconsciously or not! The evocation of the old dramas and perils called forth her gestures, resuscitated her love. That was why she had told her story.

And he was impelling her towards the madness of love. Their early ardour was being reborn, and now their words were looking for the most poignant memories before turning into deeds.

'It was sad when, the day after the day you became mine, I saw you again at your house, at a reception—inaccessible, surrounded by people. An accomplished hostess, as gracious to one person as to another, and a little shy, you distributed common-place words to everyone, you casually lent us all—me like the rest—the beauty of your face.

'You were wearing that very bright green dress of yours, and everyone was teasing you about it . . . I remembered, while you were passing and I didn't dare to follow you with my eyes, how mad we had been in our first raptures. I told myself: "I have had the great necklace of her bare legs round my neck; I have held her supple, rigid body in my arms; I have caressed her until I drew blood." I had a feeling of triumph, but it was not a calm triumph, because at that moment I wanted you and I could not have you. Our embrace had been, and no doubt would be, but it was not, and although the treasure of your body belonged to me, I was a poor man at that moment. Besides, when a man lacks something, who knows if he will have it again?'

'No,' she sighed, in the growing beauty of her memories, of her thoughts, of her whole soul, 'love isn't what people say it is! I too suffered anguished torments. How carefully I had to hide my feelings, concealing every sign of happiness, hurriedly lock-ing it up in my heart! At the beginning, I didn't dare to fall asleep for fear of saying your name in my dreams, and often, shaking off the approaching madness of sleep, I would prop myself up on my elbows and lie there with my eyes open, heroically watch-ing over my heart.

'I was afraid of being recognized. I was afraid that someone would see the purity in which I was bathed. Yes, purity. When, in the midst of life, you wake up from life, when you see a new brightness in the daylight, when you recreate everything, I call that purity.'

◐

'Do you remember that mad cab-race across Paris—the day he thought he recognized us from a distance, and jumped into an-other cab which set off in pursuit of ours?'

She gave a start of excitement and ecstasy.

'Oh, yes!' she murmured. 'That was the wonderful time!'

He spoke in a trembling voice, a voice mingled with his heart-beats, and his heart said:

'Kneeling on the seat, you looked out of the rear-window while I caressed your body, with my hands inside you. You kept crying out: "He's getting nearer . . . He's falling behind . . . We've lost him . . . Ah!"'

And in a single movement their lips came together.

She said in a whisper:

'That was the only time I have ever come.'

'We shall always be afraid,' he said.

Their words were drawing closer together, embracing, turning into kisses, whispered by their flesh. He was hungry for her; he was drawing her towards him, his mouth summoning her with all its might. Their hands were motionless, all their life rising to their lips. And everything else vanished in the face of this desire of theirs reconstructed by the spirit of evil.

Yes, they had to resuscitate their past in order to love each other; they had to reassemble it continuously, piece by piece, to prevent their love from being destroyed by habit—as if they were enduring, in darkness and dust and icy enfeeblement, the oppression of old age and the imprint of death.

They clasped each other tightly. The pale patches of their faces came together. I could not tell them apart, but I had the impression that I could see them better, for I understood the great inner motive of their coupling.

They were shutting themselves up in the night; they were falling, falling into the shadowy gulf they had chosen; they were sinking into the darkness which they had sought and implored here on earth.

He stammered:

'I shall always love you.'

But she and I knew very well that he was lying as he had lied a little earlier; there was no deceiving us. But what did it matter? What did it matter?

With her lips on his, she murmured like a piercing caress inside a caress:

'He will be here soon.'

How little they were united! Only their terror was common to them both, and I could understand why they fanned it so desperately . . . But their immense effort to partake in something together was about to achieve success.

At the approach of the dark festival, the woman was assuming a sublime importance, and her face which was smiling and weeping with shadow was taking on an expression of supreme resignation.

There were no more words; these had done their work of renewal . . . There were only embraces and flesh, the great ceremony of silent ardour which was beginning; sighs, clumsy gestures, human sounds of materials.

She was standing now; she was half-undressed; she had become white . . . Was it she who was undressing, or was it he who was divesting her of things? . . . I could see her broad thighs, her silvery belly in the room like the moon in the night . . . There was a thick black line across that belly: the man's arm. He was holding her, clasping her, as he clung to the divan. And his mouth was near the mouth of her sex, and they drew together for a monstrously tender kiss. I saw the dark body kneeling before the pale body—and she was gazing fervently down at him . . .

Then, in a radiant voice, she murmured:

'Take me . . . Take me once again after so many other times. My body belongs to you and I give it to you. Why shouldn't I? It doesn't belong to me. That is why I offer it to you so joyfully.'

Now he had stretched her out on his knees . . . I had the impression that she was naked; I couldn't make out lines and shapes very well. But her head was thrown back in the light from the window, and I could see that evening face in which the eyes were shining, in which the mouth was shining too like the eyes, that face starlit with love . . .

He pulled her on to him, the naked man in the darkness. Even in the midst of their mutual consent, there was a sort of struggle; the atmosphere was one of extraordinary emotion, at once savage and holy, and, although I saw nothing, I knew the moment when his flesh entered the woman's.

. . . My prolonged immobility was torturing the muscles in my back and shoulders, but I flattened myself against the wall, pressing my eyes to the hole; I crucified myself to enjoy the cruel, solemn sight. I drank in that vision with my whole face, I embraced it with my whole body. And the wall seemed to echo the sound of my heartbeats.

. . . The two creatures locked in each other's arms were trembling like two entwined trees. Pleasure, going beyond the law, beyond everything, even the lovers' sincerity, was frantically preparing its sweet masterpiece. And it was such a frenzied, wild, fateful movement that I realized that even God could not stop what was happening, unless he killed his creatures. Nothing could stop it, and that makes one doubt the power and even the existence of a God.

Above the entanglement of their bodies he raised his head and threw it back, and there was just enough light left for me to see his face, the mouth open in a broken, sing-song groan, waiting for the approaching pleasure.

It came, overwhelming, indescribable. I felt it coming like an event.

I counted up to four. During that fragment of time I did not take my eyes off the face of the man who was there before me, beating the air with one hand, his body slavering. He was grimacing, smiling, dark with blood, like a divine martyr, an archangel wallowing and soaring at the same time. He was uttering staccato cries of surprise, as if he were dazzled by something magnificent and unexpected, as if he had not expected it to be so beautiful, as if he were astonished by the prodigies of joy which his body contained.

Now they were communicating together. Perhaps she was not experiencing any pleasure, but I could tell, I could see, I could feel that she was taking pleasure in his: and therein lies an ineffable feminine miracle.

'Are you happy?'

I had the extraordinary impression that it was I whom she was addressing . . . I was right in a sense. Since I was close to her bare lips, it was to me that she was speaking.

His eyes cast upwards, still chained to her by the flesh, he murmured:

'I swear that this is everything in the world to me!'

Then, immediately afterwards, as she sensed that the moment of happiness was over and had already ceased to live except in memory, that the ecstasy which had settled between them for a moment was going to escape, and that her illusions were going to vanish and abandon her, she said almost plaintively:

'May God bless what little pleasure we have!'

A pathetic cry, the first sign of a great fall; a blasphemous prayer, but none the less a divine prayer . . .

The man repeated automatically:

'Everything in the world to me! . . .'

. . . The carnal group subsided. The man was seated. With my own eyes I gradually saw a feeling of regret, of remorse, harass him and draw him away from the burden of the woman who did not understand this withdrawal from her flesh: unlike him, she was not all of a sudden emptied and rid of pleasure.

But she could feel that he had not sought or looked any further than that and that he had reached the end of his dream . . . Already she was probably thinking that one day it would be over for her too and that a destiny begun again would be no better than the first.

And at that moment when it seemed to me, in my eagerness as an almost creative visionary, that I could follow this ebb-tide of distress on their faces, in the air still full of the words 'This is everything in the world to me,' he groaned:

'Oh, it's nothing, it's nothing!'

Strangers to one another, they were visited by the same thought.

. . . While she was still resting completely on him, I saw his neck twist and his eyes turn towards the clock, towards the door, towards escape. Then, when his mistress's mouth was close to his, his face drew gently away from it (I was the only one to see this) with a slight grimace of distaste, almost of disgust: he had been touched by a breath tainted by all the kisses recently shut up in that mouth as in a coffin.

Only now did she proffer, with her poor mouth, the answer to what he had said before possessing her:

'No, you won't love me for ever. You will leave me. But in spite of that, I regret nothing and will regret nothing. When, after "us," I return to the great sadness which, this time, will not let me go again, I shall say to myself: "I have had a lover!" and I shall emerge from my nothingness to be happy for a moment.'

He did not want to, indeed could not very well, make any further reply. He stammered:

'Why don't you trust me?'

But they turned their eyes towards the window. They were frightened, they were cold. They were looking at a last vestige of twilight, in the hollow between two houses, disappearing like a fire-ship.

It seemed to me that the window beside them was coming on to the scene. They were gazing at it, pale, huge, dispelling everything around it. And after the sickening carnal tension and the disgusting brevity of their pleasure, they remained crushed as it were by an apparition, before the immaculate blue and the light unstained by blood. Then their gazes returned to one another.

'You see, we stay here,' she said, 'looking at each other like the two poor animals we are.'

Their hands untwined, their caresses parted and collapsed, their flesh drooped. They drew away from each other. The movement cast her against the side of the divan.

He sat on a chair, sad-faced, his legs apart, his trousers un-buttoned, panting slowly, soiled by all the pleasure which had died and gone cold.

His mouth was half-open, his features drawn, his eye-sockets and his jaw prominent. It was as if he had grown thinner in a few moments and I had the eternal skeleton before me. He gave the impression of making an immense, painful, laborious effort. He seemed to be crying out and remaining silent, in the depths of the dusty evening.

And the two of them resembled each other at last in the midst of things, in their misery no less than in their human features.

. . . I could not see them any more in the darkness. It had finally swallowed them up. Indeed I was astonished that I had been able to see them until then. The frenzied ardour of their bodies and souls must have cast a sort of light over the group they had formed.

◖

Where is God, then, where is God? Why doesn't he intervene in the appalling regular crisis? Why doesn't he prevent by some miracle the horrifying miracle by which what is adored becomes suddenly or slowly hated? Why doesn't he save man from the quiet bereavement of all his dreams, and also from the distress of that pleasure which bursts forth from his flesh and falls back on him like spittle?

Possibly because I am a man like that one, like the rest, possibly because what is bestial and violent tends to monopolize my attention just now, I am horrified above all else by the inescapable defeat of the flesh.

'It is everything! It is nothing!' The echo of those two cries, which were not screamed out but uttered in a low, barely audible voice, resounds in my ears. Who can ever tell of the grandeur of them, and the distance which separates them?

Who can ever tell of it? Above all, who will ever know of it? You have to be placed like myself above mankind, you have to be at once among human beings and separated from them, in order to see an embrace break up, a smile turn into a death-agony, joy become satiety. For when you are in the midst of life, you don't see those things, you don't know anything of them; you pass blindly from one extreme to another. The man who uttered those two cries which I can still hear: 'Everything! Nothing!' had forgotten the first when he was carried away by the second.

Who can ever tell of it? I would like somebody to do so. What do the words matter, or the proprieties, or the age-old habit of talent and genius of stopping on the threshold of such descriptions, as if they were prohibited from going any further? Somebody must tell of it in a poem, in a masterpiece, describing it all, to the very depths, if only to show the creative power of our hopes and dreams, which, while they shine forth, transform the world and overwhelm reality.

What richer gift could anybody bestow on these two lovers when, once again, their joy has died between them? For this scene is not the last in their dual story. They will begin again, like all who live. Once again they will try by means of each other, as best they may, to defend themselves against the defeats of life, to exalt themselves, to avoid dying: once again they will seek, in their mingled bodies, a relief and a liberation . . . They will be caught up again by the great mortal vibration, by the force of the sin which clings to the flesh like a scrap of flesh. And once again the fulfillment of their dream and of the genius of their desire will postpone parting and make them doubt its existence, will uplift all that is base, will perfume all that is foul, will sanctify the darkest and most accursed parts of their bodies, which also serve the dark accursed functions, and will invest them for a moment with all the consolation in the world.

And then again and again, when they see that they have vainly sought the infinite in desire, they will be punished for their noble aspirations.

Oh, I don't regret having exposed this simple awe-inspiring secret; perhaps my only title to fame will be to have witnessed and contemplated this sight in all its grandeur, and to have realized that the living truth was sadder and more grandiose than I had hitherto been capable of believing.

S I X

Everything fell silent. They left; they went off to hide somewhere else. I didn't really understand. Did I even really know what they said?

The room was alone . . . I prowled around my own. Then I dined, as in a dream, and went out, attracted by my fellow creatures.

Outside, steep, shuttered houses. The passers-by went away from me; everywhere I saw walls and faces.

A café in front of me. Its crude lighting invited me to go inside. That artificial brilliance appealed to me, reassured me, and yet bewildered me; sitting down, I half-closed my eyes.

Quiet, simple people, without any cares, and who didn't have, as I have, a sort of task to perform, were scattered about in groups.

All alone with a full glass in front of her, looking this way and that, was a whore with a painted face. She had a little bitch on her lap whose head poked out above the table and which amusingly solicited the glances and even the smiles of the passers-by for her mistress.

This woman gazed at me with interest. She saw that I wasn't waiting for anybody, that I wasn't waiting for anything.

A gesture, a word, and she, who was waiting for everybody, would come forward, smiling with her whole body. But that wasn't what I wanted. I was simpler than that. I didn't need a woman. If I was disturbed by contact with love, it was on account of a lofty thought and not of an instinct.

She came over to me. She didn't know what sort of person I was. I turned my head away. What did I care about the quick, coarse ecstasy, the sexual comedy? I enjoyed a view over humanity, over men and women, and I knew what they did.

The smell of coffee and tobacco, combined with the warm air, produced a drowsy atmosphere. The sounds of the café—the clatter of a saucer, the opening and shutting of the street door, a card-player's exclamation—merged together. The faces were lit by a greenish glow. Mine must have been more impressive than the rest: it must have appeared ravaged by the pride of having seen, and by the urge to see more.

. . . Earlier on, he had called her 'Aimée.' I didn't know whether that was her name or a declaration of love. I didn't know the names, I didn't know the details, I didn't know anything of that sort. Mankind showed me its innermost secrets; I spelt out the depths of life; but I felt lost on the surface of the world. I had had to make an effort, just before, to slip in between the passers-by, to sit down in this public place, and to ask for what I wanted.

. . . I thought I recognized the silhouette of one of the other residents at my hotel, passing along the street, past the window of the café. I drew back quickly. I was in no condition to chat about this and that; later on, I would resume that dismal habit. I bowed my head, with my elbows on the table and my hands in my hair, to avoid being recognized by the people who knew me, if any of them should happen to pass by.

◐

Now I was walking through the streets. A woman passed me. Automatically I followed her . . . She was wearing a dark-blue dress and a big black hat; she was so distinguished that she seemed a little awkward in the street. She lifted her skirt rather clumsily and I could see her small boots fitting tightly round her slim legs in their sheer black stockings . . . Another woman passed me; I stared ardently into her face . . . Farther on, a grey feminine shape crossed the street; my heart started pounding as if it were waking up.

Curiosity? No, desire. A little earlier, I had had no desire; now, I was dazed with it . . . I stopped . . . I was a man like the rest; I had my appetites, my unspoken cravings; and in the grey street along which I was walking aimlessly, I felt a longing to approach a woman's body.

. . . I pictured to myself the pure nudity of that little figure hugging the walls not far from me . . . She had dainty feet which I could scarcely see. She drew a shawl more tightly round her shoulders. She was holding a bundle. She was leaning forward, she was in such a hurry, as if, like a child, she were trying to outstrip herself. Under that poor shadow there was a body of light, which shone before my eyes in the murky gloom into which she was disappearing . . . I thought of the starry beauty she would have, of the radiance of her hair which was concealed and diminished under her skimpy hat, of the happy smile which she was hiding on her solemn face.

I stood rooted to the spot for a moment, motionless in the middle of the road. The ghost-woman is already far away. If I had met her gaze it would have been really painful. I could feel a puckering of my features which was disfiguring me, transfiguring me.

Up there on the top of a tram, a young girl was sitting; her dress rose a little and billowed out . . . From underneath, it must have been possible to see right inside her. But a traffic jam separated us. The tram moved on, vanished like a nightmare.

Wherever I turned, the street was full of dresses, swaying, offering themselves, so light that they nearly took flight at the edges; dresses which looked as if they were going to fly up but didn't.

In the depths of a tall narrow mirror in a shop-window, I saw myself walking forward, a little pale, with rings round my eyes. It wasn't one woman that I wanted, it was all of them, and I looked for them, all around me, one by one. They passed by and went off, after seeming to approach me.

Defeated, I obeyed my instincts, at random. I followed a woman who was watching for me from her corner. Then we walked side by side. We exchanged a few words; she took me home. On the landing, when she opened the door, I was shaken by a fit of idealism. Then I went through the commonplace scene. It passed as quickly as a fall.

◗

Now I am back on the pavement. I am not feeling any calmer, as I hoped I would. A terrible bewilderment comes over me: it is as if I can no longer see things as they are; I see too far and I see too many things.

What is the matter with me? I sit down on a bench, tired out, exhausted by my own weight. It starts raining again. The passers-by hurry along, becoming scarcer, and then it is all streaming umbrellas, gutters overflowing, roadways and pavements black and shining, a vast half-silence, all the mournful paraphernalia of rain . . .

The trouble with me is that I have a dream bigger and more disturbing than I can bear. Woe to them who think about what they lack! They are in the right, but they are too much in the right, and consequently they are unnatural. The simple, the weak, the humble, pass unconcernedly by what is not for them; they brush past everything and everybody without so much as a hint of anguish (although even those little souls want little things, minute by minute). But it's a different matter for the rest, for me!

Wanting to take what one lacks . . . stealing . . . It has been enough for me to see a few human beings struggling in the depths of their reality to become convinced that man moves in that direction as surely as the earth moves in its own.

Unfortunately, I haven't only learnt this appalling, simple truth: I have been caught up in it, infected by it. My own desire is growing wider and stronger; I should like to live every life, lie heavy on every heart, and it seems to me that whatever is not for me is withdrawing from me, and that I am alone, deserted.

And huddled on this bench, in the vast empty street awash with rain, lashed by every squall of wind, hunching my shoulders to shelter myself more, I am in despair because I love everything as if I were overflowing with kindness.

Oh, now I begin to see how I am going to be punished for penetrating the raw secrets of mankind. My punishment will be made to fit my offence. I shall suffer all the infinite misery which I discover in others. I shall be punished in every mystery which remains silent, in every woman who passes by.

The infinite is not what people think. People tend to see it in the poetic soul of some legendary or literary hero; they clothe the extraordinary extravagance of some romantic Hamlet with it as if it were a theatrical costume . . . The infinite lives quietly in that man whose dim reflection I saw earlier on in the café window, and in myself as people see me, with my commonplace features and my ordinary name, longing for everything I lack . . . For there is no reason why this should stop; I am treading step by step the path of the infinite, and this progress without any horizon is akin to the stars in the sky. I raise anguished eyes towards them. I am miserable. If I have committed an offence, this misery of mine, full of the sorrow of the impossible, redeems me. But I don't believe in redemption, in all that moral and religious rubbish. I am miserable, and doubtless I look like a martyr.

I must go back to live out this martyrdom to its full extent, to its full pathetic extent; I must go on contemplating. I ma wasting my time here in everybody's space. I turn back towards the room which opens up like a human being.

●

I spent two empty days, looking without seeing.

I had hurriedly resumed my round of calls and succeeded, not without difficulty, in obtaining a few more days' respite, in making people forget me.

I remained between these walls, feverishly calm, and as un-occupied as a prisoner. I walked up and down my room for much of the day, attracted by the opening in the wall, and not daring to leave it any more.

The long hours went by, and by the evening I was exhausted by my tireless hope.

During the night of the second day I awoke suddenly. With a shudder I found myself outside the narrow refuge of my bed; my room was as cold as the streets. I drew myself up against the wall which, to my trembling hands, felt dead and icy.

I looked. The moonlight was pouring into the next room, whose shutters were not closed like mine. I remained standing in the same place, still full of sleep, hypnotized by that bluish light, not clearly aware of anything but the cold . . . Nothing . . . I felt as lonely as somebody who has been praying.

Then a storm which had been threatening at the end of the day finally broke. Drops of rain started falling, and the wind came in sudden drawn-out gusts. Rumbles of thunder shook the sky.

Every minute the rain became heavier, the wind blew more

gently and steadily. The moon was hidden by the clouds. Around me there was complete darkness.

The register in front of the fireplace trembled, then fell silent. And, without knowing why I had awoken and why I was standing there, I remained in the presence of that endless darkness, of the whole night, of the world which was like a wall before me.

◐

Then, into the black emptiness, there stole a tiny sound . . .

Probably some distant noise of the storm. No . . . a murmur quite close to me; a murmur, or a sound of footsteps.

Somebody . . . somebody was there . . . At last! The instinct which had snatched me from the embrace of my bed had not been mistaken.

I strained my eyes desperately, but the darkness was impenetrable. At the very most the window was tinged with blue in the dense gloom, and even then I didn't know if it was the window or whether I was imagining it.

◐

The sound came again, slightly more drawn-out . . .

Footsteps—yes, footsteps . . . He was walking about . . . Then came a breath, some objects being moved around, furtive, indefinable sounds, broken by silences, which seemed to have no reason.

The next moment, I had doubts . . . I wondered if it hadn't been an hallucination, an imaginary buzzing created by the pounding of my heart.

But like a divine reassurance the sound of a human voice reached my ears.

◐

How low that voice was at first, above all how curiously monotonous! It seemed to be reciting a litany or a poem. I held my breath so as not to banish that approach of life . . .

. . . It split into two . . . Now there were two voices answering each other. They were overflowing with an ineffable sadness like all voices kept very low . . . a musical sadness . . .

No doubt I had another two lovers before me, who had taken refuge for a few moments in the empty room. Two human beings attracted by each other were there in that compact solitude, in that colourless abyss; and, although I was incapable of making them out, I could feel them growing excited like my heart in my breast.

I searched for the lost couple. The whole of my attention groped towards those two bodies. In vain. The night entered my eyes and blinded me; the more I looked, the more the darkness hurt me. At one moment, however, I thought I saw a figure take shape, very dark, against the dark window . . . It stopped . . . No . . . the night; the shadows as motionless as an idol . . . What were they, those living creatures, what were they doing, where were they, where were they?

●

And all of a sudden I heard coming from the mass of shadows a distinct word, a word in human form, the word: 'Again!'

'Again!' That word came from their flesh. It showed them to me at last. It seemed to me that their faces, emerging from the mist, were stripped bare.

Then, in the midst of hurried stammering, in the midst of a sort of struggle, another exclamation burst forth, uttered in a muffled, happy voice:

'If they knew! If they knew!'

And these words were repeated with a restrained passion, in an ever lower voice, until there was complete silence.

Then they came out, very loud, in a burst of laughter. And the sound of a kiss spread throughout the room, covering everything. In the midst of the heaped-up shadows, that kiss emerged like an apparition.

◐

A flash of lightning shone, transforming the room for a fraction of a second into a pale refuge; then the black night returned.

The flash of electricity had raised my eyelids which I instinctively kept half-closed, since my eyes were useless. My gaze had invaded the room, but I had seen nothing living . . . Had the two people it contained huddled in some corner, then, concealing themselves even in the dark?

They did not seem to have noticed the sheet of lightning. With heartbreaking regularity the same words assailed me, but heavier, rarer, fainter:

'If they knew! If they knew!'

And I listened to that cry, bending over them with devout attention, as over a dying couple.

◐

Why that perpetual fear which was shaking them and trembling in their voices? What desperate reason had they for being alone and hidden, for uttering that pitiful cry of pride which resembled a cry for help? What abominable crime were they committing? What vice was concealed in their embrace?

I received a sharp stab in the heart. The two voices were too similar. I understood: these were two women, two lovers who came in the night to join in a strange union.

◐

Oh, how I listened! . . . Never had I pressed so hard upon the night, and it was really with my whole life that, with folded hands and empty eyes, I questioned the dark lovers who lay there in the bed of shadows . . .

I could feel that a tremulous apotheosis had taken hold of them:

'God can see us! God can see us!' stammered one of the mouths.

They too needed God to see them, in order to become more beautiful; like those in distress, they were imploring his help!

●

. . . I doubt now whether they are two women. I have the impression of having caught the deep sound of a male voice. I listen, I compare, I turn over these scraps of voices, trying once again, in a supreme effort, to rid myself of the darkness.

Now I distinctly hear the ardent prayer which is beginning to open out, very quietly, the words pressed one on top of another, crushed by two mouths, moistened, drenched with the blood of kisses.

'Do you want to? Do you want to?'

And the question assumes an immense, trembling importance, the question of a whole person being offered, open or rigid with desire.

Then a great voice rises with the beat of a wing:

'Yes.'

'Ah!' stammers the other body.

What strange, mysterious means are they using to know each other and touch each other? What form does this couple have?

What form? What does the form of love matter? I abandon this anxiety, and it seems to me that the whole tragedy of love is promptly revealed to me.

They love each other; the rest is nothing. Whether they are normal or depraved, whether they are blessed or accursed, they love each other and possess each other as far as that is possible on this earth.

They hide from everyone else after summoning each other; they roll in the shadows as in sheets or shrouds; they shut themselves up; they hate and shun the daylight as if it were a punishment inflicted by decency and peace. 'If they knew!' they cried, wept and laughed; they pride themselves on their solitude, whip themselves with it, caress themselves with it. They have hurled themselves outside the law, outside nature, outside normal life composed of sacrifice and emptiness. They try to come together; their marble brows collide. Each is preoccupied with his body, each feels himself embracing a body devoid of thought. Oh, what does the sex matter of their hands groping for sleeping pleasure, of their two mouths seizing upon each other, of their two hearts so blind and silent?

All the lovers in the world are alike: they fall in love by chance; they see each other, and are attached to each other by the features of their faces; they illuminate each other by the fierce preference which is akin to madness; they assert the reality of illusions; and for a moment they change falsehood into truth.

Just now, I heard a few fragments of their confidences:

'You are mine, you are mine . . . I possess you, I take you . . .'

'Yes, I am yours!'

Here is love in its entirety; here it is, close to me, sending into my face, like incense, with its to-and-fro motion, the smell and warmth of life, and performing its task of madness and sterility.

◑

The dialogue begins again, quieter and calmer, and I hear it as if it were being addressed to me.

First of all a trembling phrase passes by as in a dream:

'I adore our nights, I dislike our days.'

And the voice continues, slowly, listlessly giving reasons, in a gentle, satisfied tone, the words occasionally mingling and losing their shape, the two mouths as close together as two lips:

'During the day we dissipate and waste ourselves. It's at night that we can really offer ourselves.'

'Oh,' says the other voice, 'how I wish that we could make love during the day.'

'That may come . . . Later on, though, later on.'

The words linger on in a long, distant echo.

Then the voice says:

'Soon . . .'

'Heavens!' says the other, with a shudder of hope.

I have already heard an identical complaint—it is the same one, as if there were few subjects for complaint on earth—when the adulterous wife groaned: 'I who would have loved a destiny in the broad daylight!'

Now, in phrases whose beginnings I can't make out and which I can't link together, they talk about sunlit bowers, about parks with dark lawns and broad golden paths, and about large, curved, ornamental pools so bright and sparkling at noon that nobody can look at them any more than at the sun.

Lost in the darkness, shadows themselves, they create light; they think about the daylight, they take it for themselves, and it is a sort of monument of summer skies which emerges from them.

And the more they talk about sunshine, the lower and fainter their voices become.

After a more solemn and tender silence I hear these words:

'If you knew how beautiful love makes you, how your smile lights up your face.'

All the rest fades away, and I can no longer see anything but that smile.

Now the melody of their dream changes in character though not in clarity. They talk about drawing-rooms, mirrors, and lamps wreathed with flowers . . . They talked about parties given at night on the supple water covered with boats and coloured balloons—red, blue, green—like women's parasols in the sunshine in a park.

Once again a pause, then one of them continues in a tone of entreaty, revealing an immense obsession, an immense longing to fulfil their dream, almost to the point of madness:

'I feel feverish. It is as if I had sunshine on my hands.'

●

And the next moment, in a rush of words:

'You are crying! Your cheek is as moist as your lips.'

'We shall never have all that,' groans one of the voices. 'We shall never have that light except in the dreams we have at night, when we are together.'

'We shall have it!' cries the other. 'One day, all this sadness will come to an end.'

The voice adds superbly:

'We almost have it. You know that for yourself!'

'Oh, if they knew!' they continue, with a sort of remorse that others shouldn't know. 'They would all be jealous of us, even lovers, even people who are happy!'

Once again they say that God can see them.

This group of shadows, carved out of the shadows, dreams of God discovering them and touching them with light. Their entwined souls live more deeply and more nobly. I catch this word: 'Always!'

Crushed, reduced to nothingness, these creatures whom I imagine crawling up and down each other under the sheets like grubs said: 'Always.' They uttered the superhuman word, the extraordinary, supernatural word.

All hearts are identical with their creation. The mind full of
mystery, the blood of the night hours, and desire akin to darkness, utter their cry of victory. Lovers, when they clasp each
other, fight each for himself, and say: 'I love you'; they wait,
weep and suffer, and say: 'We are happy'; they let go of each
other, already faltering, and say: 'Always!' It is as if, in the depths
to which they have sunk, they, like Prometheus, had stolen the
fire of heaven.

And I go looking for them, breath to breath . . . How I should
love to see them at this moment! I want that as much as I want
to live: to discover the gestures, the rebellion, the paradise, the
faces, from which all this is coming. But I can't penetrate as far
as the truth. I can scarcely see the window in the distance, as
vague as a milky way, in the vast darkness of the room. I can no
longer hear any words but only a murmur from which I can't
tell whether these are words of consent exchanged once more,
or complaints torn from the open wound of their mouths.

Now the murmur itself ceases.

Perhaps, still clasped together, they have begun sleeping far
away from each other; perhaps they have left to dazzle themselves elsewhere with their unique treasure.

The storm, which I thought had fallen silent, begins again,
goes on.

◖

For a long time I fight against the darkness, but I am no match
for it, and it buries me. I collapse on my bed, and I stay there
in the darkness and the silence. I prop myself up on my elbows,
I spell out some prayers, I stammer: *'De profundis.'*

De profundis . . . Why does that cry of terrible hope, that cry
of misery, torment and terror rise tonight from my heart to my
lips?

It is the confession of all creatures. Whatever the words uttered by those of whose destiny I have caught a glimpse, that is what they were really crying out—and after these days and nights spent listening, that is what I hear.

That call from the abyss to the light, that effort by hidden truth to reach hidden truth, rises on all sides and falls back on all sides, and, haunted by mankind, I am still full of the sound of it.

For my part, I don't know what I am, where I am going, what I am doing, but I too have cried out, from the depths of my abyss to a little light.

S E V E N

The room is in the morning state of moist untidiness. Aimée is there with her husband. They have arrived from a journey.

I didn't hear them come in. I was probably too tired.

He has his hat on; he has sat down on a chair by the bed, which is not unmade, but where I can make out the long imprint of a body or of a couple.

She is dressing. I have just seen her disappear through the door of the dressing-room. I look at the husband, whose features strike me as possessing great regularity and even a certain nobility.

The line of the forehead is clear-cut; only the mouth and the moustache are a little common. He looks healthier and stronger than the lover. His hand, which is toying with a stick, is delicate, and his whole person is endowed with a certain forceful elegance. It is this man that she deceives and hates. It is this head, this face, this expression, that are spoilt and disfigured in her eyes, and are identified with her unhappiness.

Suddenly she is there; she arrives right in the centre of my field of vision. My heart stops, then grips me and draws me towards her.

She is half-naked: a mauve chemise, short and light, stretched and swollen by her breasts, clings gently to the curve of her belly as she walks.

She is coming back from the dressing-room, a little languid and weary of the countless trivialities she has already undertaken, a toothbrush in her hand, her lips all moist and red, her hair undone. Her legs are slim and pretty, her dainty feet steeply arched on the high, pointed heels of her shoes.

The room, which is in utter chaos, is full of a mixture of smells—soap, face-powder, the sharp scent of eau de Cologne—in the heavy atmosphere of the musty morning.

She has disappeared; she comes back warm and soapy; then, all fresh-looking, her face turning pink, she wipes away some little drops of water.

He is talking, explaining a business deal. He has half stretched out his legs. Sometimes he looks at her, sometimes he looks elsewhere.

'You know, the Bernards haven't agreed to the station contract . . .'

This time he follows her with his eyes while he speaks, then he looks away, gazes idly at the carpet, and clicks his tongue in disappointment, completely absorbed in his thoughts—while she goes to and fro, showing the curve of her hips, her sinewy back, her pale belly, and the dark shadow below her belly.

My temples are throbbing; all my flesh is straining towards this woman, almost naked and so lovely in the morning light and in the transparent garment which encloses the sweet smell of her . . . And I can still hear the echo of the husband's commonplace phrase, a phrase which is foreign to her, a phrase which is blasphemous in this room into which she has brought her nakedness.

She puts on her corset, her suspenders, her drawers, her petticoat. The man remains plunged in his brutish indifference; he returns to his thoughts.

. . . She has installed herself in front of the mantelpiece mirror, with some boxes and other things. The mirror in the dressing-room probably strikes her as inadequate for what she wants to do.

Beginning her toilet, she talks to herself, gay, loquacious, lively, because this is still the springtime of the day.

. . . And she works hard and exerts herself; she takes a long time over her appearance, but this time is important and not wasted. Besides, she is hurrying.

Now she goes to open a wardrobe, and takes out a frail, light dress which she holds out in her arms, like a nestful of birds.

She puts on this dress. Then all of a sudden an idea strikes her and her arms stop moving.

'No, definitely not,' she says.

She takes off her dress and goes to get something else to wear: a dark skirt and a chemisette.

She takes a hat, ruffles the ribbon on it a little, then holds the roses trimming this hat close to her face, in front of the mirror, and, doubtless satisfied, she starts humming to herself . . .

◐

. . . He doesn't look at her, and when he looks at her, he doesn't see her.

Oh, that is a serious matter! It's a tragedy, a dismal tragedy, but all the more distressing for that. This man is not happy, and yet I envy his happiness. What can you say to that, except that happiness is in ourselves, in each one of us, and that it is the desire for what we lack?

These two people are together, but in fact absent from each other; they have parted without parting. They are caught in a sort of web of nothingness. They will never come together again, since their dead love stands four-square between them. This silence, this mutual indifference are all that is cruellest on earth.

To love no more is worse than to hate, for, whatever people may say, death is worse than suffering.

I pity those who go through life two by two, chained together by indifference. I pity the poor heart which has what it has for so short a time; I pity the men who have a heart which no longer loves.

And, for a moment, faced with this simple, pitiful scene, I have endured a little of the vast, incalculable martyrdom of those who suffer more.

◐

She has finished dressing. She has put on a jacket of the same colour as her skirt, revealing a great deal of her bodice, the upper part of which is transparent and pink, right at the beginning and so to speak at the dawn of her body—and she leaves us.

He for his part gets ready to go off. The door opens again. Is it Aimée coming back? . . . No, it's the maid. She makes as if to withdraw.

'I was coming to do the room, but if I'm in your way . . .'

'You can stay.'

She moves some things about, closes some drawers . . . He has raised his head, is watching her out of the corner of his eye.

He has stood up, is approaching clumsily, as if fascinated . . . A stamping of feet, a shriek drowned by a coarse laugh; she drops her brush and the dress which she was holding. . . . He seizes her from behind, his hands gripping the girl's breasts through her bodice.

'Oh, no! What's got into you?'

He makes no reply, his face masked with blood, his eyes staring blindly; at the most he has given an inarticulate cry, the mute utterance in which only the body speaks; from his inflamed lips, drawn back tightly over his teeth, comes a machine-like breath

. . . He has clutched hold of this flesh, his belly pressed against this rump, like a sort of monkey, like a kind of lion.

Her big ruddy face creases into a laugh; her hair, half undone, falls over her forehead; her buxom breasts are pushed in by the clenched fingers gripping her.

He tries to pull at her skirt, to lift it. She squeezes her legs together and presses her hands against her thighs to keep her dress in place. She is only partly successful. I catch a glimpse of the wrinkled stockings on her thick round legs, a bit of her chemise, her old shoes. They trample on Aimée's dress which the girl has dropped and which has fallen gently to the floor.

Then she decides that this has lasted long enough.

'Now, that's enough, my lad! Lay off!'

As he still says nothing, simply pushing his jaw towards the nape of her neck, like the maw of desire, she loses her temper:

'No, stop it! Lay off, I tell you!'

. . . He has ended up by letting go of her, and he goes off laughing a diabolic laugh, full of shame and effrontery, almost staggering as he walks, under the impulse of a great inner force.

He goes off among the women passing by, his eyes obsessed with a nightmare which throws their skirts up over their heads.

The sap is rising in him and wants to burst out. If what is obsessing him is not released, it will go to his head like a mother's milk. There he goes, that casual progenitor, groping forward with his arms held out for an embrace, eaten away by a wound which is coming to a head, stumbling towards a bed, strong in the weight of his body.

But he is not impelled simply by a powerful instinct, since a little while ago an exquisite woman was moving about in front of him (and the light playing in her ethereal veils showed the whole of her body in a radiant halo), and he did not desire her.

Perhaps she would have refused to give herself; perhaps some

pact had been concluded between them . . . But I saw quite
clearly that his very eyes didn't want her: those eyes which lit up
as soon as that girl appeared, that ignoble Venus with dirty hair
and muddy fingernails, and which were filled with hunger for
her.

Because he doesn't know her, because she is different from
the woman he knows. To have what one lacks . . . So, strange
though it may seem, it is an idea, a lofty, eternal idea, which
directs instinct. It is an idea which, in front of an unknown
woman, rouses a man like that, like a wild beast, watching her
with rapt attention, with eyes like claws, driven by a passion as
tragic as if he needed to murder her to live.

I understand, I to whom it is given to survey these human
crises—crises so frenzied that God seems useless beside them—
I understand that many things which we place outside ourselves
are within us, and that that is the secret. When the veils fall,
what simple truths appear, how simple things are seen to be!

◑

Lunch at the common table has a magical attraction for me at
first: I examine every face in an attempt to catch out the two
human beings who made love together last night.

But however closely I scrutinize the faces around me, two by
two, trying to discover a point of resemblance, I find nothing to
guide me. I cannot recognize them any more than I could when
they were plunged in utter darkness.

. . . There are five girls or young women. One of them, at
least, holds the living, burning memory of last night imprisoned
in her body. But a will stronger than mine keeps her face in-
scrutable. I don't know, and I am appalled by the nothingness
offered to my eyes.

They have left one by one. I don't know . . . I clench my fists in the infinity of uncertainty and clasp emptiness between my fingers; my face, precise and well-defined, is confronted with everything that is possible, with everything that is vague, with everything.

◖

That lady over there! I recognize Aimée. She is talking to the proprietress, near the window. I didn't see her at first, because of the other people between us.

She is eating some grapes, quite daintily, with somewhat affected gestures.

I turn towards her. She is called Madame Montgeron or Montgerot. This name strikes me as curious. Why should she be called Montgeron or Montgerot? It seems to me that this name doesn't suit her or that it serves no useful purpose. I am struck by the artificial character of words and signs.

It is the end of the meal. Nearly everybody has left. The coffee cups and the sticky liqueur glasses are scattered about on the table, where a ray of sunshine is dappling the cloth and making the glassware sparkle. A pungent stain of spilt coffee is drying up.

I join in the conversation between her and Madame Lemercier. She looks at me. I scarcely recognize her gaze, which I have seen in its entirety.

The waiter comes up and whispers a few words to Madame Lemercier. She gets up, excuses herself, and leaves the room. I am sitting beside Aimée, having come over to her a few minutes ago. There are only two or three other people in the dining-room, discussing how they are going to spend the afternoon.

I don't know what to say to this lady. The conversation between us languishes and dies. She must imagine that she doesn't interest me—this woman whose heart I can see, and whose destiny I know as well as God could know it.

She reaches out for a newspaper lying on the table, becomes engrossed in it for a moment, then folds it up, gets up in her turn, and leaves the room.

Disgusted by the banality of life, and dulled by the hour, I drowsily lean my elbows on the table, the endless, sunlit, vanishing table, making an effort not to lower my arms, drop my chin and close my eyelids.

And in this untidy room, already discreetly besieged by servants in a hurry to clear away and lay the table for dinner, I remain almost on my own, not knowing whether I am very happy or very unhappy, not knowing what is real and what is supernatural.

Then, slowly, dully, I begin to understand . . . I glance around me, I gaze at everything which is quiet and simple, then I close my eyes, and I say to myself, like one of the elect gradually becoming aware of his revelation:

'But the infinite is here: I can't doubt that any more.' It becomes clear to me that there is nothing strange in this world: the supernatural doesn't exist, or rather it is everywhere. It is in reality, in simplicity, in peace. It is here, between these walls which are waiting with the whole of their weight. The real and the supernatural are the same thing.

There can no more be any mystery in life than there can be any more space in the sky.

I, who am like other men, am steeped in the infinite. But how vague and confused all that seems to me! And I think about myself, about myself who can neither know myself well nor get rid of myself; about myself who am like a heavy shadow between my heart and the sun.

EIGHT

The same setting surrounded them, the same twilight darkened them as on the first occasion I saw them together. Aimée and her lover were sitting side by side, not very far from me.

They had probably been talking for some time when I bent down to listen to them.

She was behind him, on the sofa, hidden by the shadows of the evening and the shadow of the man. He, a pale, vague figure, with his hands on his knees, was leaning forward into space.

The night was still dressed in a grey, silky evening softness; soon it would be naked. It was going to come upon them like a sickness which may be fatal. I had the impression that they could sense this, that they were trying to defend themselves, that they would have liked to take precautions in word and thought against the fateful shadows.

They were in a hurry to talk about this and that, without enthusiasm, without interest. I heard names of people and places; they spoke of a station, of a public walk, of a flower-seller.

Suddenly she stopped, seemed to become sad, and buried her face in her hands.

He took hold of her wrists, with a melancholy slowness which showed how accustomed he was to her moments of weakness— and he spoke to her without knowing what to say, drawing as close to her as he could and stammering:

'Why are you crying? Tell me why you are crying.'

She made no reply; then she took her hands away from her eyes and looked at him.

'Why? How do I know?' she said. 'Tears aren't words.'

◐

I watched her crying, drenching herself with tears. It is an important experience to be in the presence of a thinking creature who is crying. A weak, broken creature who is crying creates the same impression as an omnipotent god whom one implores; for in its weakness and defeat it rises above the human condition.

A sort of superstitious admiration took hold of me at the sight of that woman's face bathed in the inexhaustible spring, that face which was at once sincere and truthful.

◐

She had stopped crying. She raised her head. Without his questioning her this time, she said:

'I am crying because everybody is alone in the world.

'Nobody can get out of himself; nobody can even admit anything; everybody is alone. Besides, everything passes, everything changes, everything escapes; and as soon as everything escapes, one is alone. There are some moments when I see that better than at others. And then, what could possibly prevent me from crying?'

In the melancholy into which she was sinking further every moment, she had a little burst of pride; on the mask of sadness I saw a smile appear like a gentle grimace.

'I am more sensitive than other people. Things which would go unnoticed by others have a considerable effect on me. And in these lucid moments when I look at myself, I see that I am alone, all alone, all alone.'

Uneasy at the sight of her growing distress, he tried to revive her spirits:

'We can't say that, we who have reshaped our destiny . . . You who have made a great show of willpower . . .'

But these words were carried away like wisps of straw.

'What's the use? Everything is useless. In spite of what I have tried to do, I am alone. Committing adultery won't change the face of things—however sweet the word itself may sound!

'It isn't through evil that one can attain happiness. It isn't through virtue either. Nor is it through that sacred fire of great instinctive decisions which is neither good nor evil. It isn't with any of those things that one can attain happiness; one never attains it.'

She stopped and, as if she could feel her destiny falling on her again, she said:

'Yes, I know that I have done wrong, that those who love me most would hate me in many ways if they knew. My mother, who is so indulgent, would be so unhappy if she knew. I know that our love is made up of the reprobation of all that is wise and just, and with my mother's tears. But this shame no longer serves any useful purpose! My mother, if she knew, would pity my happiness!'

He murmured in a faint voice: 'That's unkind of you . . .'

This was ignored as an insignificant remark.

She stroked the man's forehead with a light touch of her hand, and, in an unnaturally assured voice, said:

'You know perfectly well that I don't deserve that word. You know perfectly well that I am talking of more than ourselves.

'You know perfectly well, you know better than I do, that everybody is alone. One day when I was talking about the joy of living and you were imbued with sadness as I am today, you told me after looking at me that you didn't know what I was thinking, in spite of my words; that you couldn't be sure that the blood rising to my face wasn't a living rouge.

'All our thoughts, the greatest and the smallest, belong only to ourselves. Everything turns us in upon ourselves and condemns us to ourselves alone. You said that day: "There are things which you hide from me, and which I shall never know—even if you tell them to me." You showed me that love is only a sort of celebration of our solitude, and you ended up by crying out to me, as you engulfed me in your arms: "Our love is me!" And I returned the, alas, inevitable answer: "Our love is me!"'

He tried to say something. In a friendly, desperate gesture she put her hand on his mouth, and said in a louder, more trembling, more penetrating voice:

'Look here . . . Take me, squeeze my fingers, raise my eyelids, press the whole weight of your breast on mine; explore me with your hands or your flesh; kiss me for a long, long time, until you breathe with my mouth, until we can no longer tell our mouths apart; do what you like with me to come nearer, to come nearer . . . And then reply: "I am here to suffer. Can you feel my suffering?"'

He said nothing, and in the twilight shroud which enveloped them, vainly enfolding one on top of the other, I saw his head make the futile gesture of negation . . . I saw all the misery expressed by that couple which, for once, in the dark, couldn't lie any more.

It was true that they were there, and that there was nothing to unite them. There was an emptiness between them. However much people may talk, act, rebel, rise in fury, struggle and threaten, isolation defeats them. I could see that there was nothing to unite them, nothing.

◐

'Oh,' she said, 'let's not talk any more, let's never talk again about suffering and joy; it's really quite impossible to distinguish between them. But even the penetration of one mind by another is forbidden. There aren't two human beings in the world who speak the same language. At certain moments, for no particular reason, two people may draw together; then, for no adequate reason, they move far away from each other. They clash, they caress each other, they hurt each other, they mutilate each other; they laugh when they ought to weep, without ever being able to do anything about it. A couple is always mad. I didn't invent that phrase: you said it yourself. You who are so intelligent and know so much, you told me that two people talking together are two blind creatures face to face, and almost two mutes, and that two lovers clasped in each other's arms remain as foreign to each other as the wind and the sea. A personal interest, or a different orientation of feelings and ideas, a momentary weariness or, on the other hand, a sharp stab of desire, spoil concentration and prevent it from being absolutely pure. When you listen, you don't really hear; when you hear, you don't really understand. A couple is always mad.'

He seemed to be accustomed to these melancholy monologues, uttered in a monotonous voice, long litanies to the impossible. He no longer made any reply. He held her in his arms, rocked her to and fro, soothing her tenderly and cautiously. He seemed to be behaving with her as with a sick child whom one cares for without explaining anything to him . . . And like that, he was as far away from her as it was possible to be.

But he was disturbed by her nearness. Even dejected, downcast, desolate, she palpitated warmly against him; even wounded, she was a prey he desired. I saw the eyes he laid on her glisten while she gave herself up to her sadness in complete abandonment. He bent over her. What he wanted was her. The words she was saying he tossed aside; they were of no importance to him, they didn't caress him. He wanted her, her!

How separate they were! They were very much alike in thought and spirit, and at that moment they were helping each other intimately. But I, a spectator divorced from mankind and looking at them from above, could clearly see that they were strangers to each other, and that in spite of appearances they could neither see nor hear each other . . . She was sad and perhaps vaguely prompted by pride in persuading, while he was excited and lustful, tender and bestial. They answered each other as best they could, but they couldn't give in to each other and were trying to conquer each other; and this sort of terrible conflict tore my heart.

●

She understood his desire. She said in a plaintive voice, like a child caught out:

'I'm not well . . .'

Then she was gripped by a dismal frenzy. She threw aside, pulled up, tore open her clothes, freed herself from them as from a living prison, and offered herself to him, stripped and sacrificed, with her woman's wound and her heart.

. . . The great dark span of her clothes opened and closed.

Once again the mingling of bodies and the slow, rhythmical, endless caress took place. And once again I watched the man's face while he was preoccupied with his pleasure. Oh, it was obvious that he was alone!

He was thinking of himself, loving himself; his face, swollen with veins, gorged with blood, was in love with itself. He was working himself into a frenzy by means of the woman, a carnal instrument equal to himself. He was thinking of himself, marvelling at himself. He came with his whole body and his whole mind. His soul burst from him, lit up the whole of his face . . . He was completely carried away by joy . . . He murmured words of adoration; deified by her, he was blessing her.

They were not united because they quivered and swayed at

the same time, or because they had a little of their flesh in common. On the contrary, they were alone to the very end; both fell, neither knew where, lips and arms open. To come together was to be utterly separate.

●

Now they picked themselves up, freeing themselves from the dream which had suddenly weakened and flung them to the ground.

He was as dejected as she was. I bent forward to catch his words, as faint as a sigh. He said:

'If I had known!'

The two of them, prostrate but more suspicious of each other, with a crime between them in the heavy darkness, in the murk of the evening, seemed to drag themselves slowly towards the grey window cleansed by a little light.

How similar they were to what they had been the other evening. It *was* the other evening. Never before had I had so strongly the impression that all actions were vain and passed away like ghosts.

The man was affected by a fit of trembling. Conquered and stripped of all his pride, of all his masculine modesty, he no longer had the strength of mind to refrain from expressing shame and regret.

'We can't help it,' he stammered, bowing his head even further. 'It's the hand of fate.'

They took each other's hand and gave a faint shudder, breathing hard, their hearts pounding in their breasts.

The hand of fate!

They saw further than the flesh and the act of intercourse, to speak like that. Mere sexual disillusionment would not have crushed them to such a degree, would not have reduced them to such utter remorse and disgust. They saw further. They were overwhelmed by an impression of empty truth, of aridity, of growing nothingness, at the thought of having so often adopted, rejected and returned to their fragile carnal ideal.

They could feel that everything passed on, that everything wore out, that everything came to an end, that everything that was not dead would die, and that even the illusory bonds that existed between them were not lasting. The echo of the woman's inspired words lingered on like an unforgettable memory of splendid music: 'As soon as everything escapes, one is alone.'

This common dream did not bring them together. On the contrary. Both of them were bent at the same time in the same direction. The same shudder, inspired by the same mystery, impelled them towards the same end. They were parted by the whole extent of their sufferings. To suffer together was to be utterly separate.

And the condemnation of love itself came from her, flowed and fell from her, in a cry of agony:

'Oh, our great love, our boundless love! I can feel that I am gradually recovering from it!'

●

She had thrown her head back, raised her eyes.

'Oh, the first time!' she said.

She went on, while both of them recalled that first time, when, in the midst of people and things, their two hands had found each other:

'I knew perfectly well that all that emotion would die one day, and in spite of all the exciting promises of the future, I would have liked time to stand still.

'But time went by. Now we scarcely love each other any more . . .'

He made a gesture which went unfinished.

'It isn't only you, my dear, who are drifting away; I am too. I

thought at first that it was only you, but then I understood my
poor heart which, in spite of you, could do nothing against time.'

Looking at him, then turning her eyes away only to look at
him again, she said slowly:

'Alas, one day I may say to you: "I don't love you any more."
Alas, alas, I may say to you one day: "I have never loved you."'

●

'That is the trouble: time which goes by and changes us. The
separation of two people in conflict with each other is nothing
in comparison. One could bear that at a pinch. But time going
by! Growing old, thinking differently, dying! I am growing old,
I am dying now. It took me a long time to realize that, you know.
I am growing old; I am not old, but I am growing old. I already
have a few white hairs. What a shock the first white hair gives
one! One day, peering into my mirror, just before going out, I
saw two white threads above my temple. That's a serious matter,
you know, a clear, direct warning. That time, I sat down in one
corner of my bedroom, I saw the whole of my life at one glance,
from beginning to end, and I decided that I had been mistaken
every time I had laughed. White hairs—me! Me, yes, me. I had
seen death around me, but I couldn't imagine my own death.
And now I saw it, I realized that it was a question of it and me!

'Oh, to escape from that discolouration which settles upon
you and takes you, like a puppet, by the top! To escape from that
extinction of the colour of the hair which covers you with the
pallor of the shroud, of bones and flagstones . . .'

She raised herself slightly and cried out in the darkness:

'Oh, to escape from the net of wrinkles!'

●

She went on:

'I said to myself: "Little by little you are coming to that, you are going that way. Your skin will dry up. Your eyes, which smile even at rest, will cry by themselves . . . Your breasts and your belly will wither, like rags over your skeleton. Weariness with life will slacken your jaw, which will yawn continuously, and you will shiver continuously on account of the cold. Your face will be ashen-coloured. Your words which everybody used to consider charming will sound odious when they are uttered in a worn-out voice. The dress which concealed you too well, in the opinion of the male hordes, will not conceal your monstrous nudity well enough, and men will turn their eyes away and not even dare to think of you." '

Gasping for breath, she put her hands to her mouth, choking with truth, as if she really had too much to say. It was a splendid, terrifying sight.

He clasped her desperately in his arms. But she seemed delirious, carried away by a universal sorrow. It was as if she had just learnt the dismal truth like sudden bad news, like a fresh bereavement.

'I love you, but I love the past even more than you. I long for it, I long for it, I am eaten up with desire for it. Oh, the past! You know, I shall weep and suffer as long as the past is no more.'

◑

'But however much one may love it, it will not stir again . . . Death is everywhere: in the ugliness of what has been beautiful too long, in the dirtiness of what was pure and undefiled, in the forgetfulness of what is far away, and in habit, that forgetfulness of what is close. We catch a glimpse of life—morning, spring-time, hope—but it is only death that we really have time to see . . . Since the world began, death has been the only palpable thing. It is on death that we walk and towards death that we move. What is the use of being modest and beautiful, when others will one day walk on us? There are far more dead under

the earth than there are living on its surface; and we have more
of death in us than life. It is not only the others—our fellow-
creatures—whose voices used to be complete around us and
have now fallen silent; it is also, year by year, the greater part of
ourselves. And what does not as yet exist will also die. Almost
everything is dead.

'A day will come when I shall no longer exist. I weep because
I am sure to die.

'My death! I wonder how we can live, dream, sleep, when we
are doomed to die: because we are tired, because we are drunk.

'In spite of all our vast, patient, continued efforts, and the
strong, determined onslaughts of our energy, we can hear—or
at least, I can hear—the lies of destiny in the promises we make.
Every time we say *yes*, a *no* intervenes, infinitely louder and
truer, rises up and carries all before it.

'Oh, yes, there are moments, especially in the evening, when
it seems that time hesitates, softened and worn down by our
hearts; and we have the delightful impression that the hours are
standing still. But that isn't so. There is an invincible emptiness
in everything, and it poisons us as we pass by.

'You see, my dear, when one thinks of that, one smiles, one
forgives, one no longer bears a grudge against anyone, but that
sort of resigned kindness is the heaviest of burdens.'

◐

He kissed her hands, bending over towards her. He was covering
her with a warm, respectful silence; but, once again, I felt that
he was in complete control of his emotions . . .

She was speaking in a changed, lilting voice:

'I have always thought about death. Once I admitted this obsession to my husband. He exploded in a furious outburst. He
told me that I was neurotic and that I ought to see a doctor. He

urged me to be like him who never thought about such things, because he was healthy and well-balanced.

'That wasn't true. It was he who was ill with calm and indifference, suffering from a paralysis, a grey sickness; and his blindness was an infirmity, and his peace was that of a dog which lives for the sake of living, of an animal with a human face.

'What is a person to do? Pray? No: the eternal dialogue in which one is always alone is overwhelming. Throw oneself into some task, and work? That's useless: isn't work something which always has to be done again? Have children and bring them up? That gives the impression both that one is finished and that one is starting again in vain. And yet, who knows?'

It was the first time that she had relented.

'I have never known the assiduity, the submission, the humiliation of being a mother. Perhaps that would have guided me in life. I am the orphan of a little child.'

For a moment, lowering her eyes, dropping her hands, giving free rein to her maternal instincts, she thought of nothing but loving and regretting the absent child—without realizing that if she regarded it as her only hope, that was because it didn't exist . . .

'Charity? They say that helps you to forget everything.'

While we felt the damp chill of the evening and of all the winters of the past and future, she murmured:

'Oh, yes, being kind! Going to give alms with you along the snow-covered roads, with a thick fur coat!'

She gave a weary gesture.

'I don't know. I don't think that's the answer. All these things are just ways of numbing the mind; they don't alter the truth because they aren't the truth . . . What can save us? And even if we were saved, what difference would that make? We shall die, we are going to die!'

She cried out:

'You know very well that the earth is waiting for our coffins and that it is going to have them. And that won't be long from now.'

She emerged from her tears, dried her eyes, and adopted a tone of voice which was so calm and reasonable that it gave an impression of madness:

'I should like to ask you a question. Answer me truthfully. Have you ever dared, my dear, even in your most secret thoughts, to take a date, a fairly remote date, but precise and definite, with four figures, and say to yourself:

' "However long I may live, when that year comes I shall be dead—while everything else will continue, and, little by little, my empty places will have been destroyed or filled"?'

He stirred uncomfortably at the preciseness of this question. But it seemed to me that he was trying above all to avoid giving her a reply which might stimulate her obsession. Obviously he understood all these things (among which, as she had said, he could sometimes hear the echo of his words), but he gave the impression of understanding them theoretically, in the light of the great ideas of mankind, and in a philosophical or artistic fever distinct from his sensibility; whereas she was completely shaken and overwhelmed by personal emotion, and her reasoning was stained with blood.

◗

She remained attentive, motionless; then, after a moment's hesitation, she went on, in a lower voice, speaking faster, in a more desperate outburst of her exalted misery:

'You know what I did yesterday? You mustn't scold me. I went to the cemetery, to Père-Lachaise, I walked along the paths, then between the tombs, as far as my family vault, the one into which, after removing the stone, they will lower my coffin with ropes.

I said to myself: this is where my funeral procession will come one day, a day which may be close or distant, but one day for sure—about eleven o'clock in the morning. I was tired and I was obliged to lean on a tomb; and by a sort of contagion spread by the silence, the marble and the earth, I had a vision of my burial. The road rose steeply. The horses had to be pulled along by the bridle (I have seen that happen several times at that spot). It was pitiful, that road which had to be climbed like that in such circumstances. All those who knew me and loved me were there, in mourning; and they had collected in scattered groups among the tombs (how stupid it is to have those heavy stones on top of the dead!) and the monuments, which are locked up like houses, in the shadow of that tomb which is in the form of a chapel, and brushing against that other one which is covered with a slab of new marble—it will still be new enough to produce an identical bright patch. I was there . . . in the hearse—or rather it wasn't me. *She* was there . . . And all of them, at that moment, loved me with a sort of terror; and all of them were thinking about me, thinking about my body; there is something indecent about a woman's death, because it involves the whole of her.

'And you were there too, with your poor little face contorted with mute grief and passion—and our vast love was no longer anything but you and the thought of me, and you were scarcely entitled to talk about me . . . When it was all over, you went away, as if you had never loved me.

'And, coming home, chilled to the marrow, I told myself that that nightmare was the most real of realities, that it was the simplest, truest thing in the whole world, and that all the actions which I was living through in real life were mirages in comparison.'

She gave a stifled cry which sent a long shudder through her whole body.

'What misery I dragged home with me! Outside, my sadness

had darkened everything, although the sun was shining. What havoc we wreak on the whole of Nature around us, and what a world of suffering we bring into the world! There is no fine weather which can hold in face of our sadness.

'Everything seemed to me to be stricken and doomed by the evil angel of truth whom no one ever sees.

'My home appeared to me as it really is in fact: bare, white, empty . . .'

●

And all of a sudden she remembered something he had said to her; she remembered it with a sort of extraordinary ingenuity of admirable skill, in order to silence him in advance and torture herself more.

'Ah, listen . . . Do you remember . . . One evening, next to the reading-lamp, I was leafing through a book, and you were watching me. You came over to me and knelt down. You put your arms round my waist, you laid your head in my lap, and you wept. I can still hear your voice: "I am thinking," you said, "that this moment will never exist again. I am thinking that you are going to change and die, that you are going away—and that, all the same, you are here now . . . I am thinking, with an immense, genuine fervour, how precious every moment is, how precious you are who will never again be as you are now, and I implore and adore your indescribable presence at this moment." You looked at my hand, you found it small and white, and you said that it was an extraordinary treasure which would disappear. Then you repeated: "I adore you," in such a tremulous voice that I have never heard anything truer or more beautiful, for you were right after the manner of a god.

'And another thing: one evening when we had stayed together a long time, and nothing had succeeded in banishing your gloomy thoughts, you buried your face in your hands and you said this terrible thing to me which pierced my heart and has remained ever since in the wound: "You are changing; you have already changed; I dare not look at you, for fear of not seeing you!"

'It was that evening, you know, that you spoke to me about cut flowers: the corpses of flowers, you called them, and you likened them to little dead birds. Yes, it was the evening of that great curse which I shall never forget, and which you cried out all at once, as if your heart were aching because of cut flowers.

'How right you were to feel defeated by time, to humiliate yourself, and to say that we were nothing, since everything passes and nothing is unattainable.'

◑

Dusk was entering the room, and like a high wind was bending the heads of that poor couple busy examining the causes of suffering, and studying misery to find out what it was made of.

'Space is always between us, and time is installed inside us like a disease . . . Time is more cruel than space. Space has something dead about it, while time has something murderous. Every silence, you see, every tomb, has its tomb in time . . . Those two things, which are so invisible and so real, meet in us at the very point where we are . . . We are crucified, but not like God who was physically crucified on a cross;'—she pressed her arms against her body and curled up small—'we are crucified on time and space.'

And she did in fact seem to me to be crucified in those two senses, bearing in her heart the bleeding stigmata of the great agony of living.

She was in the full flight of her yearning. She resembled all those whom I had seen where she was, and who, like her, wanted to break away from their nothingness and live a fuller life, but what she wanted was complete salvation. Her great, humble heart was turning in its effusion from absolute death to absolute life. Her eyes were gazing in the direction of the white window, and it was the most immense of all longings, the most immense of human desires which quivered in that sort of assumption of her face to heaven.

'Oh, stop time from passing! You are nothing but a poor man, a little thought and existence lost in the corner of a room, and I am telling you to stop time, and I am telling you to prevent death!'

Her voice trailed off, as if she could not say anything more, all her supplication spent, worn out, used up; and she sank into a pitiful silence.

'Alas!' said the man.

He looked at the tears in her eyes, the silence of her mouth . . . Then he bowed his head. Perhaps he was giving way to utter discouragement; perhaps he was awakening to the great inner life.

When he raised his head, I had a vague intuition that he knew what to say, but that he didn't know yet how to put it—as if anything he said was bound to be inadequate to begin with.

'This is what we are!' she repeated, raising her head and looking at him, hoping for an impossible contradiction, as a child asks for a star.

He murmured:

'Who knows what we are?'

●

She interrupted him, with a gesture of infinite weariness which in its unconscious pride imitated the scythe-stroke of death, and with unseeing eyes she said in an expressionless voice:

'I know what you are going to say. You are going to speak to me of the beauty of suffering. Oh, I know your fine ideas. I love

them, my beloved, your fine theories; but I don't believe them.
I would believe them if they consoled me and abolished death.'

Unsure like her, and feeling his way, he murmured with an
obvious effort:

'They might abolish death if you believed them.'

'No, that isn't true, they won't abolish it. Whatever you may
say, one of us will die before the other, and then the other will
die. What do you say to that, tell me, what do you say to that?
Oh, answer me! Don't avoid the question, but answer it honestly. Oh, disturb me, change me, with a reply which concerns
me personally, just as I am here and now.'

She had turned towards him and had taken one of his hands
in hers. Her whole body was questioning him, with a pitiless
patience; then she slipped onto her knees in front of him, like a
lifeless body, crumpling up on the floor, shipwrecked in the
depths of despair and at the very foot of heaven; and she begged
him:

'Oh, answer me. I would be so happy to think that you could
do that!'

She stretched out her hand and pointed at the haunting vision, the pitiful truth whose name she had discovered, the widest
description of evil: space which conceals us, time which rends
us.

In the room which dusk had made low and narrow, in which
the poor sky revealed space and the monotonous clock represented time, he repeated, bending over her as over the edge of
an abyss of interrogation:

'Do we know what we are? Everything we say, everything we
think, everything we believe is uncertain. We know nothing;
there is nothing solid and sure.'

'Yes there is,' she cried; 'you are wrong. There's our suffering,
alas, and our need, perfect and absolute. Our misery is here: we

can see it and touch it. You can deny all the rest, but who could deny our wretchedness?'

'You are right,' he said, 'that's the only absolute thing in the world.'

It was true that it was there; and it was true that one could see it and touch it on their wide-open faces.

◐

He repeated:

'We are the only absolute thing in the world.'

He was clinging to that. He had felt a point of support in the flight of time. 'We . . .' he said. Having found the war-cry against death, he repeated it. He tried it out: 'We . . . We . . .'

In the now total twilight of the room I gazed at the man and the woman at his feet, like a cloud and a pedestal . . . His forehead, his hands, his eyes, the whole of his luminous personality emerged like a constellation.

And it was magnificent to see him beginning to resist.

'We are what remains.'

'What remains! On the contrary, we are what passes.'

'We are what sees things pass. We are what remains.'

She shrugged her shoulders, with an expression of protest and disagreement. Her voice was almost vicious.

'Yes . . . No . . . Perhaps, if you like . . . After all, what does it matter to me? That's no consolation.'

'Who knows if we don't need sadness and darkness, to make joy and light.'

'Light would exist without darkness.'

'No,' he said gently.

She replied a second time:

'That's no consolation.'

◐

Then he remembered that he had had already thought about all these things . . .

'Listen,' he said, in a trembling, rather solemn voice, as if he were making a confession. 'I once imagined two people at the end of their lives who remember all that they have suffered.'

'A poem,' she said with an air of discouragement.

'Yes,' he said: 'one of those which could be so beautiful!'

Strangely enough, he appeared to be gradually coming to life; he seemed sincere for the first time, now that he was abandoning the quivering example of their fate in favour of the figments of his imagination. Speaking of that poem of his, he had trembled. I could tell that he was going really to become himself and that he had faith. She had raised her head to listen to him, tormented by her relentless longing for an answer, even though she had no confidence.

'There they are,' he said. 'The man and the woman. They are believers. They are at the end of their lives, and they are happy to die for the same reasons that people are sad to live. They are a sort of Adam and Eve thinking about the paradise to which they are going to return.'

'And are we going to return to our paradise?' asked Aimée. 'Our paradise lost: innocence, freshness, whiteness! As if I believed in that paradise!'

◗

'Whiteness, that's it,' he said. 'Paradise is light, life on earth is darkness: that's the theme of the poem I've sketched out—light which they want, darkness which they are.'

'Like us,' said Aimée.

. . . They were there too, close to the shifting darkness, a pale movement towards the almost vanished pallor of the skies, with their invisible thoughts and voices . . .

'These believers are asking for death as people ask for food.

On this supreme day, one word has at last been changed in the daily prayer: death instead of bread.

'When they know that they are finally going to die, they offer thanks. I should like this thanksgiving to light up right at the beginning—like the dawn. They show God their dark hands and mouths, their shadowy heart, their gazes which give no light, and they beg him to cure their incurable darkness.

'An elementary reasoning appears in the midst of their supplication. They want to escape from the darkness because it intercepts the divine light; through their humanity they have seen only reflections or fugitive flashes of that light, and they want the whole of that God of whom they have glimpsed only the pale gleams in the sky.

' "Give us," they cry, "give us the charity of the ray whose light sometimes covers us like a veil, and which, from infinity, falls as far as the stars!"

'They lift up their pale arms like two poor, heavy, stunted branches . . .'

And I for my part wondered whether the couple I had before me weren't already in the darkness of death; whether it wasn't the sound of their common soul breathing its last sigh which I could hear . . .

The poetry was translating them, marking them out; it was withdrawing their lives, fragment by fragment, from silence and the unknown. It was perfectly suited to their profound secrecy. The woman had, once again, bent her head, already more splendidly bowed. She listened to him; he was more important than she, he was more splendid than she was beautiful.

'They ponder upon themselves. On the threshold of eternal bliss they look back on the life's work which they have completed. What a succession of bereavements, anxieties, fears! They describe everything that was against them, forgetting nothing, missing nothing, wasting nothing of the frightful past. What a poem that makes—all that misery returning at once!

'The brutal necessities first of all. The child is born; its first cry is a complaint: ignorance is similar to knowledge; then illness, grief, all those laments with which we feed the indifferent silence of Nature; work against which we must fight from morning till night, in order to stretch out our hands, when we have scarcely any strength left, towards a heap of gold crumbling like a heap of ruins; everything, down to our pitiful excrement, down to the pollution, the contamination of the dust which lies in wait for us and from which we must constantly cleanse ourselves—as if the earth were trying to seize us, never pausing until our final burial; and fatigue which degrades us, banishing the smiles from our faces, and making the home almost deserted in the evening, with its ghosts preoccupied with rest.'

. . . Aimée listened, accepted. At one moment she put her hand on her heart and said: 'Poor people!' Then she stirred slightly; she considered that he was going too far; she didn't want so much gloom—either because she was tired or because, done by another voice, the picture struck her as exaggerated.

And, by an admirable coincidence of dream and reality, the woman in the poem also protested at that moment.

'The woman raises her eyes and says in timid protest: *"The child who came to help us . . ."* *"The child to whom one gives life and whom one allows to die!"* replies the man . . . He wants no suffering to be concealed, and in the past he finds even more unhappiness than they had thought; there is a sort of perfection in his search, and his judgment on life is as beautiful as the Last Judgment: *"The child through whom the human wound bleeds once more. Creating, beginning a heart all over again, resurrecting a misfortune; having a child means sacrificing a human being. Engendering, with a scream, another complaint. Oh, the pain of having a child! It never ends; it grows immeasurably in fears and wakeful nights . . ."* And he goes on to speak about the passion of motherhood, the self-sacrifice of the parents, their heroism at the bedside of the vacillating little soul, scarcely daring to live, looking happy when they are worried to the point of tears, and smiling bravely . . . And their perpetual uncertainty: *"Remember the end of the working day, and in the evening, at sunset, the melancholy bliss of sitting down . . . Oh, how many times, in the evening, looking at my trembling brood, narrowly saved from disaster again and again, my shaking hands would pass over beloved brows, and then I would drop my arms in discouragement and remain there weeping, defeated by the weakness of my family! . . ."'*

Aimée could not help making a gesture at this point; it seemed to me that she was going to tell him that he was being cruel . . .

'They grow up, and then . . . His eyes ablaze, he says: *"Cain!"* and she says in a choking voice: *"Abel!"* She suffers at the memory of the two children who hated each other and struck each other. They had struck her too, since they were in her heart; it was as if they were still in her flesh. Then another memory calls to her in a whisper; she thinks of the little child who is dead: *"The little one, the best of them all . . . He is dead and I go on looking at him!"* She holds her arms out to the impossible and, heartbroken by the empty kiss, groans: *"He is dead, and I go on caressing him!"* And the man growls: *"Death, curse of the beloved, sinister bounty which leaves us,"* and she gives this supreme cry: *"Oh, the sterility of being a mother!"'*

I was carried away by the voice of the poet who was declaiming with his shoulders swaying slightly, possessed by the harmony of his words. I was carried away to the point of the dream's fulfillment . . .

'Then they remember how they were deserted by their children, as soon as those children had grown up and fallen in love.

"*Living or dead, the child leaves us, because it is good to hate old age when one is young and strong and bright, because the terrible spring buries the winter, and because a kiss is passionate only on new lips. You shall leave your father and your mother, and flee from the sterile, heavy embrace of their arms . . .*'"

I thought about the scene which I had seen the other evening, the same one in which that man was speaking, about that drama in my life. Yes, it had been just like that. The old woman had enveloped the young, mysteriously liberated couple in a useless embrace, a wasted embrace. He was right, that vague poet, that vague singer, that thinker.

'There is no defense against the tireless unhappiness of life, not even sleep: "*Sleeping . . . At night, we used to forget . . .*"— "*No, we dreamt; rest is remembrance, full of real ghosts; our sleep is never sleep but a death-agony . . .*"—"*Sometimes the dream we dream caresses us with its grey forms.*"—"*It always hurts us; when it is sad it wounds our nights, and when it is sweet it wounds our days . . .*"

'"*Yet we were two,*" murmurs the wife . . . And they consider love. When work was done, they used to go together to mingle rest and tenderness all night long . . . "*But at night we belonged to each other for a moment . . . When we searched among all the roads for ours, and hurried, two dark figures, towards the half-open door of our home, as towards a raft in the midst of the waves; when shadows mingled, in the depths of the valley, with your worn, humble, as it were flagellated dress, my eyes, in the rays of light fading in unison, used to see the almost naked beating of your heart. When we were all alone, what did we say?*"—"*We used to say to each other: I love you . . .*"

'But those words, alas, are meaningless, since each person is alone, and two voices, whatever they are, murmur incomprehensible secrets to each other. And there follows an outburst against the solitude to which they are condemned: "*Oh, sepa-*

ration of hearts, earth heaped up on each and every one, horrible silence of thought! Lovers, we searched endlessly for each other; we were there with nothing to unite us, and close and trembling under the stars, with our fingers intertwined, we were nothing but a couple of almsgivers."'

'Ah!' said Aimée. 'So you admit that in your poem. You shouldn't . . . It's too true.'

'Then came the moment of the kiss and the embrace. But bodies cannot penetrate each other any more than hands, in spite of all the audacities of thought, and this was not union, but two deliriums superimposed one another.'

'I know,' said Aimée, shuddering from head to foot with a twofold shame.

'And at times of despair, pleasure only accentuated their twin solitudes: *"Wrapped in our bodies as in our shrouds, our eyes mingled their tears, our hearts wept by themselves; I used to see you, infinitely fragile and profound; you were weeping . . . I realized that each person is a world in himself."'*

◐

'Thus misery and evil appear in their entirety in a great conscience which forgives nothing. The imprecation is over. For that matter, life is over too. This is the last time that they will recall these things.

'The woman looks straight ahead, with the same curiosity she showed on entering life. Eve ends as she began. Her whole, subtle, sensitive woman's soul is rising towards the secret like a sort of kiss towards the lips of her life. Already she yearns to be happy . . .'

Aimée was paying greater attention to her companion's words. The imprecation so similar to her own had given her confidence. But it seemed to me that she had diminished in stature before us. A little earlier she had dominated everything; now she was listening, she was waiting, she was captivated.

'We too, don't you think?' she had said at one moment.

It was moving, that sort of dual work of life and art. He was lyrical; she was dramatic. They were at one and the same time creators, actors, victims. It was no longer possible to tell what they were. There was nothing but a great truth, which was the same for both words and fate. Where did the drama they were playing begin, and where the drama which was playing with them?

◑

'An immense piety fills them with hope: "*I believe in God, I no longer believe in myself!*" But tireless curiosity intervenes. What will paradise be like? *How* can everybody stop suffering?

' "We have caught scanty glimpses of paradise," he said, "on earth. Our hopes, our emotions, the splendid effusions and interior rewards of pride—all that was a little of paradise. They were like brief moments of God . . . But that was quickly hidden by our ignominy, by our human baseness. Now our sad veil is going to fall and we shall have God without end." And the woman asks: "*But what shall I be?*" '

Aimée said: 'She is right. For after all, what can he say in reply?'

'He shows her that perfect happiness is an entity whose nature escapes our comprehension. We can't touch eternity, still less experiment with it. We must trust in God, and go to sleep like children in the evening of our evenings.'

'All the same . . . ,' said Aimée.

'But in the grip of an anxiety which is gradually obsessing her, the woman asks once again the unanswerable question: "*What shall we be?*"

H E L L

112

'And, once again, he answers her by saying what they will not
be. In spite of the fact that he would like to say something positive, the truth takes hold of him and turns him towards negation: "*We shall no longer be the rags, the flesh, the sobs we are
. . .*" And he plunges into his darkness in order to deny it. "*What
shall we be?*" she cries, trembling with emotion—"*No more
darkness, no more separation, no more fear, no more doubt. No
more past, no more future, no more desire: desire is poor because
it has not. No more hope.*"'

'No more hope?'

'Hope is unhappy, because it hopes. No more prayer: prayer
too is indigent, because it is a cry which rises and abandons us
. . . No more smiles: isn't a smile always half-sad? We smile at
our past melancholy, anxiety, solitude, at our passing grief; a
smile doesn't last, for if it lasted it wouldn't be; its nature is to
be dying . . .—"*But what shall I be? I! I!*" This cry of "I!" gradually fills the air, resonant, demanding. And yet again he throws
her phantom words, since she is asking him what will be and he
is offering in reply what will no longer be. He sets out once more
the ills they have endured, like a row of scarecrows. He draws
them out of the shroud of mystery. He admits what he has never
admitted before. "*There is this and that which I have always concealed from you. I told you that, but I was lying.*" He would
almost invent things, in his need to find some reply to her all
too simple question. He lists his desires, and every scrap of
speech conjures up an agony. He has desired everything: the
property of others, the fate of others, fame, an immortal audience. He even affords a glimpse of a whole play killed, convulsed, immobilized within him, a whole great poem in em-
bryo: "*A still more terrifying, more horrible hell: our daughter,
who resembled your dawn!*" He has not succumbed to his desires;
he has only suffered them more grievously as a result. He has
borne within him, beneath a calm exterior, eternal temptation:

"Nailed inside me, but huge and whole . . . nestling in my heart . . . the hidden torment, the inadmissible agony of not having sinned!"

'Above all else he has desired the past, and he recalls that simple, certain source of suffering—the past which is dead. He would have liked to enter into the past as into the future, as into a beloved heart. But memory is implacable. It is nothing; it is nevermore; and he who remembers, suffers and feels remorse for the past, as if he were a criminal. Moreover he, and indeed both of them, in spite of their piety which has grown into them with their old age, were obsessed by the idea of death. The idea of death was everywhere. For what is horrifying is not death itself but the idea of death, which ruins all activity by casting a subterranean shadow. The idea of death: death which is alive . . . *"Oh, how I have suffered! . . . How I must have suffered!"*

'There you have all that was and that will finally cease to be. There you have all the different kinds of darkness which have defended us against the prolongation of happiness. Everything comes down to an invasion of gloom from which life wishes to escape. *"We are those,"* he cries as he did at the beginning, *"who have never had any light, those whom the universal darkness enfolds anew every evening, those whose deep, living blood is black, those whose obscure dream sullies everything it touches; and our eyes are as dark as our mouths. Black and empty, our eyes are blind, our eyes are dull: they need the succour of the skies . . . Remember how, when we stood together beneath the calm tempest of the evening, a ray of light lingered on our heads, and for a long time we hoped that night would never fall. Your weak arm trembled as it pressed hard upon mine . . . Crushing our dismal aspirations, the night took back from us the stolen light . . ."*

'Night pours from them as from a wound in their sides; they literally make darkness . . . And limited, dazzled by his childish reasoning, he cries out: *"Night will be swallowed up; you shall be light!"* But this vast, pitiful promise has no effect on the woman's terror, and she goes on asking what she herself will be: for light is nothing. Nothing, nothing . . . She tries in vain to fight against that word.

'He reproaches her for contradicting herself by demanding both happiness on earth and happiness in heaven; she replies, from the very depths of her being, that the contradiction lies not in herself but in the things she wants.

'Then he snatches at another straw, and with desperate eagerness he explains, he screams: *"We cannot know! How could we possibly know? What madness, what sacrilege, to try! We are concerned with an order of things totally different from that with which we are familiar. Divine happiness does not have the same form as human happiness. Divine happiness is outside us."*

'She stands up, trembling. *"That isn't true! That isn't true! No, my happiness is not outside me, since it is my happiness . . . The universe is God's universe, but my happiness is myself who am God as a result of it. What I want,"* she adds with final simplicity, *"is to be happy myself, such as I am and such as I suffer."* '

Aimée had given a start: she was doubtless thinking of what she had said a little earlier: 'An answer which involves me personally, such as I am here and now." And she resembled that woman more than herself . . .

' *"Myself such as I suffer,"* repeats the man.

' "Those are significant words. They confront us directly with this great law: happiness is not an object, nor a mathematical term; it is born of misery and it is entirely contained in misery, for we can no more separate joy and suffering than light and shade. To separate them is to destroy them both. 'Myself such as I suffer.' How could we be happy in a perfect calm and a pure light as abstract as a formula? We have too many needs, too irregular a heart. If everything that hurt us were taken from us, what would be left? And the happiness which came then would not be for us; it would be for *another*. The vague cry which, thinking to be logical, says: *We have had a glimpse of happiness obscured by darkness; when the darkness goes, we shall have happiness itself in its entirety* is a mad lie. And it is another mad lie to say: *We shall have a pure happiness such as we cannot imagine.*

'And the woman says: "Lord, I want no part of heaven!"'

'Why!' exclaimed Aimée. 'We would have to be able to be miserable in paradise!'

'Paradise is life,' he said.

Aimée fell silent and remained there, her head erect, realizing at last that with all these words he was simply answering her, and that he had refashioned a loftier, truer concept in her soul.

◑

'The man is now in agreement with her,' he went on . 'Besides, he had been conscious for a few moments of the mistake he was making in her anger. Now he underlines and perfects the dramatic truth glimpsed in the light of the woman's words. "*And God? What of God?*" she asks.—"*God can do nothing for mankind. There is nothing to be done. He is not the impossible; he is only God.*"

'So what do they do, these two believers who can find no comfort in spite of God? . . . They clumsily reconstruct their life, memory by memory, and they worship that life in its misery in which everything was to be found. Beside each of those flashes of joy or pride which they earlier described as fragments of God, they see the shadow which permitted it, the weakness which prepared it, the danger and the doubt which surrounded it like delicate attentions, the trembling which gave it life . . . This vision of their fate melts into that of their love, all the more dazzled in that it was more agonized. If he had not been poor, he would not have endured all the charity she heaped upon him, when he drew near to her light which was necessary to him, and to her woman's mouth with its silent appeal.

'They seem to be reliving, imitating that . . . It is as if they didn't know each other and were gradually recognizing each other, judging each other and embracing each other. They say that they were looking for the dark. They see each other searching, during the day, for the dusk in the midst of the bedrooms, in the depths of the woods. They used to contemplate and understand Nature. They understood it too well and gave it something which did not belong to it, when their mortal emotion granted a last smile to the evening . . . *"And all around us, the day was dying, alas!"* '

I could no longer tell in whose name this human being was speaking before me, and whether he was talking about himself or the others. Shut inside these walls, tossed into this room like a wet rag, the man seemed to be creating one of those great works in which music mingles with words:

' *"We were frightened and cold . . . You were surrounded by shadows: our evening, your dress, your modesty . . . But what a dawn broke when I went towards you! Oh, when I took your precious head in my arms under the veils of evening; when I glimpsed in your broken gestures your mouth and its silence rich in kisses, your flesh which is white as an angel in the darkness . . . When I drew near to your face as to the mirror of my smile; when, standing beside you, supporting you and being supported by you, I plunged my closed eyes into the sunshine of your hair, to dazzle myself; when I caressed your shadow with my heavy hands.*

' *"We needed each other, we suffered through each other . . . Oh, doubting, not knowing, hoping, weeping! And it was always like that. In spite of lapses and weaknesses, forgetfulness and indigence, the grand poverty of our love triumphed!"* '

'Ah!' said Aimée. 'One mustn't curse, one mustn't have any regrets, one must love one's heart.'

He went on without listening to her: 'And the dying couple say: "*And when life, in the end, without bringing us closer together than is possible, alas, without turning two human beings into one, nonetheless fashioned us similar enough for affection to make us miraculously sensitive to each other, we won together a respect and a cult—a trembling religion—for our very misery. We found it everywhere with death; we worshipped human weakness in the tremulous breeze which approaches—and goes on blowing; in the setting sun which turns bare; in the summer which can be seen suffering and declining; in the autumn whose beauty is full of presentiments, and whose dead leaves sadly muffle the sound of footsteps; in the starry skys whose grandeur looks like madness; and indeed it was difficult to believe that stone had a heart of stone and that the future was not innocent and liable to error. And we resisted, and we grew big with hope.*

'*"Remember how, when the evening in which we felt old age approaching descended on the great slopes, we joined our inadequate hands together and, in spite of everything, turned our eyes towards the future. The future! On your infinitely beautiful cheek a wrinkle smiled. Everything was tremulous and magnificent, the wise truth fell from the splendid sky, and its last gleam settled on your white brow. Weary and miserly, barely able to open our eyes, full of the poor past which can never be cured, we hoped: evening softened the stones, your eyes were golden, I felt you dying!*

'*"Life rises to a sort of perfection as it draws to a close. It is a beautiful thing,*" he declares in an even deeper voice, "*It is a beautiful thing to reach the end of one's days . . . This is how we have experienced paradise.*"

'And they reach the point of saying shyly, awkwardly to each other: "*I love you.*" On the threshold of eternity they try to carry out the humble beginnings of the expiatory life. And they go so far as to maintain that it hurts God to see them die, and they pity him. Then this couple, who are going to suffer no more, bid each other a heartrending farewell which brings the play to an end.'

'They are right,' said Aimée in a cry which expressed her while being.

'That is the truth,' said the poet. 'It doesn't abolish death. It doesn't diminish space or delay time. But it turns those things and the concept we have of them into the sombre, essential elements of ourselves. Happiness needs unhappiness; joy is partly composed of sadness; it is thanks to our crucifixion on time and space that our heart beats in the midst of it all. We mustn't dream of some sort of ridiculous abstraction; we must retain the link which chains us to the earth and the flesh. Remember: "Such as we are." We are a great amalgam; we are more than we think: who knows what we are?'

On the woman's features, which the fear of death had contracted, a smile had begun to live again. She asked with childish simplicity:

'Why didn't you tell me that straight away, as soon as I asked you?'

'You couldn't understand me then. You had led your dream of distress into a blind alley. I had to take truth a different way in order to present it to you again.'

◐

Something else which I could see in them made them vibrant with life: the beauty, the joy of having spoken. Yes, that created a halo around them for the few moments before they descended from their dream.

'It is good,' she sighed, 'to have all those words there which say exactly what is against us.'

'To express oneself, to awaken what is alive,' he said, 'is the only thing which really gives the impression of justice.'

After these great words they fell silent. For a fraction of time they were as close together as it is possible to be on this earth—because of their noble assent to the sublime truth, to the hard truth (for it is difficult to understand that happiness is at once happy and unhappy). Yet she believed this—she the rebel, she the unbeliever to whom he had given a real heart to touch.

N I N E

The window was wide open. The evening was coming in, rich and vibrant, like a season. In the dusty light of the setting sun I saw three people with their backs to the long reddish rays. An old man, with a downcast, broken look and a face furrowed with wrinkles, sitting in the armchair drawn up to the window; a tall young woman with very fair hair and the face of a Madonna; and, sitting a little to one side, a pregnant woman who seemed to be staring into the future.

The latter was taking no part in the conversation, either because she was of humbler rank than the others, or because her thoughts were completely devoted to the event of her flesh. In the half-light into which she had withdrawn, I could see her swollen, sweetly monstrous figure, and her tender, absorbed smile.

The others were chatting together. The man had a tired, uneven voice. His shoulders occasionally gave a feverish shudder, and now and then he would make abrupt gestures which were quite involuntary; he had slit eyes, and he spoke with a foreign accent. The young woman sat quietly beside him, with her Nordic brightness and gentleness, so white and golden that the daylight seemed to die more slowly than anywhere else on her pale silvery face and the diffused radiance of her hair.

Were they a father and his daughter, a brother and his sister? It was obvious that he adored her, but that she was not his wife.

He looked at her with his dull eyes in which the sunlight falling upon her was reflected.

He said:

'Someone is going to be born; and someone is going to die.'

The pregnant woman made a movement. The other woman leant sharply towards him and cried out softly:

'What are you saying, Philippe!'

He seemed indifferent to the effect produced by his words, as if this protest were futile or insincere.

Perhaps he was not an old man; his hair seemed to me to be scarcely turning grey. But he was in the grip of a mysterious ailment which he was finding hard to bear, in a state of continuous tension. He had not long to live. That was obvious from the traditional signs around him: a frightened, excessively discreet pity in his companions' eyes, and already an unbearable atmosphere of mourning.

◐

He began speaking after a physical effort to break the silence. As he was sitting between the open window and me, his words were partly lost in space.

He spoke about his travels. I think that he also spoke about his marriage, but I didn't hear what he said about it.

He came to life again, and his voice rose; now it had a deep, disturbing sonority. He was quivering with emotion; a restrained passion was quickening his looks and gestures, warming and ennobling his words. Through him I could see the brilliant, active man he must have been before he had been sullied by illness.

He turned his head slightly and I heard him better.

He listed and recalled the towns and the countries he had visited. They were like sacred names he was invoking, different, distant skies he was imploring: Italy, Egypt, India. He had come here between two stops, in order to rest; and he was resting uneasily, like a fugitive in hiding. Soon he would have to set off again and his eyes lit up at the thought. He spoke of all that he still wanted to see. The twilight gradually deepened; the warmth in the air disappeared like a pleasant dream; but he thought only of all that he had seen:

'All that we have seen, all the space we carry with us!'

They gave the impression of a group of travellers who had never found contentment, of eternal fugitives, halted for a moment in their insatiable flight, in a corner of the world which seemed small because of them.

◐

'Palermo . . . Sicily . . .'

He was trying to intoxicate himself with his spacious memories, since he did not dare to venture into the future. I could see the effort he was making to draw closer to some luminous point in the past.

'Carpeia, Carpeia!' he exclaimed. 'Do you remember, Anna, that morning with the magical light? The ferryman and his wife were at table in the open country. What a flame was burning in Nature! . . . The table was round and pale like a star. The river was gleaming. On the bank there were tamarisks with rose-laurels. Not far away there was the dam in the sunshine: the long sparkling curve of the river . . . The sunlight was decking out every leaf. The grass was shining as if it were covered with dew. The bushes seemed to be studded with jewels. The breeze was so gentle that it was a smile rather than a sigh.'

She listened to him, taking in his words, his revelations, as placid, deep and limpid as a mirror.

'The ferryman's family,' he went on, 'were not all there. The young daughter had withdrawn a little way from her parents, far enough not to hear them, and was sitting dreaming on a rustic bench. I remember the soft green shadow the great tree cast over her. In her poor dress she was on the edge of the violet mystery of the wood.

'And I can still hear the flies buzzing in that Lombardy summer, around the winding river which spread out gracefully as we walked along its banks.

'Who can describe,' murmured the man, 'who can render in words the buzzing of a fly? It's impossible. Possibly because that buzzing was never isolated, and every time we heard it, it was mingled with the universal music of a moment.'

◐

'Where I had the strongest impression of the southern sun,' he continued, considering another memory, 'was in London, in a museum; in front of a picture showing a sunlit scene in the Roman campagna, a little Italian in fancy dress, a model, was craning his neck. In the midst of the immobility of the gloomy attendants and the current of raindrenched visitors, in the greyness and the damp, he shone out; he was silent, deaf to everything, full of secret sunlight, and he had his hands joined, almost folded; he was praying to the divine picture.'

'We saw Carpeia again,' said Anna. 'Chance ordained that our travels should take us there in November. It was bitterly cold; we were wrapped in all our furs; the river was frozen.'

'Yes, and people were walking on the water! It was strange and melancholy. All the people who earned their living from the water—the ferryman, the fishermen, the bargees, the washerwomen and their husbands—all those people were walking on the water.'

He paused for a moment, and then asked:

'Why do certain memories remain imperishable?'

He buried his face in his sad, sensitive hands, and gasped:

'Why? Why?'

◐

'Our oasis,' she went on, either to help him in his work of recollection, or else because she herself shared his obsession for reliving the past, 'was that corner with the lime-trees and acacias at your castle in Kiev. A whole side of the lawn is always strewn with flowers in summer and with leaves in winter.'

'It's there,' he said, 'that I can still see my father. He had a kindly look on his face. He was dressed in a thick coat of fluffy cloth, and was wearing a felt cap pulled down over his ears. He had a long white beard, and his eyes were watering slightly on account of the cold.'

He returned to his idea:

'Why have I kept that memory of my father rather than some other? What extraordinary sign marks out that memory alone for me? I don't know, but that is how he endures in me; that is how he hasn't died.'

Then he almost trembled as he said:

'I love Baku. I shall never see that country again. In any case, I don't know anybody there any more. Last year that old miser Borin was still there amassing money and counting it.'

'When he felt death coming,' said the young woman, 'he said: "I'm going to be ruined."'

The light was fading. The woman looked more and more visible among the others, and more and more beautiful.

'He too had great kindness in his face. Why shouldn't misers, who love something, have a kindly look?'

A shiver shook the dying man's shoulders.

'Shut the window, please,' he said. 'I'm cold.'

When it had been shut, silence fell. She said:

'I've had a letter from Catherine de Berg.'

'Still the same?'

'Yes, she's dying of grief. It's no use her going from one country to another—last week she was in the Balearics—wherever she goes, she takes a sort of indolence with her, her inconsolable widowhood. What strength it must take to be as inconsolable as that! She's fighting her youth and her beauty. She doesn't travel to reduce her grief, but to increase it, to spread it all over the world. The truth is that she doesn't want any distractions. She's upset when life takes its revenge and she forgets for a moment. One day I saw her crying because she had laughed. And yet her grief is a peaceful thing to see, as peaceful as the beauty in her face.'

I could see the man's silhouette against the white curtains— bent back, nodding head, thin neck. He raised his hands.

'Real grief remains inside us,' he said. 'It's something you can scarcely see or hear. But it stops everything easily, even life. Real grief takes on the imposing appearances of boredom.'

With almost clumsy movements he took a cigarette-case out of his pocket.

He lit a cigarette. As the bright little glow fastened itself on them like a brilliant mask, I saw his ravaged features. Then he started smoking in the half-light, and I could see nothing but the burning cigarette, moved by an arm as light and indistinct as the smoke it was giving off. Whenever he put the cigarette to his lips, I saw the light of his breath, whose mist I had seen earlier in the cool of the room.

. . . It was not tobacco that he was smoking: a pharmaceutical smell made me feel slightly sick.

He stretched out a limp hand towards the closed window—a humble casement with its little panes slightly raised.

'Look . . . That's Benares and Hallihabad . . . A blaze of red-dish gold against a grey background, a sparkling of strange human beings. They aren't people, they are statues of gods under the purple evening sky. They are moving . . . No, they aren't . . . Yes, they are. It's a lavish ceremony, a medley of tiaras, banners and women's jewels. On the edge, the high priest, with his complicated tiered headdress and his curved hands—an indeterminate pagoda, architecture, period, race. How different we are from those creatures! Who is in the right?'

Now he was widening the circle of the past. He seemed to be doing it with a strong, ponderous effort, as if he were widening a circle of hell and supplication.

'Travel: all those places one has to leave! And it's all useless. Travel doesn't broaden the mind; why should the mind be broadened by the steps one takes? In any case, who has the time to lay down the burden of his soul in order to see properly what he is passing? And even if he had the time, the traveller would know only one point of the surface of the present moment; nobody travels in the past. Everything has already been. Last night, while the memory of the cliffs and moors and forests of Wales was haunting me, I thought of the Knights of the Round Table. King Arthur and his companions . . . I had the impression of being close to them and walking towards them. I could see only one of them, who was wearing a strange helmet; his emerald eyes gazed at me and chilled my blood. The others were vague, ghostly figures. The stone table was round in the autumnal clearing, where the grey mist mingled with the reddish veil of the forest. The table was round so that when they stood around it, none of them took precedence over the rest. It was like a gigantic millstone. It was very white. The edges were very sharp. It had not been cut very long before; it was quite new.

'A thousand years! . . . Two thousand, three thousand years, and the shores of Troy . . .

'Do you remember, Anna, that line of gold off which we cruised?

'The Greek hero walks along the sands tinged with red by the dawn. I can see the broad, regular, firm footprint which he leaves in the sand. On the edge of each of these footprints, after he has gone, a little golden sand collapses. The sea comes to die beside him. I can see the trace—a thin fold of foam—which the last wave has just left on the wet sand, darker than the sand on which he is walking. A pebble has grated under the bronze of his sandals and has rolled away. I can hear the sound of his footsteps. Think of that, Anna: his footsteps, the sound of his footsteps, which vanished so many thousands of years ago. Think of the timespan we must cover to approach those footsteps of which no trace remained the next day, and which none the less exist. Where do they exist? Where do they exist? They exist in us, since we can see them. Time is not time; space is not space.'

Silence fell upon that admirable phrase, that mystery of lucidity. The woman did not feel capable of breaking the silence which was imbued with a truth to which she doubtless could not attain.

'His sword has knocked against a rock, and the blade can be heard rattling in the scabbard. In order to climb a steep slope, his strong hand has seized the trunk of a young pine from which a few dry needles have fallen behind him. What's that running in the pinewood nearby? An animal, a dog: this man's dog. He is bringing something back in his mouth: a leather belt hardened and shrunk by the salt and the wind, a Trojan belt, an already half-destroyed relic of the carnage about which Homer will sing hundreds and hundreds of years from now.

'The warrior has arrived on a promontory. He turns his head and looks out to sea. His nose is straight and thin; the line of his forehead falls sharply from his iron helmet; his eyebrows are curiously prominent; his lashes flutter over flashing eyes; but it is his hand which I examine most closely—a half-closed hand, with the back and the fingers a burnt, slightly reddish colour, as if they were carved out of brick, and the nails short and bulging, like encrusted pebbles.

'He sees the shore. The sailors are busy putting the countless hulls into the water. They are dragging them and then pushing them right out to sea to avoid the sharp reefs along the coast. The Greek fleet is going to put out this evening, since it is only possible to navigate under the stars, and it is getting under way while the morning is shining on the blue sea.'

After this contemplation of the sun, the man lowered his ravaged head.

'I have a vision of a stretch of water. I can see this water from close quarters, these grey and silver waves lapping in absolute silence, under a strange light. Why this infinite silence? They are on another planet, heaven knows how many hundreds of centuries away from us.'

●

I looked at what he was saying, and I looked at him: the sight which did not exist and the man who in the shadows scarcely existed any longer. The evocation and the man evoking it . . . I thought of that ineffable difference in grandeur which exists between him who thinks and what he thinks. His face is a tiny, vague, shadowy patch at the beginning of the unfolding of periods and countries.

More memories, and still more, came crowding in, piling up. I could tell that he was being assailed by a whole world, that he was a prey to too many memories: those he had stammered out, and those he hadn't the leisure or the power to recount. He could not rid himself of the luminous grandeur that was in him.

He had thrown his head back; he had probably closed his eyes . . . And I could count and measure his memories, from the expression of suffering worn by a face which allowed itself to be looked at like that.

Now he who had gone into ecstasies a little earlier started complaining.

'I remember . . . I remember . . . My heart has no pity for me.

'Ah,' he groaned immediately afterwards, with a gesture of resignation, 'one can't bid farewell to everything.'

She was there, and she could do nothing, although she was adored. She was helpless against that endless farewell which filled the man's last glances. She could offer nothing but her beauty, her smile . . . And the superhuman vision was imbued in vain with regret, remorse, desire. He did not want it to be over. He was calling for what he had evoked; he wanted to take it back. He loved his past.

Inexorable, immobile, the past offers the characteristics of a divinity—because for those who believe as for those who deny, the supreme characteristic of God is to allow men to implore him.

●

The pregnant woman had gone. I had seen her steal away towards the door, with tender, motherly solicitude for herself.

The two of them remained . . . The evening had an impressive reality: it seemed to be alive, to be rooted there, to be omnipresent. The room had never been so full.

He said:

'Another day coming to an end.'

And, as if continuing this train of thought, he added:

'All the preparations must be made for the marriage.'

'Michel!' the young woman blurted out, as if she could not hold back the name.

'Michel won't be angry with you,' the man replied. 'He knows that you love him, Anna. He won't be alarmed by the mere formality'—the speaker stressed these words, smiling to console himself—'of a marriage *in extremis.*'

The darkness presented them gently, in unique fashion, to each other, keeping them together. They gazed at one another.

He was thin and feverish; his words came echoing from the hollow of his life. As for her, white and majestic, she was vibrant with flesh and light.

With his eyes fixed upon her, he was making a visible effort as if he did not dare to touch her with his words. Then he let himself go.

'I love you so much,' he said simply.

'Ah,' she said, 'you won't die!'

'How kind you were,' he replied, 'to deign to be my sister for so long!'

'How much you have done for me!' she said, joining her hands and bending her magnificent bust towards him, as if she were prostrating herself.

It was obvious that they were speaking openly to each other. What an admirable thing it is for two people to talk frankly together, without the slightest reticence, without a shamefaced, guilty ignorance of what one is saying, and to be perfectly straightforward with each other! It is almost a miracle of radiance, peace and life.

He was silent. He had closed his eyes, but he could still see her. He opened them to look at her.

'You are my angel and you don't love me.'

As he said this his face clouded over. This very ordinary spectacle filled me with distress: the infinity of the heart participating in Nature: his face clouded over.

I could see how lovingly he felt towards her. She knew this; in her words, in her attitude beside him, there was an immense gentleness which knew it in every detail. She didn't encourage him, didn't lie to him, but every time she could, with a word, a gesture, or a beautiful silence, she tried to console him a little for herself, for the suffering she caused him with her presence, with her absence.

After looking at her once again, while the darkness brought him even closer to her in spite of himself, he said:

'You are the sad confidante of my love for you.'

He spoke of the marriage again. Since all the arrangements had been made, why shouldn't it take place straight away?

'My fortune, my name, Anna, the pure link with me which will remain for you when . . . when I have passed on.'

He wanted to endow the vague future with a lasting benefit, a light caress—too light, alas—like a blessing. For the present, he aspired to nothing more than the weak, fictional union of the word 'marriage.'

'Why talk about that?'

She did not reply directly, seized by an almost insurmountable repugnance, doubtless on account of that love which she had in her heart and which the man had admitted for her. Although she had agreed in principle and had allowed things to go ahead—since the formalities had been concluded—she had never given a clear reply to that supplication, which, every time they were alone together, went from him to her like a glance.

But, this evening, wasn't she on the brink of consent, of the decision which she would take in spite of the material advantage it might bring her, which she would take in her white, open soul —to submit to him and allow him a pathetic degree of intimacy?

'Tell me,' he murmured.

We looked at her mouth . . . Already it was almost smiling, that mouth implored like an altar, like the face of a god, rich in the hopes which were addressed to her alone, as well as with all the beauty of the evening.

The dying man, sensing that agreement was coming, murmured:

'I love life . . .'

He shook his head.

'I have so little time left, so little time of my own, that I would like to sleep no more at night.'

Then he fell silent in order to hear her.

She said: 'Yes,' and lightly—very lightly—touched the old man's hand with hers.

And in spite of myself, my pitiless gaze noticed that this gesture was marked by a theatrical solemnity, a self-conscious grandeur. Even when it is honest, chaste and disinterested, self-sacrifice contains a vainglorious pride which I can see, I who see everything.

◗

In the hotel, the talk is all about the foreigners. They have taken three rooms and have a considerable amount of luggage: and the man, it seems, is very rich, although very simple in his tastes. They are going to stay in Paris until the young woman's confinement, which is to take place a month from now, in a local nursing-home. But the man, so they say, is very ill. Madame Lemercier is extremely annoyed about this. She is afraid of his dying in her house . . . She is ashamed of his death in advance. The rooms were reserved by post, otherwise she would not have taken these people in—despite the cachet which their wealth lends her hotel. She hopes that he will last long enough to be able to set off again; but whenever anyone runs into her, she looks preoccupied.

. . . When I see him again, I think that he really is going to die before long. He is slumped in his chair, with his elbows on the arm-rests and his hands dangling limply. He seems to be pushing his gaze forward with an effort. As his head is bowed, the light from the window, falls, not on his pupils, but on the edge of his lower eyelids, so that his face looks as if it had been flayed. A recollection of something the poet said makes me tremble before this man who has finished, who dominates nearly the whole of his existence with a horrifying supremacy which is endowed with a beauty before which God himself is powerless.

TEN

He was talking about music.

'Why,' he said, 'are we captivated by rhythm? In the midst of the disorder of Nature, human creation introduces, wherever it appears, its great principle of regularity and monotony. It is only by obeying this hard law that the work, whatever it may be, can arise and be firmly established. It is this austere virtue which distinguishes the street from the valley and builds a staircase with equal steps up the mountain of noise. For disorder has no soul, and regularity thinks.'

Then he spoke about the harmony and proportion of unity. I could hear only fragments of his sentences as if the wind were bringing me whiffs of the scent of the country and the open sea.

There was a knock at the door.

It was the doctor's time to call. He rose unsteadily to his feet— degraded and defeated in front of this master.

'How have you been feeling since yesterday?'

'Bad,' said the sick man.

'Come, now!' the newcomer said calmly.

The two of them had been left alone together. The man had sat down again with a ridiculous slowness and awkwardness. The doctor was standing between him and me. He asked him:

'Well, and what about this heart of yours?'

By an instinct which struck me as tragic, they had both lowered their voices, and it was in an undertone that the sick man recounted his day of illness to his doctor.

The man of science listened, interrupted, nodded his head approvingly. He brought this confession to a close by repeating, this time in a loud voice, the commonplace, reassuring interjection which he had already used, with the same sweeping, stagnant gesture:

'Come, now, I see that there's nothing new . . .'

He moved, and I saw the patient: his features drawn, his eyes haggard, shaken to the core from having talked about the grim mystery of his disease.

He calmed down, and chatted with the doctor, who had settled cheerfully in a chair. He broached a few different subjects of conversation, and then returned in spite of himself, like a criminal to the scene of his crime, to the sinister thing he carried within him: his illness.

'What a disgrace!' he said.

'Nonsense!' said the doctor with a blasé air.

Then he stood up.

'Well, I'll see you tomorrow.'

'Yes, for the examination.'

'That's right. Well, goodbye for now.'

The doctor went off with a light step, with his bloody memories, that whole burden of misery whose weight he had forgotten.

◐

The examination had probably just finished. The door had opened. Two doctors came in; they seemed to me to be embarrassed. They remained standing. One was a young man, the other an old man.

They looked at each other. I tried to penetrate the silence of their eyes, the darkness inside their heads. The older man stroked his beard, stood with his back to the fireplace, stared at the floor. He murmured:

'*Casus lethalis* . . . and I would add: *properatus.*'

He had lowered his voice, for fear of being heard by the patient, and also because of the solemnity of the death sentence.

The other nodded in agreement—one might almost have said in complicity. Both men fell silent like a couple of children who had been up to some mischief. Once again their eyes met.

'How old is he?'

'Fifty-three.'

The young doctor remarked:

'He's lucky to have lasted as long as this.'

To which the old man retorted philosophically:

'He has *been* lucky. But he's no better off for that now.'

☾

There was a pause. The man with the grey beard murmured:

'I felt the sarcoma just behind the carotid.'

He put his finger on his neck.

'It's there that I *saw* it.'

The other nodded—since he had come into the room, his head seemed to have been nodding all the time—and muttered:

'Yes . . . It's quite inoperable.'

'Of course it's inoperable,' said the old doctor, his eyes gleaming with a sort of sinister irony. 'There's only one operation that could get rid of that for him: the guillotine! Besides, metastisis is far advanced. There are cancerous cells in the submaxillary, the subclavian, and probably the axillary glands. It's a lightning process. The respiratory, circulatory and digestive tracts are all going to be obstructed before long; strangulation will follow quickly.'

He heaved a sigh and stood there, an unlighted cigar in his mouth, his features rigid, his arms folded. The young man had sat down and was leaning against the back of his chair, tapping the marble mantelpiece with his idle fingers. One of the two men said:

'When you are faced with a case like that, you have the impression that the cancer has chosen where to strike!'

◐

'Chief, what am I to tell the young woman?'

'Say that it's serious, very serious, with a defeated air. Talk about the infinite resources of Nature.'

'It's a familiar phrase . . .'

'So much the better,' said the old man.

'What if she insists on knowing?'

'You mustn't reply but just turn your head away . . .'

'Can't we give her a little hope? She's so young!'

'No . . . precisely because her hopes would rise too easily. My boy, you must never say anything so useless. It would just give us a reputation for ignorance and make people hate us.'

'And what about him? Does *he* know?'

'I don't know. While I was examining him—you heard me— I tried to find out from his answers to my questions. Once I had the impression that he suspected nothing; another time, it seemed to me that he saw himself as I saw him.'

◐

Once again they remained for a few moments without saying a word. It seemed as if these two doctors had come there more to keep silent than to speak. They had scarcely moved, and they had exchanged their rare words with difficulty and caution.

Then, in the presence of the hideous wound seen again at close quarters, they raised themselves to loftier, more general thoughts. I could sense this development taking place in their minds; finally I heard these words:

'It takes shape like a child.'

●

The old man began to speak.

'Like a child. The germ acts upon the cell, as Lancereaux has observed, like a spermatozoon. It's a micro-organism which penetrates the anatomical structure, chooses it and impregnates it, places it under vibratory control, gives it *another life*. But the excitant agent of this intra-cellular activity, instead of being the normal germ of life, is a parasite.

'Whatever the nature of this *primum novens* may be, whether it is the *micrococcus neoformans* or the as yet invisible spore of the Koch bacillus, the fact remains that the cancerous parasitic tissue develops at first like foetal tissue.

'But the foetus reaches a conclusion. There comes a moment when the embryonic mass encysted in the womb has, so to speak, become adult. It has formed its superficial membranes, which Claude Bernard, in his illuminating terminology, calls limiting membranes. The foetus is complete; it is going to be born.

'The cancerous tissue, on the other hand, isn't completed; it goes on, without ever reaching its limits. The tumour (I'm not, of course, talking about fibromas, myomas and simple cancroids, which are benign tumours) remains eternally embryonic; it can't develop in a complete, harmonious way. It spreads—spreading is all that it can do—without managing to acquire a shape. Cut out, it starts to proliferate all over again, or at least ninety-five per cent of it. What can the whole of our body do against that flesh which won't take shape and won't get out? What can the delicate, fragile balance of our cells do against that chaotic vegetation which introduces into our blood and our organs, through the bone-structure and all the various systems, an insoluble, unlimited mass?

'Yes, in our system, cancer is infinity in the strict sense of the word.'

The young doctor nodded his agreement, and said with a profundity derived from heaven knows where, under the impulse of the idea of infinity:

'It's like a rotten heart.'

●

Now they were sitting facing each other. They drew their chairs closer together.

'It's even worse than anything we say,' the younger of the two men went on, in a shy, reserved voice.

'Yes, yes,' said the other, nodding vigorously.

'We aren't faced with a local disease introduced by some mysterious agency; it isn't, as the public imagines, a matter of a sinister internal accident. Cancer isn't even contagious. We are faced with a swift, acute, pathological attack of a whole species of weaknesses, one of the elementary forms of human illness.

'It's a general condition which necessitates and chooses the disease; it's the patient himself, you might say, who calls for the ravages of the parasite. It's his system which *wants* it!

'That parasite! Perhaps there's only one, which changes its characteristics according to environment, and engenders the various diseases in the appropriate organic localities. Bacteriology is still in its infancy; when it has learnt to talk, it will doubtless announce this piece of news which will give medicine an even more tragic grandeur than it has at present.

'I for my part believe in parasitic unity.'

'It's the fashionable theory of the moment,' said the old doctor. 'It's certainly tempting, and it must be admitted that medicine,

chemistry and physics, the deeper they go, are everywhere leading towards a unity of forces and material elements. In view of
that, and although there's no irrefutable proof, what could be
more probable than that terrible simplification you mention?'

'Yes,' said the other man in an undertone, as if he were thinking. 'All diseases are composed of the same elements. It's the
same invisible life which leads us all to death.'

'All of us,' murmured the other man, likewise lowering his
voice, 'are probably brothers in illness as we are brothers in
nothingness.'

'The one and only germ of death, the infinitely tiny germ
which sows the dreadful crop in our flesh, is probably that mi-
crobe whose role previously seemed fairly neutral, and which
we passed almost without seeing it: the *bacterium termo*.

'It is present in enormous numbers in the large intestine; it
exists in thousands of millions in every healthy human being.

'It is the germ which, in a phosphated terrain, probably becomes the golden staphylococcus, the agent of the furuncle and
the anthrax which mortify patches of flesh.

'It is the germ which, in the small intestine, probably becomes
the Eberth bacillus, the cause of the typhous pustule . . .'

The man of science took on a more earnest, solemn expression as he came closer to uttering the name of the as yet un-
conquered enemy:

'Finally, it is the germ which, in a dephosphated terrain,
probably becomes the Koch bacillus.'

◖

'The Koch bacillus isn't simply tuberculosis, in its pulmonary,
laryngeal, intestinal and osseous forms. Landouzy has reported
its presence in the pleuritic fluids, Kuss in cold abscesses.'

'Besides,' the old doctor broke in, 'who has listed all the huge
variety of lesions of tubercular origin?'

'Let's consider it in the lungs—seeing that the lungs are always affected in the adult patient. Its appearance leads to the formation of tubercles, small tumours which necrotize in consequence of the absence of vessels, and whose softening and expectoration result in the disappearance of the organ and death by asphyxia. The tubercle is essentially a neoplasm. The Koch bacillus is *neoformans*: the source of a new formation. For that matter, any micro-organism is *neoformans* in the organism; the word is not so much a scientific term as a sort of Homeric epithet referring to the creative power of the bacillus. The tubercle multiplies, but remains small. That's why Virchov described it as a poor neoplasm.'

◑

'But in the case of arthritics in a state of depression and with low temperatures, the parasite fails to produce tuberculosis.

'It passes into the blood with the peptones by way of the chyliferous vessels. The blood is filled with glycogen, and this human sugar, which is no longer used up by the high temperature, is deposited by venous stasis in large quantities in the anatomical elements of the glandular or passive tissues. It's then that there develops in a cold state what you might call a rich neoplasm; instead of several tubercles, there is only one, which grows enormously. This is the cancer, in all its various forms, with all its various names: sarcoma, carcinoma, epithelioma, scirrhus, lymphaderoma.

'So cancer is the incoherent result of the accumulation of glycogen in an arthritic adult in a state of debility and free from fever.'

'Yes, yes,' said the old man, 'that's quite possible, but where's your proof? It's an attractive theory, but where's your practical confirmation? For after all, there's a morphological difference between the tumour and the tubercle.'

He seemed to have become sarcastic and hostile, ready to rise up in protest and to draw on his knowledge and experience.

'If we examine a certain number of types of tumour,' replied the other man, 'we shall find that their number is directly proportional, and their volume inversely proportional, to the temperature of the subject producing them.'

He drew facts and figures from his memory. He threw them forward like weapons. He was fired by an ardent desire to present a complete, irrefutable case, to defend his broad simplification, which embraced the whole of mankind in a single dramatic theory:

'From 44° to 45° aviary tuberculosis develops with its countless numbers of almost microscopic tumours. From 40° to 41° you have the tuberculosis known as military because its products are the size of millet seeds. From 39° to 40° you have granulated tuberculosis, from 38° to 39° lenticular tuberculosis, from 37° to 38° a slow tuberculosis, with big superficial ganglions, at 37° extremely large ganglionic tumours culminating in cold abscesses (this category includes coxalgia, white swellings, and Pott's disease), at 36. 5° the big tumours of cow-pox, and at 28°, as Dubard has shown, you have the huge dark lumpy tumours which deform fishes' sides.'

He paused after piling up these examples, then went on:

'We can produce experimentally the retrocession of one infection into another; we take a rabbit which we inoculate with tuberculosis, and when it shows unmistakable signs of consumption we turn it into a cold-blooded animal by means of a swift section at the level of the last cervical vertebra and the first dorsal vertebra. If the animal doesn't die of paralysis, we soon see a large tumour with all the appearance and characteristics of a cancer taking form in its abdomen or on one of its joints.'

He looked his colleague straight in the face.

'I remember what De Backer says: "We have observed the

progress of tuberculosis and cancer simultaneously and we have always seen the cancer ceasing to subsist and drying up as soon as the tubercles asserted themselves and developed at a temperature exceeding 38°. Generally speaking," he adds, "it was the tuberculosis which dominated the situation."

'The main thing is the formation and internal distribution of sugar. This distribution is governed by the body's heat, which steadily burns it up in the tubercular patient; in the cancer patient, where there is an absence of heat, the glycogen accumulates. Cancer is sugary. De Backer has drawn attention to this process which shows cancer to be a sort of localized diabetes.

'The presence of sugar has been proved by manufacturing liqueur brandy with cancerous fluids. I have repeated this experiment myself. I obtained twenty-two pounds of cancerous matter from operations performed during two mornings in the Paris hospitals. Crushed in a press, this mass provided me with nearly four pints of a cloudy, fetid liquid which contained more sugar than most diabetic urine. When ferments had been added, the liquid yielded a strong and highly aromatic fermentation. The alcoholometer registered 6°. Using a still, I obtained alcohol at 60°, from which I extracted this laboratory liqueur brandy.

'Thus, invaded and conquered by the same pathogenic germ, men develop according to their temperaments: the feverish depressives, who spend more than they acquire, develop tuberculosis—dwarf tumours; the cold-blooded arthritics, who acquire more than they spend, develop cancer—giant tubercles.

'The two diseases sometimes exchange victims. Most cancer patients are tubercular patients who have been cured and have cooled down. Dubard was the first to notice this. What is a safeguard for one group (richness in glycogen or over-feeding) is a threat to the other group.'

The old doctor nodded; he was listening carefully again, but his face was expressionless, and he clearly had his own ideas.

The speaker stopped for a moment, and then said:

'We must look at the truth without flinching (that's what we are here for, after all) and not be afraid of opening this mysterious, awe-inspiring door to the cure of tuberculosis.'

'Whatever the truth of the matter,' said the old doctor, 'this resemblance and this inverse ratio which you claim to see between the two diseases are indicated to a certain extent by the figures we have. It is obvious that the two sets of statistics correspond. In Paris there is one cancer patient for every four tubercular patients. When two hundred and sixty tubercular patients die here in one week, there are sixty-five deaths from cancer. In France as a whole, there are a hundred and eighty thousand deaths caused every year by tuberculosis, and thirty-six thousand victims of cancer: a proportion of five to one. Five hundred French people die every day of tuberculosis; a hundred die every day of cancer.'

'And how many are going to die of it tomorrow?' said the young man, raising his cold, lucid eyes in a prayer which he knew to be futile.

'For we have lifted only a corner of the veil and admitted only a small part of the truth . . .'

'Yes,' said the old doctor, 'there is much more to it than that.

'The ravages of cancer are increasing day by day. Without the slightest doubt, modern life is multiplying the cases of morbid receptivity which are especially favourable to the disease.

'The general condition gives the lesion its fatal quality. As I said before, it is because of the patient that the disease is incurable. What is the use of obtaining a local cure by cutting away harmful matter, if the patient, left to himself, revives the disease? We can only stand by helplessly! A tubercular patient whose tubercles we removed, without doing any more for him, would be doomed to suffer a relapse. Similarly the scalpel isn't an adequate means of defence against malignant tumours. The facts are there to prove it: out of a hundred patients operated on for cancer of the bones, there are ninety-two recurrences; for cancer of the breast, the same percentage of recurrences—ninety-two; for uterine epithelioma, ninety-six; for cancer of the rectum, ninety-eight; for cancer of the tongue,' (he nodded in the direction of the door), 'ninety-nine.'

During these last few sentences, he had taken a sheet of notepaper and a pair of scissors from the mantelpiece and had started automatically cutting up the paper. Suddenly realizing the vague instinct behind his gesture, he tossed the two objects aside. He drew himself up.

'It is beginning to attack the young . . . Oh, I can still see in my mind's eye the inexorable picture of a little bright-eyed angel with a breast as huge and purple as a red cabbage! . . . Cancer is spreading through mankind as it does through a human being. If we don't stop it,' he added with the grim irony I had already heard in his voice, 'there'll be no need to wonder any more whether the world is going to die as the result of the extinction of the sun!'

'What other relationships,' said the young doctor, putting his hands to his forehead, 'are linked to this fantastic relationship between the two greatest living scourges? Syphilis, which I haven't mentioned so far. What others? Where will the research take me that I shall be continuing when I leave here? What will it condemn me to? I don't know . . . To be seeing in a single glance the whole pestilential side of our misery, all the distress into which the human race is slipping, and which is such that one wonders how anybody dares speak of other dramas!'

All the same, after saying that, and stretching out his hands, which by a sort of sublime contagion were shaking like a sick man's, he added:

'Possibly—probably—the diseases of mankind will be cured one day. Everything may change. They will find a suitable diet to avoid what can't be checked. Then and only then will they dare to admit the massacre perpetrated by the diseases which are now incurable and on the increase. We may indeed be already curing certain incurable diseases; the remedies haven't had time to show their worth.

'We shall cure other people—that's certain—but we shan't cure *him.*'

Instinctively his arms fell to his sides, and his voice stopped in the silence of mourning.

The dying man was taking on a holy grandeur. In spite of them, all the time they had been there, he had been dominating their words, and if they had generalized the question, it had perhaps been in order to rid themselves of the particular case . . .

●

'Is he a Russian or a Greek?'

'I don't know. After spending so much time looking at men's insides, they all seem very much alike to me!'

'They are most alike,' murmured the other man, 'in their odious insistence on being different and hostile.'

The speaker seemed to shudder as if this idea had aroused a passion in him. He stood up, full of anger, transformed.

'Oh,' he said, 'what a disgraceful spectacle mankind offers!

'It fights against itself, in spite of the appalling wounds it bears. We whose task it is to examine wounds are struck more than other people by all the harm men deliberately inflict on one another. I'm not a politician or a revolutionary. It isn't my job to busy myself with social theories; I've plenty of other things to do; but now and then I have feelings of pity as lofty as dreams. There are times when I should like to punish men, and times when I should like to implore them!'

The old doctor smiled sadly at this vehemence, but then his smile disappeared in the face of such obvious, undeniable shame.

'That's true, alas! Wretched as we are, we go on rending ourselves with our own hands. War, war . . . To anyone looking at us in the future from afar, and to anyone looking at us now from above, we are lunatics and barbarians.'

'Why? Why?' said the young doctor, becoming increasingly agitated. 'Why do we remain mad, when we can see our madness?'

The old man shrugged his shoulders, as he had done a few moments earlier when they had been talking about incurable diseases.

'The force of tradition, helped by interested parties . . . We aren't free; we are tied to the past. We listen to what has always been done, we do it again, and the result is war and injustice. Perhaps some day mankind will succeed in ridding itself of the obsession with what it was. Let us hope that we shall finally emerge from the long ages of massacre and misery. What more can we do than hope for that to happen?'

The old doctor stopped there. The young one said:

'We can want it to happen.'

The other made a vague gesture with his hand.

The young man exclaimed:

'For the world's ulcer there is a great overall cause. You have just said what it is; subservience to the past, time-honoured prejudice, which prevents mankind from beginning everything all over again in accordance with reason and morality. The spirit of tradition pollutes mankind; and the names of two of its appalling manifestations are . . .'

The old man straightened up on his chair, already beginning to make a gesture of protest, as if to signify: 'Don't say it!'

But the young man couldn't help speaking out.

'Property and patriotism,' he said.

◖

'Hush!' cried the old doctor, 'I can't go along with you there. I recognize the evils of the present day. I long for a new era with all my heart. I do more than that: I believe in it. But don't talk like that about two sacred principles!'

'Ah!' said the young man bitterly. 'You talk like the others, Chief . . . But we have to go to the root of the evil, you know that perfectly well . . .'

He went on violently:

'Why do you act as if you didn't know it? . . . If we want to cure mankind of oppression and war, we are right to use every possible means—I repeat, every possible means—to attack the principle of personal wealth and the cult of the mother country.'

'No, you aren't right!' said the old man, standing up in a state of great agitation, and casting a hard, almost savage glance at his companion . . .

'We are right!' cried the other.

All of a sudden, the grey head drooped once more, and the old man said in an undertone:

'Yes, it's true, you are right . . .

'I remember . . . one day, during the war, we were gathered round a dying man. Nobody could recognize him. They had found him in the debris of a dressing-station which had been shelled—deliberately or not, it came to the same thing—and his face had been mutilated. Nobody knew what he was: he be-

longed to one of the two armies, that was all that anybody could
say. He was groaning, weeping, howling, inventing horrible
cries. We tried to distinguish in his death-agony some word,
some accent, which would at least have indicated his national-
ity. We didn't succeed; we were unable to hear anything distinct
coming from the figure panting on the stretcher. We followed
him with our eyes and listened to him until he fell silent. When
he died and we stopped trembling, I saw and I understood for a
moment. I understood deep inside me that man is more closely
attached to man than to his fellow countrymen. I understood
that every word of hatred and revolt against the army, every insult to the flag, and every antipatriotic appeal was a call for idealism and beauty.

'Yes, you are right, you are right! And since that day, I have
had occasion to penetrate to the truth several times. But what
can I do? . . . I'm an old man, I haven't the strength to stay with
the truth.'

'Chief!' murmured the young man in a tone of tender respect.

The old doctor went on, opening his heart and growing in-
toxicated with truth:

'Yes, I know, I know, I know, I tell you! I know that, in spite
of the maze of arguments and special cases in which it's easy to
lose one's way, nothing can shake the simple truth that the law
which makes some men rich at birth and the others poor, and
which maintains a state of chronic social inequality, is a supreme
injustice which has no more validity than that which formerly
created races of slaves, and that patriotism has become a narrow,
offensive feeling which, as long as it exists, will feed loathsome
war and advance the exhaustion of the world; that neither work,
nor material and moral prosperity, nor the noble refinements of
progress, nor the marvels of art have any need of hostile emu-
lation—and that all these things, on the contrary, are crushed
by warfare. I know that the map of a country is made up of con-

ventional lines and disparate names, that innate self-love brings us closer to man himself than to those who belong to the same geographical area; that we are more truly the compatriots of those who understand and love us, and are on the level of our souls, or of those who are suffering the same slavery, than of those whom we meet in the street . . . National groups, units of the modern world, are what they are—agreed. But by the monstrous, growing deformation of patriotic feeling, mankind is killing itself, mankind is dying, and the present period is a death-agony.'

They both had the same vision and said at the same time:

'It's a cancer, it's a cancer.'

The old doctor became excited, falling a prey to the evidence.

'I know as well as you do that posterity will judge severely those who have cultivated and spread the fetichism of ideas of oppression. I know that the cure of an abuse begins only when people refuse to subscribe to the cult which consecrates that abuse . . . And I who have spent half a century studying all the great discoveries which have changed the face of things—I know that when one begins something, one has to face the hostility of everything in existence.

'I know that it is a vice to spend years and centuries saying about progress: "I would like it to happen but I don't want it to happen," and that if, in order to bring about certain reforms, universal consent is required, well, the universe too can be seeded! I know all that!

'Yes . . . But what about me? I am beset by too many cares, overwhelmed by too much work; and then, as I have already said, I am too old. These ideas are too new for me. A man's mind is capable of absorbing only a certain *quantum* of creation and novelty. When that amount has been exhausted, however much progress is being made around him, he refuses to see or go forward . . . I am incapable of contributing any fruitful exaggeration to the discussion. I am incapable of the audacity of being logical. I admit to you, my dear boy, that I haven't the strength to be right!'

●

'My dear Chief,' said the young man, in a tone of reproach which had grown stronger and more heartfelt in the face of his sincerity, 'you have publicly expressed your disapproval of those who had publicly attacked the idea of patriotism. Your name has been used as a weapon against them.'

The old man drew himself up. His face coloured.

'I can't agree with people putting the country in jeopardy!'

I could no longer recognize him. He had fallen from his lofty heights, and already he was no longer himself. This made me sad at heart.

'But,' the other murmured, 'everything you have just been saying . . .'

'It isn't the same thing. The people you are talking about have hurled challenges at us. They have taken their stand as enemies and have justified every insult in advance.'

'Those who insult them are guilty of the crime of ignorance,' said the young man in a trembling voice. 'They fail to understand the superior logic of what is going to happen.'

He bent close to his companion, and in a steadier voice asked him:

'How could the movement which is beginning fail to be revolutionary? Those who have been the first to cry out are alone, and therefore either hated or ignored—you have just said so yourself!—But posterity will pay tribute to this vanguard of martyrs, will salute those who have cast doubt upon the ambiguous notion of patriotism, and will compare them to the precursors to whom we ourselves have rendered justice!'

'Never!' cried the old man.

He had listened to these last words with anguish in his eyes. A line of stubborn impatience had furrowed his forehead, and his hands were clenched in hatred.

He corrected himself. No, it wasn't the same thing; in any case, these arguments served no useful purpose, and, pending the day when everybody would do his duty, it would be best for them to do theirs and tell that poor woman the truth.

'And who is going to tell *us* the truth?'

The question came out unexpectedly; the young man had hesitated, anxiety written all over his face, and then this great appeal, of universal significance, had burst forth from his lips.

'What is the use of anyone telling us the truth, seeing that we think we know it?'

'Ah,' said the young man, abruptly gripped by an invisible terror which I did not understand and which seemed to throw him suddenly off his balance, 'how I should like to know what I am going to die of!'

He added with a shudder which I saw:

'I should like to be sure about it . . .'

His illustrious colleague looked at him in surprise, halting a gesture in mid-air:

'You have some symptoms that are worrying you?'

'I'm not sure . . . It's just an impression I have . . . All the same, I don't think . . .'

'Is it what we have been talking about?'

'Oh, no! It's something entirely different,' the young man replied, turning away.

Just as a sort of ardour had transfigured him a little earlier, now certain signs of weakness had turned him once again into another man.

'Chief, you were my teacher. You witnessed my ignorance, and now you witness my weakness.'

His hands were twitching nervously, and he was blushing like a schoolgirl.

'Come, now!' said the old doctor, without asking him any more questions. 'I know all about that. I've been afraid myself in the past—afraid of cancer, then afraid of madness!'

'You, Chief—afraid of madness!'

'All that disappeared, year by year . . . And now,' he said, in a voice which changed in spite of himself, 'all that I'm afraid of is old age.'

'There's no denying, Chief,' said his disciple, who had regained some of his composure and thought himself entitled to smile in face of the facts, 'that that disease is the only one you have any reason to fear!'

'What's that you say?' exclaimed the old man with a violence which he could not restrain and which took the young man aback.

He was ashamed of the pitiful naïvety of this protest, and stammered:

'Oh, if you only knew! If you knew what it was like, this simple, simple disease, this gentle, inevitable erosion and general infection! Oh, if only someone could come along before we die, to cure our decrepitude!'

The young doctor did not know what to say to this man who was suddenly disarmed, as he himself had been a moment before. A word trembled on his lips; then he looked at the old doctor, and what he saw both disturbed and calmed a little his own distress. I followed with my eyes this rapid exchange of torments, and I found it hard to tell whether the feeling which had relieved his anguish in the face of his master's was base or sublime. . . .

'There are some people,' he ventured at last, 'who maintain that Nature knows what she is doing.'

'Nature!'

The old man gave a derisive laugh which sent a chill down my spine.

'Nature is a curse,' he said. 'Nature is evil. Illness is Nature too. Since the abnormal is inevitable, isn't it as if it were the normal?'

All the same, moved by his defeat, he added:

' "Nature knows what she is doing." Oh, at bottom that's an unhappy phrase for which men can't really be blamed. They hope to dazzle themselves and comfort themselves with the idea of an inevitable fate. It's because that isn't true that they insist that it is.'

They looked at each other as they had done at the beginning. One of them said:

'We are a couple of poor wretches.'

'Of course,' the other said gently.

They made for the door.

'Let's go. She's waiting for us. Let's take her the irremissible sentence. Not simply death, but immediate death. It's like two sentences.'

The old doctor added between his teeth:

' "Sentenced by science." What a stupid phrase!'

'Those who believe in God ought to place the responsibility higher than that.'

They stopped near the door, at the word 'God'. Once again their voices dropped, and became scarcely audible, fierce and trembling.

'As for him,' the old man exclaimed in a low voice, 'he's mad, he's mad!'

'Oh, it's a good thing for him that he doesn't exist!' muttered the other with vindicative irony.

And I saw the old man turn round at the far end of the grey room, to face the whitening window and to shake his fist at the sky, on account of the realities of life.

. . . The sick man's face was concealed behind the railing of his long fingers. A splendid, precise dream was coming from his decomposing mouth, which was nourishing the abject disease, and this pure torrent of thought was flowing over the woman, to whom the doctors had presumably spoken.

'Architecture! . . . What can I say about it? Listen to this, for example . . . A huge site: a sheet, a plain of colossal paving-stones, spread over the heights of the city, in the direction of the suburbs. Then a portico takes shape. Columns spring up. Soon they crowd together, increase in number, rising to such dizzy heights that their long, fleeting lines give them the appearance of narrowing at their summits, and the roof looks like the shadow of the evening or the night. A quarter of the site is covered like that. It is like an enormous, wide-open palace, invested with a sort of seminatural grandeur, worthy of receiving the rising sun and the setting sun as guests. At night the vast, pale forest sheds over its stone soil a diffused light: the aurora borealis of a firmament of lamps.

'It is here that a large part of public activity is concentrated: trade, finance, art, exhibitions and ceremonies. It is swarming with a huge crowd which keeps forming eddies and currents, which swirl around slowly at the crossroads; and the eye loses itself in its midst, in this dream of vertical lines.

'On one side, the colonnade plunges straight into the next district of the city, like a cliff. There is no style about all this. Large-scale architecture has a simple appearance. But the proportions are so vast that they strain the eyes and grip the heart.'

I gazed intently at this man in whom, hour by hour, death was extending its hold, and all of a sudden I noticed his neck. It was swollen by the sort of creature which was growing inside it . . . While he was talking I had the impression that I might almost have been able to see it, deep, deep down in the darkness of his mouth.

'From a long way off,' he went on, 'when you arrive by train, you can see that the colonnade is built on a mountain, and on the side facing the line of gateways, a staircase leads down to the gardens on the plain. That staircase! It's like nothing else in the whole world, except perhaps the ruins of the Pyramids in Egypt. It's so wide that it takes an hour to walk the length of one step. It's broken up by lifts going up and down like slender chains; it's dotted with moving platforms, hoists and trains. It's a staircase as big as the mountain itself. Nature martyred over an area of several square miles, refashioned by geometrical drawing, harmoniously presented—because, from above or below, you can take in the whole staircase with a single glance—and also reshaped in new designs; great blocks, whole hills which weigh upon it and dominate it are astir with a strange life: they are statues . . . That smooth, polished slope, turning and bending in a curve which you don't understand straight away—that's an arm.'

His voice had a piercing quality which fore-shadowed and emphasized the beauty of his dream.

He went on talking about magnificent things, with only a few days between him and the grave. And I, listening to him with only half an ear, overwhelmed by the contrast between his body and his soul, would have dearly loved to know whether he knew . . .

'A sculptor is a child: he works with white, elementary ideas, in simple lines, rigid and all of a piece. It's a difficult ideal that he pursues, almost disarmed in the face of the commonplace, with his rudimentary tools. Sculptors are children, and few sculptors are child prodigies.'

He searched for statues in his dream:

'A piece of sculpture must be dramatic, theatrical, even when it depicts only one character. I can't understand the concept of the bust, which has no more soul than it has limbs and which is the equivalent in stone of a picture—which indeed would be truer to nature, for the picture, like the model, possesses light and shade.'

He appeared to look at something and to say what he could see:

'The marble statue of the Fall. Where is that immobility for-ever falling?

'A splendid subject for a piece of sculpture: a beloved person you have lost, raising his tombstone and showing you his face. This face is at once infinitely desirable and infinitely terrifying—because of him and because of his death. It comes from the depths of the earth, a death's-head, and yet it is on earth, since it is there and you are looking at it. Behind the shadow of the head, the shadow of the hand is supporting the tombstone.

'I don't know whether the beloved is a dead man or a dead woman; the face is a dear face, whose features strike the heart as poignantly alive and possess a miraculous kindliness; but it is motionless and muddy like the earth, and although its gaze is directed at you, it can hear nothing. The mouth smiles, and the smile is an ineffable combination of love and horror—because it is his smile, but also the grimace of the last moment of his death-agony. Why this moisture on the lips? What infinity of tiny particles, what vast icy breath are they exhaling? The eyes are weeping a little, but the tears are also liquefaction. You think of the memory whose imprint remains on this face, and of the body beneath it. The body is alone in the darkness, disappear-ing, spreading out into the hiding-places of the earth; and the head is here, white, everlasting flotsam, coming towards you, looking at you, smiling and grimacing at you . . . Sweet, ter-rifying monster, opening the mouth of the tomb and coming out! . . . Friend remaining within! . . . Enemy! . . .'

●

Then he talked about painting; he said that it had a relief which sculpture lacked. He spoke of the incredible immobility of fine portraits and the jealous authority of the painted face as it catches the eye.

He sighed: 'Artists deserve our pity; they have to create the world all over again. Everything depends on them. How can anybody ever know what the fragment of reality which offers itself contains? You need clairvoyance for that—a clairvoyance verging on hallucination. The great artists go outside Nature: Rembrandt has visions, just as Beethoven hears voices.'

This last name brought him to the subject of music.

He said that although music had attained a perfection without parallel in the history of man's pursuit of art in all its countless forms—on account of Beethoven alone—there none the less existed a hierarchy among the arts, according to the contribution which thought made to them; that for that reason literature occupied a place above the rest: whatever the number of masterpieces created so far, the harmony of music was not to be compared with the whispered voice of a book.

◗

'Anna,' he said, 'which is the better poet—the one who translates into fine, sonorous phrases the beautiful pictures which present themselves to us, crowded, majestic and triumphant like colours in broad daylight, or the poet of the North who, in the bleak, bare setting of grey corners, in the smoky yellow light from the windows, shows in a few words that faces can be transfigured and that the only true infinity is in the shadows separating two people.'

'Both of them are probably right.'

'For my part, although all my childhood I was drawn to the poets of exuberance and sunshine, I prefer the others now, to

the extent of believing only in them. Colour is empty and superficial. Anna, Anna, the soul is a night-bird. Everything is
beautiful, but dark beauty is primeval and maternal. Light
shows appearances; the darkness reveals ourselves. Darkness is
the miraculous reality which renders the invisible.'

A movement which placed him in semi-profile showed me
clearly the swollen thickness of his neck.

'Yes, yes,' he went on, with a slight gesture which none the
less had a certain solemnity, a pitiful, prophetic gesture, 'it is in
literature that you will find the loftiest and fullest acceptance of
what is; it is literature which provides in the most perfect fashion—almost perfection itself—the reward of self-expression.
Yes . . . although Shakespeare has afforded glimpses of the interior world, and although Victor Hugo has created a verbal
splendour such that after him the setting of the world seems to
have changed, the art of writing has not had its Beethoven. That
is because the scaling of the highest peak is more difficult here;
it is because here form is only form, and we are concerned with
truth in its entirety. Nobody has ever expressed in a great work—
secondary works don't exist—truth itself, which so far, through
the ignorance or the timidity of the great writers, has remained
an object of prayer or of metaphysical speculation. It is still confined and confused in treatises of a scientific appearance or in
pitiful religious books which are restricted to ethical considera-
tions and which wouldn't be understood if certain people didn't
adopt their dogmas for supernatural reasons. In the theatre, writers rack their brains to find amusing formulas; in books they
show themselves as caricaturists of a sort.

'Nobody has ever combined the drama of human beings with
the drama of everything. When will profound truth and lofty
beauty finally be united? They must be united, those two ab-
solutes which both already unite men—for it is through the ad-

miration of beauty that we enjoy pure moments which have no limits and no country, and it is through truth that the blind see, that the poor are brothers, and that all men will one day be right. The book of poetry and truth is the most sublime discovery which remains to be made.'

E L E V E N

The two women were alone together at the wide-open window, drawn to it by the vast space beyond. In the clear, bright light of the autumn sun, I saw how withered the pregnant woman's face was.

All of a sudden, that face took on a frightened expression; the woman fell back towards the wall, leant against it, and collapsed with a stifled cry.

The other woman took her in her arms; she dragged her over to the bell, and rang it again and again . . . Then she remained there, not daring to move, holding in her arms the frail, heavy woman, her face close to that face whose eyes were rolling and whose cry, dull and walled in at first, finally soared upwards in a scream.

The door opened. People came hurrying in. New faces appeared. Outside the door, the staff of the hotel were on the watch. I caught a glimpse of the proprietress who was finding it hard to conceal her comical disappointment.

The woman had been laid on the bed; vases were moved about, towels unfolded, hurried instructions given.

The woman's pain abated, fell silent. She was so happy to have stopped suffering that she laughed. A somewhat strained reflection of her laughter appeared on the faces bending over her. She was carefully undressed . . . Like a child, she offered no resistance . . . The bed was prepared. Her legs looked quite spindly; her face stagnated, reduced to nothingness. All that anybody saw was that huge belly in the middle of the bed. Her hair was undone and lay inert around her face like a puddle. A pair of woman's hands nimbly plaited it.

Her laughter stopped, broke off miserably.

'It's beginning again . . .'

A groan which grew louder, a fresh scream.

The young woman—the young girl—her only friend, had remained with her. She looked at her and listened to her, deep in thought; she was thinking that she too contained similar sufferings and similar cries.

. . . This lasted all day; for hours on end, from morning till night, I heard the heartrending complaint of the pitiful dual creature rise and fall. I saw flesh split asunder; I saw supple flesh break like stone.

At certain moments I fell back, exhausted, incapable of looking or listening any longer; I could not bear so much reality. Then once again, making an effort, I pressed against the wall, and my gaze pierced it.

The two legs were scarlet. They were being held straight and apart. They looked like two streams of blood flowing from her belly—women's blood, so often shed . . . Her modesty, her religious air of mystery had been thrown to the winds. The whole of her flesh was offered to view, red and gaping, exposed as on a butcher's stall, naked to the very depths.

The young girl kissed her on the forehead, bravely coming right up to the vast cry.

When that cry assumed a shape, it was: 'No! No! I don't want to!'

Faces which had almost grown old in a few hours, with fatigue, nausea, and gravity, passed to and fro.

I heard somebody say:

'We mustn't help her, we must let Nature take its course. Nature knows what she is doing.'

This phrase had a familiar ring. Nature! I remembered that the doctor, the other day, had cursed her.

And my lips repeated in surprise the old lie, while my eyes considered the fragile, innocent woman at the mercy of immense Nature which was crushing her, rolling her in her blood, extracting from her all the suffering she could provide.

The midwife had rolled up her sleeves and pulled on some rubber gloves. I could see her moving these huge, shining, red and black hands about like a washerwoman's beetles.

And the whole thing became a nightmare in which I only half believed, my head aching, my throat filled with a bitter smell of murder, and with that of the carbolic acid which was being poured out by the bottleful.

Basins full of red water, pink water, yellowish water. A pile of dirty linen in a corner, and more towels all over the room, spread out like white wings, with their fresh smell.

At one moment when my attention had wandered, I heard the cry separated from her. A cry which was scarcely more than the sound of an object, a tiny noise. It was the new human being which was breaking away, which so far was simply a piece of flesh taken from her flesh—her heart which had just been torn out of her.

This cry made a profound impression on me. I who am the witness of all that men endure, felt within me some indefinable paternal or fraternal response to this first human signal.

She smiled.

'That was over quickly!' she said.

The light faded. The voices around her fell silent. An ordinary night-light; the fire, stirring slightly now and then; the clock, that poor soul. Scarcely anything around the bed, as in a real temple.

She was there, stretched out, fixed in an ideal immobility, her open eyes directed towards the window. She could see the evening gradually falling on the most beautiful of her days.

On that inert mass, on that drawn face, there shone the glory of having created, a sort of ecstasy which was offering thanks to suffering, and one could see the new world of thoughts which was inhabiting her.

She was thinking about the growing child; she was smiling at the joys and sorrows he was going to bring her; she was smiling too at the brother or sister who would come into the world.

And I thought about all that at the same time as she did— and I saw her martyrdom more clearly than she did.

That massacre, the tragedy of the flesh, is so ordinary and commonplace that every woman carries the memory and the mark of it. And yet nobody knows it properly. The doctor, who sees so much suffering of the same kind, is incapable of being moved by it any longer; the woman, who is too full of tenderness, can no longer remember it. Between sentimental involvement on the one hand and professional disinterestedness on the other, the pain fades and is forgotten. But I who see in order to see have experienced the full horror of that agony of childbirth which, as the man said whom I overheard the other day, never ceases in a woman's body; and I shall never forget the great laceration of life.

The night-light was placed in such a position that the bed was plunged in shadow. I could no longer make out the mother; I no longer had any knowledge of her; I believed in her.

◐

Today the mother was carried with exquisite care into the next room, which she had occupied before, and which is more spacious and comfortable.

The room was then cleaned from top to bottom.

This was no easy matter. I saw the staff fold the red sheets, remove the soiled bedding in which infection would rapidly have taken hold, and wash down the bedstead and the fireplace; and the maid was hard put to it to push the pile of linen, cotton-wool and bottles out of the room with her foot. Even the curtains bore bloody fingermarks, and the bedside rug was heavy with blood like a bloated animal.

○

It was Anna who was speaking this time.

'Be careful, Philippe, you don't understand the Christian religion. You don't really know what it is. You talk about it,' she added with a smile, 'like women when they talk about men, or like men when they try to explain women. Its basic element is love. It is an arrangement of love between people who instinctively hate one another. It is also a wealth of love in our hearts which in itself answers all our yearnings when we are small, and to which afterwards every tenderness is added like one treasure to another. It is a law of effusion and the food of that effusion. It is life itself, almost a work of art, almost a person.'

'But Anna, dear, that isn't the Christian religion. That's you . . .'

○

In the middle of the night I heard somebody talking on the other side of the wall. I overcame my fatigue; I looked.

The man was alone, stretched out in his bed. A lamp with the wick half turned down had been left in the room. He was stirring slightly. He was dreaming and talking in his sleep.

He smiled and said: 'No!' three times, with growing pleasure. Then the smile he had been addressing to the vision delighting him faded and disappeared. For a moment his features remained fixed and rigid, as if in expectation, and then the lips pouted in a slight grimace. The next instant the face took on an expression of terror and the mouth opened. 'Anna! Ah, ah! . . . Ah, ah!' it cried without closing, gagged by sleep. Then he awoke and rolled his eyes about. He heaved a sigh and calmed down. He sat up in his bed, still shaken and terrified by all that had happened a few seconds before; he looked all around him, as if to soothe his eyes and rid them completely of the nightmare in which they had been involved. The familiar sight of the bedroom, in the middle of which the discreet little lamp stood utterly motionless, reassured and cured this man who had just seen something which did not exist, who had just smiled at ghosts and touched them, who had just been mad.

◖

I got up this morning feeling worn out. I am worried; I have a dull ache in my face; my eyes, when I looked at myself in the mirror, seemed red, as if I were looking through a film of blood. I walk and move about with difficulty, half-paralyzed. I am beginning to be punished in my flesh for the long hours spent pressed against this wall, with my eye to the hole. And it is getting worse.

Besides, I am plagued by all sorts of worries when I am alone, freed from the scenes and visions to which I am devoting my life. Worries about my job, which I am placing in jeopardy, and about the steps which I ought to be taking but am not taking, in my insistence on brushing aside all pressing obligations, on postponing everything, on repelling with all my strength my fate as an employee destined to be caught up in the slow, purring mechanism of an office clock.

Trivial worries too, harassing because they pile up, one after another, minute by minute: not to make any noise, not to put on a light when there is no light next door, to remain hidden, always to remain hidden. The other evening, I was choked by a fit of coughing while I was watching them talking. I grabbed my pillow, thrust my head into it, and stifled the sounds coming from my mouth.

It seems to me that everything is going to combine against me in some sort of revenge, and that I shan't be able to hold out for long. All the same, I shall go on looking as long as I have health and courage, for this is worse and more than a duty.

◐

The man was failing. Death was obviously in the house.

It was fairly late in the evening. The two of them were sitting facing each other, on opposite sides of the table.

I knew that their marriage had taken place in the afternoon. They had concluded that union which was only an additional solemnity for the approaching farewell. A few white blossoms— lilies and azaleas—were strewn on the table, the mantelpiece, an armchair; and he was as moribund as these heads of cut flowers.

'We are married,' he said. 'You are my wife. You are my wife, Anna!'

It was for the nuptial joy of uttering these words that he had hoped so fervently. Nothing more . . . but he felt so poor, with his few remaining days, that it was all happiness for him.

He looked at her, and she raised her eyes to him—he adoring her sisterly affection, and she attached to his adoration. What infinite emotion there was in these two silences confronting each other with a certain tenderness; in the dual silence of these two human beings, who I had noticed, never touched each other, even with their finger-tips.

The young girl straightened up and said in a trembling voice:
'It's late, I'm going to bed.'

She stood up. The lamp, which she placed on the mantelpiece, lit up the whole room.

She was trembling all over. She seemed to be in the middle
of a dream, and to be unsure how to obey this dream.

Standing there, she raised her arms and took the combs out
of her hair, which, as it streamed down in the darkness, seemed
to be lit up by the setting sun.

He had made an abrupt movement. He was looking at her in
surprise, without saying a word.

She removed a gold pin which fastened the top of her bodice,
and a little of her bosom was exposed.

'What are you doing, Anna? What are you doing?'

'Why, I'm undressing . . .'

She had intended to say that in a normal tone of voice, but
she had been unable to do so. He replied with an inarticulate
exclamation, a cry from a heart touched on the raw . . . He was
disturbed, excited by stupefaction, desperate regret, and also the
splendour of an incredible hope.

'You are my husband . . .'

'Oh,' he said, 'you know that I am nothing.'

In a weak, tragic voice he stammered out broken phrases, dis-
connected words:

'. . . Married for form's sake . . . I knew it, I knew it . . .
Formality . . . Our conventions . . .'

She had stopped. Her hand had settled hesitantly on her neck,
like a flower on her bodice.

She said:

'You are my husband; you have a right to see me.'

He made a slight gesture . . . She hurriedly corrected herself:

'No . . . No, that isn't your right; it is my wish.'

I began to understand what an effort she was making to be

kind. She wanted to give this man, this poor man dying at her feet, a reward worthy of her. She wanted to give him out of charity the sight of herself.

But it was even more difficult than that: it had to avoid the appearance of being the payment of a debt: he would not have agreed to it, despite the joy growing in his eyes. He had to believe that it was simply a conjugal act, willingly performed, a caress freely bestowed on his life. She had to conceal from him, like a vice, her suffering and revulsion. And foreseeing all the inspired tact and strength of mind she would have to expend in order to carry out the sacrifice, she was afraid of herself.

He was protesting:

'No . . . Anna . . . Dear Anna . . . Think of . . .'

He was going to say: 'Think of Michel.' But he lacked the strength to put forward at that moment the only decisive argument, and he simply murmured:

'You! . . . You! . . .'

She repeated:

'It is my wish.'

'I don't want you to . . . No, no . . .'

He said this more and more feebly, overcome by love and by the frenzied desire for it to happen. Out of an instinctive delicacy he had put his hand over his eyes, but his hand fell little by little, fell defeated.

She continued undressing. Her hands fumbled frantically, as if they no longer knew what they were doing, and stopped now and then, only to begin again. She was magnificently alone, helped only by a little pride.

She took off her black bodice, and her bosom emerged like the day. Her flesh quivered as soon as the light touched her, and she folded her bright, pure arms over her breasts. Then, putting her hands behind her and thrusting her flushed face forward, her lips pursed in concentration as if she were giving all her attention to what she was doing, she unhooked the belt of her skirt, which slipped down her legs. She stepped out of it with a soft rustling, like the sound of wind in the depths of the garden.

She removed the black petticoat which lent a gentle melancholy to her figure, the corset which boldly imposed its strength upon her, and the drawers which, with their shape and their folds, vaguely imitated her nakedness.

She stood with her back to the fireplace. She had fine, majestic, sweeping gestures which were none the less delicate and feminine. She unfastened one stocking, and withdrew from the dark, filmy veil a leg as firm and polished as that of a statue by Michelangelo.

At that moment she shivered, brought up short, filled with repugnance. She pulled herself together, and, to explain the shudder which had stopped her, said:

'I'm a little cold . . .'

Then she went on, revealing her immense modesty as she violated it, and took the ribbon of her chemise between her fingers.

The man cried softly, so as not to frighten her with his voice: 'Holy Mother of God!'

And he sat there, a huddled, shrunken figure, with all his life in his eyes, burning in the darkness, his love on a par with her beauty.

He was gasping: 'More . . . More . . .'

The great moment had arrived; the vast colloquy between the silences of ardour and virtue. The poor, weak eyes of the dying man were despoiling her, deflowering her—and he had to fight against the vast strength of this entreaty in order to obtain its fulfilment. His action had everything against it: him and her.

Yet, with a gentle coquetry which was simple and august, she slipped the straps of her chemise over the warm marble of her shoulders—and she was naked before him.

◗

I had never before seen a woman so radiantly beautiful. I had never dreamt of such a woman. Her face had struck me the first day by its beauty and its regularity; and tall as she was—taller than myself—she had seemed to me both graceful and majestic; but I would never have imagined her to possess a figure of such splendid perfection.

With her superhuman proportions, she reminded me of the Eve in some great religious fresco. Huge, suave and supple, she had the same ample flesh, the same simple radiance, the same solemn, measured gestures. Broad shoulders, a firm, heavy bosom, small feet and sturdy legs, with calves as round as two breasts.

She instinctively adopted the sovereign attitude of the Venus de Medici: one arm half-folded over her breasts, the other reaching down with the open hand covering her belly. Then, in a movement of rapturous giving, she raised both hands to her hair.

Everything which had been hidden by her dress she now offered to his eyes. All that whiteness which until now she alone had seen, she sacrificed to this male gaze, which was going to die, but which was still alive.

Everything: her smooth virginal belly with the broad patch of golden down; her delicate silky skin, of a colour so pure and light that here and there it had a silvery sheen, and that at the throat and groin a little of the blue of the veins showed through, introducing as it were a cold shiver into the warm flesh-tint; the fold in her waist which came from her leaning to one side, and which, with the faint living collar around her neck, was the only line on her body; her hips as broad as the world; the limpid and troubled expression which she had in her eyes because she was naked.

She spoke: in a dreamlike voice, going further still in the supreme offering, she said:

'Nobody'—and she stressed this word with an insistence

which named somebody—'*Nobody*, I tell you, come what may, will ever know what I have done tonight.'

After confiding this secret for eternity to the worshipper bowed down before her like a victim, it was she who knelt before him. She went down on her lovely knees, and in this position, truly naked for the first time in her life, blushing to her shoulders, decked out and adorned with her chastity, she stammered out incoherent words of gratitude, as if she were well aware that what she was doing went beyond her duty and was more beautiful, and as if she were dazzled by it herself.

●

And when she had dressed again and obscured her beauty for ever, and they had parted without daring to say anything to each other, I was visited by a great doubt. Had she been right or wrong? I saw the man weep and I heard him murmur to himself;

'Now I shall no longer know how to die!'

T W E L V E

The man now remains in bed. The others circle cautiously around him. He makes little gestures, utters rare words, asks for water, smiles, keeps silent as thoughts crowd in on him.

This morning he assumed the hereditary attitude and folded his hands.

They gathered around him and looked at him.

'Do you want a priest?'

'Yes . . . No . . . ,' he said.

They went out; and a few moments later, as if he had been waiting outside the door, a man in the dark robe was there. They were alone together.

The dying man turned his face towards the newcomer.

'I am going to die,' he told him.

'What is your religion?' asked the priest.

'The religion of my country, the Orthodox religion.'

'That is a heresy which you must abjure before we can go any further. The only true religion is Roman Catholicism.'

He went on:

'Make your confession . . . I will give you absolution and baptize you.'

The other man made no reply. The priest repeated his question:

'Make your confession. Tell me what evil you have done—

apart from the error of your religious conviction. You will repent and everything will be forgiven.'

'The evil I have done?'

'Try to remember . . . Have I got to help you?'

He jerked his head towards the door.

'That person who is there?'

'She is my wife,' the man said with a slight hesitation.

This had not escaped the keen ears of the man bending over him. The priest scented a mystery.

'How long have you been married?' he asked.

'Two days.'

'Oh! Two days, eh? And before that, did you sin with her?'

'No,' said the man.

'Ah! . . . I assume that you aren't lying. So why didn't you sin? That isn't natural. For after all, you are a man . . .'

And as the sick man stirred uneasily, he went on:

'Don't be surprised, my son, if my questions are blunt and direct to the point of hurting you. I am questioning you very simply, under the protection of the august simplicity of my ministry. Answer me in the same simple way, and,' he added with a certain affability, 'you will make your peace with God.'

'She is a young girl,' said the old man. 'She is engaged to be married. I look her in when she was just a child. She has shared the fatigue of my life of travel, and has looked after me. I married her before dying, because I am rich and she is poor.'

'Just because of that? There's nothing else? Nothing at all?'

He stared the other man in the face with a searching, inquiring gaze. Then he said: 'Well?' with a smile and an engaging, almost conspiratorial wink.

'I love her,' said the man.

'At last you admit it!' said the priest.

He went on, fixing the dying man's eyes with his own, and be-
labouring him with his breath:

'So you desired that woman, the flesh of that woman, and
for a long time, eh?—yes, for a long time—you sinned in
thought? . . .

'Tell me, in the course of your travels together, what arrangements did you make about rooms and beds?

'You say that she looked after you. What did that involve?'

These few questions, with which the man of God tried to
enter into the misery of the dying man, separated them like a
string of insults. Their faces were considering each other now,
watching each other closely, and I could see the misunderstanding between the two men growing.

The dying man had closed up and become hard and incredulous in the presence of this stranger with the vulgar face, on
whose lips the word *God* and *truth* took on a comic complexion,
and who wanted him to open his heart to him.

All the same, he made an effort:

'If I have sinned in thought, to use your sort of language, that
proves that I haven't sinned, and why should I repent what was
purely and simply suffering?'

'Oh, let's have no theorizing, please. We aren't here for that.
I tell you, and you must believe me, that a sin committed in
thought is committed in intention, and that it is therefore a real
sin which calls for confession and expiation. Tell me the circumstances in which desire provoked the sinful thought; and tell
me how often this happened. Give me the details.'

'But I resisted,' groaned the man. 'That's all that I can say.'

'That isn't enough. The stain—you are now convinced, I pre-
sume, of the accuracy of that term—the stain must be washed
away by truth.'

'Very well,' said the dying man, admitting defeat. 'I confess
that I committed that sin, and I repent it.'

'That is no confession, and it won't do for me,' retorted the priest. 'In precisely what circumstances did you surrender, with regard to that person, to the suggestions of the spirit of evil?'

Something in the man suddenly revolted. He propped himself up on one elbow and stared at the stranger, who stared back at him, face to face.

'Why should I have the spirit of evil in me?' he asked.

●

'All men have it in them.'

'Then God must have given it to them, seeing that it was God who made them.'

'Oh, so you're the argumentative sort, are you? Just as you like. I'll answer you. Every man has within him both the spirit of good and the spirit of evil, in other words the possibility of doing the one or the other. If he succumbs to evil, he is damned; if he triumphs over evil, he is rewarded. In order to be saved, he has to deserve salvation by fighting with all his strength.'

'What strength?'

'The strength afforded by virtue and faith.'

'And, if he hasn't enough virtue and faith, is that his fault?'

'Yes, because it means that he has too much wickedness and blindness in his soul.'

The other man asked again:

'Who was it who deposited in his soul his dose of virtue and his dose of wickedness?'

'God gave him virtue, and also left him the possibility of doing evil; but at the same time he gave him free will which allows him to choose as he wishes between good and evil.'

'But if he has more evil instincts than good ones, and if they are stronger too, how can he possibly turn towards good?'

'Through free will,' said the priest.

'But free will is just a good instinct, and if . . .'

'A man will be good if he wants to be, that's all. In any case, we'll never finish arguing about what is really beyond argument. All that we can say is that things would be different if Lucifer hadn't been damned and if the first man hadn't sinned.'

'It isn't fair,' said the sick man, revived by this fight, though doubtless only to suffer a serious relapse, 'that we should pay the penalty for Lucifer and Adam.

'Above all, it is monstrous that they should have been damned and punished in the first place. If they succumbed, it was because God, who made them out of nothing—I repeat, out of *nothing*—in other words, who gave them *everything* that was in them, gave them more vice than virtue. He punished them for falling into the abyss into which he flung them!'

The man, a thin, dark figure, still propped up on his elbow with his chin in his hand, opened his eyes wide and listened to the other one as to an oracle.

The priest repeated, as if he could understand nothing else:

'They could have been pure if they had wished; that is the meaning of free will.'

His voice was almost gentle. He did not seem to have been affected by the series of blasphemies uttered by the man he had come to help. He was not interested in this theological discussion, and was simply contributing the indispensable words to it, out of force of habit. But perhaps he was waiting for the speaker to be tired of speaking.

And when the latter was panting with exhaustion, he uttered this dictum, as cold and clear as an inscription carved in stone:

'The wicked are unhappy; the good or the repentant are happy, in Heaven.'

'And on earth?'

'On earth, the good are unhappy like the rest, indeed more than the rest, for the more one suffers in this life, the more one is rewarded in the next.'

The man propped himself up again, seized with a fresh fit of anger which was wearing him out like a fever.

'Ah,' he said, 'the suffering of the good on earth is an abomination worse than original sin and worse than predestination. There's no excuse for it.'

The priest looked at the rebel with vacant eyes . . . (Yes, I could see now that he was waiting.) With great calm he said:

'How could souls be tested otherwise?'

'There's no excuse for it. Not even that puerile explanation based on God's supposed ignorance of the true quality of souls. The good ought not to suffer, if justice existed anywhere. They ought not to suffer, even a little, even for a single moment in all eternity. "One must suffer in order to be happy." How is it that nobody has ever stood up to protest against that savage law?'

He was getting exhausted. His voice was growing hoarse. His tortured body was panting and he was speaking haltingly.

'There would have been no possible answer to the accusation of that voice. However much you may turn the goodness of God in every direction, gild it and adorn it, you will never get rid of the stain on it made by undeserved suffering.'

'But happiness won by suffering is the universal destiny, the common law.'

'It is because it is the common law that it makes men doubt the existence of God.'

'God's purposes are impenetrable.'

Hollow-eyed, the dying man threw out his thin arms and cried:

'Lies, all lies!'

◗

'That's enough,' said the priest. 'I have listened patiently to your ravings, which fill me with pity, but it isn't a question of reasoning now. You have to get ready to appear before God, whom

you seem to have ignored during your life. If you have suffered,
you will be consoled in his bosom. Let that be sufficient for you.'

The sick man had fallen back in exhaustion. For a little while
he remained motionless under the folds of the white sheet, like
a marble statue with a bronze face stretched out on a tomb.

'God cannot console me.'

'My son, my son, what are you saying?'

His voice came to life again:

'God cannot console me because he cannot give me what I
want.'

'Oh, my poor child, how blind you are! . . . And what of
God's infinite power? What do you make of that?'

'Alas, I make nothing of it,' said the man.

'What? Is man to struggle all his life, tortured by suffering,
with no consolation in the end? What can you reply to that?'

'Alas, that isn't a question,' said the man.

'Why did you send for me?'

'I hoped, I hoped.'

'You hoped for what?'

'I don't know. Man only hopes for what he doesn't know.'

His hands groped about in space, then dropped back on to
the bed.

The two men remained silent, unchanging . . . I could tell
that both of them were considering the very existence of God.
Was God non-existent? Were the past and the future dead? In
spite of everything, there was a slight rapprochement, for a fleeting moment, between these two human beings preoccupied
with the same idea, between these two supplicants, between
these two brothers in dissimilarity.

'Time is passing,' said the preist.

And taking up the dialogue where he had left it a little earlier,
as if nothing had been said in the meantime, he went on:

'Tell me the circumstances of your carnal sin. Tell me . . .

When you were alone with that person, side by side, close to her, did you talk to each other or were you silent?'

'I don't believe in you,' said the man.

The priest frowned.

'Repent, and tell me that you believe in the Catholic religion which will save you.'

But the other shook his head in utter anguish and rejected all hope of happiness.

'Religion . . .' he began.

The priest interrupted him brutally.

'Don't start that again! Be quiet. I've no time for all your quibbling. Begin by believing in religion, and you'll see what it's like later. I suppose you won't believe in it because you might like it? That's why all your talk is untimely, and why I have come here to force you to believe.'

It was a duel, a ferocious struggle. The two men were facing each other like two enemies on the edge of the grave.

'You must believe.'

'I don't believe.'

'You must.'

'You want to alter the truth by means of intimidation.'

'Yes.'

He emphasized the crude character of his command:

'Whether you are convinced or not, believe. It isn't a question of evidence; it's a question of belief. You must believe at the very beginning, otherwise you run the risk of never believing. God doesn't condescend to convince the incredulous himself. The time of miracles is past. The only miracle is ourselves and faith. "Believe and Heaven will make you believe."'

Believe! He kept hurling the same word at him, like a stone.

'My son,' he went on, more solemnly, standing up with his big plump hand raised in the air, 'I demand of you an act of faith.'

'Get out,' said the man, with hatred in his voice.

But the priest did not move.

Spurred on by a sense of urgency, impelled by the need to save this soul in spite of itself, he became implacable.

'You are going to die,' he said. 'You are going to die. You have only a few moments to live. Submit.'

'No,' said the man.

The man in the black robe grasped hold of his hands.

'Submit. No hair-splitting arguments such as those on which you have just been wasting precious time . . . Such things are unimportant. Their substance is only wind. We are alone, you and I, with God.'

He nodded his head with its little bulging brow, its round, protuberant nose with the moist, black nostrils, its thin yellow lips stretched like pieces of string over two prominent teeth isolated in the dark: a face furrowed with lines along the forehead, between the eyebrows and around the mouth, and covered with a grey scrub on the chin and the cheeks; and he said:

'I am God's representative. You stand before me as if you were standing before God. Just say: "I believe," and I will let you be. "I believe": that's the essential thing. The rest is a matter of indifference to me.'

He was bending forward more and more, almost pressing his face against that of the dying man, trying to inflict his absolution on him like a blow.

'Just recite with me: "Our Father, who art in Heaven." I shan't ask anything more of you.'

The sick man's face was convulsed with refusal, and he shook his head twice: No . . . No . . .

Suddenly the priest straightened up with a triumphant air:

'At last! You have said it.'

'No.'

'Ah!' the priest muttered between his teeth.

He was kneading the man's hands between his own, and it was obvious that he would have clasped him in his arms to embrace him, to stifle him, that he would have murdered him if he had known that his death-rattle would be a confession of faith—he was so full of desire to convince him, to extract the words which he had come to hear from his lips.

He pushed away the withered hands, paced up and down the room like a wild beast, and came back to plant himself by the bed.

'Remember that you are going to die, to rot,' he told the wretched man in a trembling voice . . . 'Soon you will be under the ground. Say: "Our Father"—just those two words, nothing more.'

He was bending over him, watching his mouth, a dark, crouching figure like a demon lying in wait for a soul, like the whole Church bending over the whole of dying humanity.

'Say it . . . Say it . . . Say it . . .'

The other tried to draw away, and croaked furiously, in an undertone, with all that remained of his voice:

'No.'

'Swine!' the priest shrieked at him.

◑

'At least you're going to die with a crucifix in your hands.'

He took a crucifix out of his pocket and placed it squarely on his chest.

The other made a sudden movement of silent horror, as if religion were a contagious disease, and pushed the object to the floor.

The priest bent down, muttering insults: 'You blackguard, you want to die like a dog, but I'm here!' He picked up the crucifix, keeping it in his hand, and with flashing eyes, certain of surviving and conquering, waited for the last time.

The dying man was panting for breath, at the end of his tether, utterly worn out. The priest, seeing that he was in his power, once again placed the crucifix on his chest. This time the other left it there, no longer able to do anything but look at it with eyes full of hatred and despair; and his glances did not make it fall.

When the man in black had gone out into the night, and the sick man gradually awoke from him and freed himself from him, I reflected that the priest, in his violence and vulgarity, was horribly right. Was he a bad priest? No, on the contrary: he was a good priest who had spoken consistently in accordance with his conscience and his belief, and who tried to practise his religion simply, such as it was, without any hypocritical concessions. Ignorant, clumsy, crude—yes, he was all that, but honest and logical, even in his appalling attempt at conversion. During the half-hour in which I had heard him, he had tried, by all the means employed and recommended by religion, to ply his trade as a recruiter of souls and a dispenser of absolution; he had said all that a priest cannot help but say. The whole dogma of Christianity was revealed, clearly and explicitly, through the brutal vulgarity of the servant and slave. At a certain moment he had groaned in despair, with genuine distress: 'What do you want me to do?' If the man was right, the priest was right too. It was the priest who was the beast of burden of religion.

◐

. . . Ah! That thing which was standing motionless by the bed . . . That big tall thing which hadn't been there a little earlier, and which was obscuring the flickering flame of the candle beside the sick man . . .

I inadvertently made a slight noise as I pressed against the wall, and, very slowly, the thing turned a face towards me, with a terror which terrified me.

I knew those anguished features . . . Wasn't it the proprietor of the hotel, a strange character who was rarely to be seen . . .

He had been hanging about the corridor, waiting for the moment when the sick man, in the confusion of this temporary accommodation, would be alone. And now he was standing beside the man as he lay asleep or exhausted.

He stretched out his hand towards a bag which had been placed by the bed. As he made his movement, he kept his eyes on the dying man, so that his hand missed the object twice.

A creaking sound came from the floor above, and both of us gave a start. A door banged; he jumped up as if to stifle a cry.

. . . He slowly opened the bag. And I for my part, completely forgetting myself, was afraid that he might not have enough time.

He took out a packet which rustled gently. And as he gazed at the wad of banknotes he was holding in his hand, I saw the extraordinary radiance which lit up his face. All the emotions of love were mingled in it: adoration, mysticism, and also brutal lust . . . a sort of supernatural ecstasy as well as a coarse satisfaction which was already savouring immediate joys . . . Yes, every kind of love was stamped for a moment on the profound humanity of that thief's face.

. . . Somebody was keeping watch outside the half-open door . . . I saw an arm beckoning.

He left on tiptoe, slowly, hurriedly.

I myself am an honest man, and yet I held my breath at the same time as he did; I *understood* him . . . Try as I may to find excuses for myself, I have to admit that, with a horror and a joy similar to his own, I stole with him.

. . . All thefts are crimes of passion, even this one, which was cowardly and vulgar. (I remember his gaze of undying love for the treasure he had suddenly seized.) All offences, all crimes, are attempts carried out in the image of the immense desire to steal which is our very essence and the form of our naked soul: to have what one lacks.

Does that mean that we should absolve all criminals, and that punishment is an injustice? . . . No, we must defend ourselves against criminals. We must—since human society is based on honesty—strike them down in order to reduce them to impotence, and above all in order to dazzle others with terror and halt them on the threshold of crime. But, once the crime has been established, we must not search for fundamental excuses for it, for fear of always excusing it. We must condemn it in advance, by virtue of a cold principle. Justice must be as icy as a sword.

Justice is not, as its name seems to suggest, a virtue; it is an organization whose virtue lies in its insensibility; it does not exact expiation. It has nothing to do with expiation. Its role is to make examples: to turn the culprit into a sort of scarecrow, to impress anyone tempted by crime with the argument of its cruelty. Nobody, nothing, has the right to exact expiation; besides, nobody can; vengeance is too far removed from the act and strikes so to speak another person. Expiation is therefore a word for which there is no possible use whatever.

THIRTEEN

He did not move, he was so weak. The sinister weight of his flesh kept him prostrate and silent. Death had already deprived him of his gestures, of his perceptible movements.

His admirable companion had placed herself exactly within the man's immobilized gaze, sitting at the foot of the bed, face to face with him; her arms were stretched out horizontally towards the bedstead, and her two beautiful hands were resting lightly on the edge. Her profile was bent slightly forward, a fine, soft outline, a luminous script in the kindly dusk. Under the delicate arch of the eyebrow, the pupil quivered, bright and pure, like an infant sky; the silky skin of cheek and temple shone softly, and her luxuriant hair, that hair which I had seen naked, crowned with its graceful curls her brow in which her thoughts were as invisible as God.

She was alone with the man lying before her, tossed there so to speak, as if at the bottom of a hole—she who had wanted to be joined to him in feeling, and to be chastely widowed if he should die. He and I could see nothing in the whole world but her face; and in fact there was nothing but that in the deep shadows of the evening: her noble, naked face, and also her two magnificent hands which resembled each other like pride and tenderness.

. . . A voice came from the bed. I could scarcely recognize it.

'I haven't finished speaking,' said the voice.

Anna bent over the bed as over a coffin, to hear the words being breathed out, doubtless for the last time, by the motionless and almost shapeless body.

'Shall I have time . . . shall I . . .'

His voice was a scarcely audible whisper which almost remained in his mouth. Then it grew accustomed once again to life and became clear.

'I should like to confess something to you, Anna.

'I don't want this thing to die with me,' continued the voice, which had almost recovered its former strength. 'I feel sorry for this memory. I feel sorry for it. I don't want it to die . . .

'I was in love with another woman before you.

'Yes . . . I was in love . . . I should like to save the sweet, sad image of that love from the clutches of death; I am giving it to you because you are here.'

He paused to look in his mind's eye at the woman in question.

'She had fair hair and a fair complexion,' he said.

'You have no need to feel jealous of her, Anna (for people are sometimes jealous, even when they aren't in love). You had been born only a few years before. You were a little child, and the only people who turned round in the street to look at you were mothers.

'We became engaged in the park of her parents' country house. She had fair hair full of ribbons. I used to caper about on horseback for her; she used to smile for me.

'I was very young and strong at that time, full of hope and ambition. I thought that I was going to conquer the world, and even that I had a choice of methods . . . Alas, I have done nothing but pass rapidly over its surface! She was even younger than I: so fresh-blown that one day, I remember, her doll was there not far from us, on the bench in the park on which we were sitting. We used to say to each other: "We will come back to this park together when we are old, won't we?" We were in love with each other . . . You understand . . . I haven't time to tell you, but you understand, Anna, that these few relics of memory which I am giving you at random are beautiful, more beautiful than you might think.

'She died that very spring, just at the time—I remember this detail—when, the date of our marriage having been officially fixed, we had decided to address each other as *tu* already. An epidemic which swept our country made victims of us both. I alone recovered. She did not have the strength to escape from the disease. That was twenty-five years ago. Twenty-five years, Anna, between her death and mine.

'And here is the most precious secret of all: her name . . .'

He murmured it. I did not hear it.

'Repeat it to me, Anna.'

She repeated it: a little collection of indistinct syllables which reached me vaguely without my being able to combine them into a word, for to catch an unfamiliar proper name one has to hear it clearly; it is possible to guess at the other parts of a sentence, or to find substitutes for them, but the name stands alone.

And, the voice of memory growing fainter like the light, he repeated:

'I confide it to you because you are here. If you weren't here, I would confide it to anybody at all, provided it were saved from me.'

◐

He added, speaking in slow, measured tones, so that his voice should serve him to the end:

'I have something else to confess, a sin and a misfortune.'

'Haven't you confessed the sin to the priest?' she asked.

'I told him scarcely anything,' was all that he replied.

And he went on in his clear, calm voice:

'I had written some poetry during our engagement, poems about us. The manuscript bore her name. We used to read those poems together, and both of us loved and admired them. "That's beautiful! That's beautiful!" she would say, clapping her hands, every time I finished reading a new poem to her; and when we were together, that manuscript—in our opinion, the most beautiful book ever written—was always ready to hand. She did not want those poems to be published and made known to others besides ourselves. One day, in the garden, she expressed her will on this point: "Never! Never!" she said. Like a stubborn, disobedient little girl she repeated that word which seemed so big for her, shaking her pretty head so that her hair danced about.'

The man's voice had become at once firmer and more tremulous as he recalled and gave life to the features of this old story.

'On another occasion, in the conservatory, when it had been raining since morning, a steady, unchanging downpour, she said: "Philippe . . ." She used to say: "Philippe" to me as you say it.'

He stopped, astonished at the all too simple simplicity of the sentence he had just uttered.

'She asked me: "Do you know the story about the English painter Rossetti?" And she told me this anecdote which had made a deep impression upon her: He had promised the lady he loved that he would always leave her the manuscript of the book he had written for her, and that if she died, he would place it in the coffin with her. She died, and true to his promise, he had the manuscript buried with her. But later, possessed by the love of glory, he violated both the promise and the tomb. "You'll leave me your book if I die before you, and you won't take it back, will you, Philippe?" And I promised with a laugh, and she laughed too.

'I recovered slowly from my illness. When I was strong

enough, they told me she was dead. As soon as I was able to go out, they took me to her tomb, the huge family monument which contained somewhere inside it the new little coffin.

'What is the use of describing the misery of my bereavement . . . Everything reminded me of it. I was full of her, and she was dead. As my memory had been impaired, every detail reminded me of something; my bereavement was a horrible recapitulation of my love. The sight of the manuscript reminded me of the promise. I put it in a box without reading it again, and yet I was no longer familiar with the contents, my convalescence having left my mind a blank. I got them to raise the tombstone and open the coffin, in order to place the book inside, in accordance with the dead girl's wishes. A servant who was present when this was done came and told me: "It was placed between her hands."

'I lived. I worked. I tried to create a body of work. I wrote plays and poems; but nothing satisfied me, and gradually I felt the need for our book.'

●

'I knew that it was beautiful and sincere and vibrant with the two hearts which had given it to each other, and so, like a coward, three years after her death, I tried to reconstruct it—in order to show it to people. Anna, you must have pity on us all! . . . But I should say that it wasn't, as in the case of the English artist, just the desire for glory and homage which impelled me to shut my ears to the voice, so gentle and yet so penetrating in its helplessness, which came out of the past: "You won't take it back, will you, Philippe . . . ?"

'It wasn't simply to flaunt before the rest of the world a work strong in the irresistible beauty of what had been. It was also to remember myself better, for all our love was in that book.

'I could not manage to reconstruct the order of the poems.

The weakening of my faculties soon after they had been written, and the three years which had gone by, during which I had taken scrupulous care not to resuscitate in my mind those poems which were not intended to go on living, had all contributed to erase the work from my memory. It was as much as I could do, and then nearly always as the result of some chance, to recall the titles of the poems and a few lines, and sometimes a sort of vague echo, a halo of wonder. I needed the manuscript itself, and that was in the tomb.

'. . . And one night I found myself going there . . .

'I found myself going there, after hesitations and mental struggles which it is pointless to describe since they were useless . . . And I thought of the other man, the Englishman, my brother in misery and crime, as I walked along by the wall of the cemetery, with the wind chilling my legs. I kept telling myself: "This isn't the same thing," and this insane observation was enough to keep me going.

'I had wondered whether to take a lamp: with a lamp it would all be over quickly: I would see the box straight away and touch nothing else—but I would see everything, and I decided I would rather grope in the dark . . . I had tied a handkerchief soaked in perfume over my face, and I shall never forget that deceitful scent. The first thing I touched on her body, I failed to recognize at first in the shock of horror . . . Her necklace . . . her filigree necklace . . . I remembered it in life. The box! The corpse gave it back to me with a moist sound. Something brushed lightly against me . . .

'I only wanted to throw you a few words, Anna. I didn't think I would have time to say how it all happened. It is better for me that you should see everything. Life, which has been so cruel to me, is sweet to me at this moment, with you listening to me, you who are alive, and this desire to describe my feelings and to revive the past, which brought me such unhappiness during the days I am telling you about, is a blessing this evening which is passing from me to you and from you to me.'

And the young woman listened attentively to him, remaining silent and motionless. What could she have said, what could she have done, that would have been more precious to him than her attention?

●

'All the rest of the night, I read the stolen manuscript. Wasn't that my only hope of forgetting her death and thinking of her life? . . .

'It was not long before I became aware that those poems were not what I had thought. I had a growing impression that they were obscure and verbose. The book I had worshipped for so long was no better than what I had written since. I remembered every detail of the bygone settings, acts and gestures from which those poems had been copied, but in spite of this resurrection, I found them painfully commonplace and excessively rhetorical.

'An icy despair took hold of me as I bowed my head before those lyrical remains. Their sojourn in the tomb seemed to have robbed my poems of life and beauty. They were as pitiful as the withered hand from which I had taken them. Yet they had been so sweet! How many times the happy little voice had cried: "That's beautiful! That's beautiful!" while her hands had been clasped in admiration.

'That was because the voice and the poems had been alive at that time, because the ardour and the frenzy of love had adorned my verses with all their gifts, because all that belonged to the past, and because in fact our love was no more.

'It was forgetfulness that I was reading at the same time as my book . . . Yes, death had proved to be contagious, and my poems had remained too long in silence and darkness. Alas, she too had remained too long in silence and darkness, she who was sleeping there with such dreadful calm—in that tomb which I would never have dared to enter if my love had kept her alive. She was truly dead.

'And I reflected that my action had been useless sacrilege— and that every promise we make and every oath we swear in this life is useless sacrilege.

'She was truly dead. Oh, how I mourned her that night! That was my real night of grief . . . When one has just lost a beloved person, there is a pitiful moment—after the brutal shock— when one begins to understand that everything is over, and then despair becomes naked, vast and omnipresent. Thus that night, as the result of the emotion of my crime and the disillusionment of my poems, was more terrible than the crime, more terrible than anything.

'I saw her again in my mind's eye. How pretty she had been, with the bright, vivacious gestures in which she expended herself, the lively grace with which she moved about, the laughter which constantly surrounded her, the countless questions she was always asking . . . I remembered, in a ray of sunshine on a bright green lawn, the silky, velvety folds of her skirt (a skirt of very pale old rose satin), one day when, bending down to smooth that skirt with both hands, she was looking at her little feet (and not far away, there was the white pedestal of a statue). Once, I had amused myself by examining her complexion at close quarters in search of some defect; and I had found none on that forehead, that cheek, that chin, on the whole of that face with the delicate, polished skin, halted for a moment in its perpetual movement to lend itself to my experiment; and I had stammered, with an emotion verging on tears, without knowing what I was saying: "*It's too much . . . It's too much . . .*" She was a princess to all who saw her. In the streets of the town, the shopkeepers considered themselves happy to be standing on their doorsteps when she passed. And everybody, even old men, approached her respectfully. Didn't she look like a queen, on the great carved stone bench in the park, half-lying, half-leaning against its broad back . . . that great stone bench which was now like an empty tomb . . .

'I had kept a few things which had belonged to her: a fan—and I opened that dead fan and waved it gently before my eyes; her little glove, which was quite cold; the letters which she had written and which exposed themselves shamelessly . . .

'Oh, for one moment in the midst of time I knew how much I had loved her, she who had been alive and was now dead, she who had been sunshine and laughter, and was now a sort of obscure underground spring.

'And I wept too over the human heart. That night my understanding matched my feelings. Then came the inevitable forgetfulness: the moments when it brought me no sadness to remember that I had wept.'

◐

'That is the confession I wanted to make to you, Anna . . . I did not want that love story which is a quarter of a century old to finish yet . . . It was so moving and so real, it was so wonderful, that I must recount it in all simplicity to the survivor that you are . . .

'Since then, I have loved you, and I love you. I offer you, as to my sole sovereign, the image of the little creature who will always be seventeen years old . . .'

He sighed, and he murmured these words which showed me yet again the poverty of religion in the human heart:

'I adore only you, I who adored her, I whom she adored. Oh, how can there be a paradise where one recaptures happiness?'

His voice rose, his inert arms quivered. For a moment he emerged from total immobility.

'Oh, it is you, it is you! You alone!'

And he made a great, impassioned appeal, an appeal which knew no bounds:

'Oh, Anna, Anna, if only I had been truly married to you, if only we had lived together as man and wife, if only we had had children, if only you had been at my side as you are this evening, but really at my side.'

He fell back. He had cried so loudly that even if there had not been a crack in the wall, I would have heard him from my room. He was expressing his dream in its entirety; he was giving it away; he was bestowing it all around him, frantically. This sincerity, indifferent to everything else in the world, had a significant finality which broke my heart.

'Forgive me. Forgive me . . . That was almost blasphemy . . . I couldn't help it . . .'

His words stopped: I could feel his will composing his features, his soul stilling his tongue; but his eyes seemed to be groaning.

He repeated in a lower voice, as if to himself: 'You . . . You . . .'

He fell asleep on that word: you . . .

●

He died last night. I saw him die. By a curious chance he was alone at the time he died.

There was no death-rattle, and indeed, no real death agony. he did not pull his bedclothes up to his chin, or speak, or cry out. No last sigh, no radiant vision. There was nothing.

He had asked Anna for a drink of water. As there was no water left, and the nurse happened to be absent at that moment, she had gone out hurriedly to get some. She had not even closed the door.

The light from the lamp filled the room.

I looked at the man's face, and I sensed, from some sign or other, that at that moment the great silence was overwhelming him.

And then, instinctively, I cried out to him. I could not help crying out to him so that he should not be alone:

'I can see you!'

My strange voice, which had lost the habit of speech, entered his room.

But he died at the very moment that I was giving him these madman's alms. His head had jerked back slightly and his eyeballs had rolled upwards.

Anna came back into the room; she must have heard me, for she was hurrying.

She saw him. She gave a terrifying cry, with all her strength, with all the force of her healthy flesh, a pure cry of true widowhood. She fell on her knees before the bed.

The nurse arrived a moment later and threw up her hands. There was a silence, the instant of incredible misery into which, whatever one may be and wherever one may be, everyone plunges completely in the presence of a dead man. The kneeling woman and the standing woman looked at the man stretched out before them, as still as if he had never lived; and the two women were themselves almost dead.

Then Anna wept like a child. She stood up; the nurse went to fetch some people. Anna, who was wearing a light-coloured bodice, instinctively picked up the black shawl which the old woman had left on an armchair and draped it over her shoulders.

◉

The room, which had been steeped in gloom for some time, now came to life.

Candles were lit everywhere, and the stars which could be seen through the window disappeared.

People knelt and wept and prayed to him. He gave the orders; everyone referred to *him*. There were servants' faces there which I had never seen before, but which *he* knew very well. It was as if all these people were begging for alms from him, as if they were suffering and dying, as if he were alive.

'He must have suffered a great deal when he died,' the doctor said in an undertone to the nurse, at a moment when he was very close to me.

'But the poor man was so weak!'

'Yes,' said the doctor, 'but it's only other people who think that weakness prevents a man from suffering.'

●

This morning, a wan light surrounds these faces and these martyred candles. The presence of the cold, subtle light of the newborn day makes the atmosphere in the room seem insipid, heavy and ambiguous.

Just for a moment, a very quiet, timid voice breaks the silence which has lasted several hours.

'We mustn't open the window; he would start decomposing earlier.'

'It's cold,' somebody murmurs . . .

Two hands draw together the ends of a fur and cross them . . . Somebody stands up, then sits down. Somebody else turns his head. A sigh is heaved.

It is as if everybody had taken advantage of the few words uttered to break out of the calm in which they had been freezing. Then they look in a new way at the man laid out on the bed—motionless, inexorably motionless, like the crucified idol which is hung up in churches.

I think that a little while ago I dropped off to sleep on my bed . . . All the same, it must be very early . . . And now, all of a sudden, the sound of church bells comes from the grey sky.

After this harassing night, a relaxation of the corpselike immobility of our attention is a relief in spite of everything, and an indescribable feeling of pleasure takes me back, with that ringing of bells, to memories of childhood . . . I think of a countryside which holds me close and which the sound of bells covers with a shrunken, palpable sky; of a calm homeland where everything is good, where snow means Christmas, where the sun is a warm disk which can be and must be looked at . . . And in the middle of all that, always in the middle of everything, the church.

The ringing has stopped. Its bright reverberations gently fall silent, and the echo of its echo . . . Now comes some more ringing: the clock striking the hour. Eight o'clock, eight loud, distinct strokes, of a terrible regularity, of an invincible calm: simple, so simple. One counts them, and when they have stopped beating the air, there is nothing to do but count them again. Time which is passing by . . . Shapeless time, and human effort which defines it and regularizes it and turns it into something like a work of destiny.

And I think of the grand symphony of those two heavenly themes.

The bright notes scatter light like seed . . . They crowd together closer and closer, and soon the starry sky turns into dawn. The church glows with the full, delicate vibration which penetrates even the walls; it lends enchantment to the familiar setting of a room, and embellishes Nature: the rain looks like pearls on the leaves, and a sort of muslin in the sky; the frost covers the windowpanes with an embroidery which seems to have been made by women's hands. The sound of the bells helps to lighten the burden of the hours and the days; sufficient unto the day is the evil thereof; when the seasons are changing, it reminds us of the different favours each of them bestows on us; it reassures the dream of its future fate; each of us is content with his life, and everyone is consoled in advance.

After the motley, varied crowd whose rejoicings are dominated and regulated by the ethereal dance of the bells, there comes a single heart, from which the cry rises into the air; this cry has a simple movement, but it is obvious that it will have no end or limits, and that it has, so to speak, the shape of the sky. Its flight merges with that of the religious voice; it rises at the same time with every shudder of the bells' three wing-beats, or in a multiple quivering when they burst into a carillon.

But there is something there which we were forgetting, something vaster than joy, and which marks its ineradicable existence with dull thuds. We sensed it, we hear it, we feel it. The pendulum is going to hammer on our dreams and break into our illusions, heedless of the tender caresses opposing it, and every blow pierces like a nail.

However powerful the song of the angelus may be, the stronger voice of the hours envelops it with its serenity; it grows into days, years, generations. It dominates the world as the church spire dominated the village. The cry of the heart puts up a passionate resistance. It is all alone: the pious song was not supported by the sky as the song of time was supported by darkness. The hour is a great monotonous rhythm whose every sonorous warning interrupts the tireless hope which rises in a perpetual movement, but does not disturb the immortal theme, the definitive adagio which comes to us from the clock . . . And the broken melody can only change sadness into beauty.

FOURTEEN

I am alone tonight. I am sitting at my table. My lamp is buzzing like summer over the fields. I raise my eyes. The stars are push-, ing the sky away above me, the city plunges down at my feet, the horizon flees eternally from me on every side. The shadows and the lights form an infinite sphere, since I am here.

These evenings I am ill at ease; a vast anguish has taken hold of me. I sat down on this chair as if I were falling. As on the first day, I look towards the mirror, attracted by myself: I examine my reflexion, and as on the first day, a single word springs to my lips: 'Me!'

I should like to know the secret of life. I have seen men, groups, gestures, faces. I have seen, shining in the dusk, the trembling eyes of creatures as deep as wells. I have seen the lips which, in a surge of pride, declared: 'I am more sensitive than others!' I have seen the struggle to love and to communicate: the mutual contradiction of two speakers and the struggle of two lovers, lovers with infectious smiles who are lovers in name only, who devour each other with kisses, who press wound against wound in order to cure themselves, who have no link between them, and who, in spite of their radiant ecstasy in the darkness are as foreign to each other as the sun and the moon. I have heard those who find a little peace only in the confession of their shameful misery, and the pallid faces which have wept with eyes like roses.

I should like to embrace all that at once. All the truths in the world make only one (I have had to wait until today to understand that simple fact): it is that truth of truths which I need.

This isn't out of love for mankind. It isn't true that one can love mankind. Nobody has loved, nobody loves, and nobody ever will love mankind. It's for my sake—purely and simply for my sake—that I want to reach and obtain that complete truth which is above emotion, above peace, above even life, like a sort of dead creature. I want to derive an aim, a faith from it; I want to use it for my salvation.

I consider the memories I have made captive since I have been here; there are so many of them that I have become a stranger to myself, and I scarcely have a name any longer; I listen to them. I recall myself, feasting myself on the sight of others, like God, alas—and, making a supreme effort, I try to see and hear what I am. It would be so wonderful to know who I am!

I think of all those who, before me, have quested—savants, poets, artists—all those who have laboured, wept, smiled in their search for reality, near square temples or under pointed arches or in dusky gardens whose soil is now nothing more than a dark perfume. I think of the Latin poet who tried to reassure and comfort men by showing them the naked truth as a statue. A fragment of his prelude comes back to me, learnt in the past, then rejected and lost like almost everything I have taken the trouble to learn until now. He says in his distant tongue, which seems barbaric in the midst of my everyday life, that he stays awake during the tranquil nights to discover in what words, in what poem, he can bring men the ideas which will set them free. After two thousand years, men still need to be reassured and consoled. After two thousand years I still need to be set free. Nothing has changed the face of things. The teaching of Christ would not have changed it even if men had not spoilt it to the extent of being unable honestly to use it any more. Will he ever come—the great poet who will limit and perpetuate belief, the poet who will be neither a madman nor an eloquent ignoramus, but a sage, the great inexorable poet? I don't know; although the lofty words of the man who has just died have given me a vague hope that he will come and the right to love him already.

But what of myself? I who am nothing but a gaze—how many destinies I have collected! And now here I am, remembering them. In spite of everything, I resemble a poet on the threshold of a work. A starcrossed, sterile poet who will leave no name, and to whom chance has lent the truth which genius would have given him; a fragile work which will pass away with me, a mortal work closed to others like myself, and yet a sublime work which will show the essential lines of life and will recount the drama of dramas.

●

What am I? I am the longing not to die. Not only this evening, when I am possessed by the urge to construct the solid, powerful dream which I shall never leave, but always. All of us, always, are the longing not to die. It is as manifold and diverse as the complexity of life, but in essence it is this: the longing to go on being, to be more and more, to blossom out and endure. All the strength, energy and lucidity we have, is used to fire our spirits, whatever the means employed. We fire our spirits with new impressions, new sensations, new ideas. We try to take what we lack in order to add it to ourselves. Humanity is the longing for novelty combined with the fear of death. That's what it is: I know, because I have seen it. The instinctive gestures and the spontaneous cries were always aimed in the same direction, like signals, and at bottom the most dissimilar words were alike.

●

But afterwards . . . Where are the words which light the way? If this is humanity, what is its place in the world, and what is the world?

I remember, I remember, as if I were calling for help . . . A landmark, a milestone, where my sacred anxiety makes a halt: the importance of a human being among things, that importance which it has taken me all my life to understand . . .

The immensity of each one of us: the first beacon in the darkness. It is true that the heart mourns or rejoices with the whole of Nature, and, in the eyes of the humblest of observers, it is true that in the skies of Provence the stars turned pale when Mireille appeared at her little window.

I am at the centre of the world. The stars crown my head. The earth bears me and lifts me up. I stand on the summit of the centuries. I see everything in terms of myself, both the vast and the little things of the mind and the heart. By putting my hand in front of my eyes, I make night during the day and hide it from view during the night; if I close my eyes, the sky can no longer exist. The further it is from me, the smaller all that is great becomes.

◗

I rest my head on my hand.

Then my fingers feel the bones in my skull: the eye-socket, the hollow at the temple, the jaw. A skull . . .

A skull! But I know that! My skull is just like the rest.

This resemblance between myself and all the rest is something which had never occurred to me. I can see it. I can see, through a little shadow, my skull, my bones. I recognize in myself my eternal phantom of dust, my skeleton, just as one recognizes an acquaintance. I touch it, I feel it, the grim white monster which I am in essence . . .

My dreams of greatness have vanished, since my skull is just like the rest, like all those which have ever existed.

How many have there been? If mankind goes back a hundred thousand years—which is probably an underestimate—and as there are one and a half milliard inhabitants on earth who are replaced every thirty years, that makes four thousand five hundred milliard skulls which have been crumbling to dust since the human race began.

●

I too shall be laid in the ground. I shall have had a disease or a wound which will make one part of my flesh rot faster than the rest. I shall probably die of some illness, some organ which is atrophied, broken or arrested—or else which goes mad, affecting all the others; I shall die of an illness, with all my blood inside me (I would rather die in the crimson torrent gushing from a wound . . .)

And I too shall be buried like the rest, strange though that may seem. Already, like a warning from the mud (the poet's words come back to me and overwhelm me), I have this dust which settles on me every day, which I am obliged to wash off, against which I defend myself, and from which I tear myself away: it is the dark angel of the earth.

In the frail coffin, my body will fall prey to the insects, to the irresistible pollulation of their grubs. A vast, ever-growing invasion—Linnaeus has observed that three flies can devour a corpse as quickly as one lion.

I open a book which I have here. I plunge into the details it provides. I learn what awaits me. I discover my future history.

The fauna of the cemeteries follow one another at periodic intervals; each species comes at its appointed time, so that it is possible to recognize the age of a corpse by the host of creatures feeding on it. Thus there are eight successive immigrations into the abandoned corpse which correspond to the eight phases of putrid fermentation by which, little by little, the inside of the body becomes the outside.

I want to know them, to see in advance what I shall not see at the time—and to touch what I shall not feel.

Little flies, the *curtonevrae*, descend on the body a few moments before death . . . I shall hear them. Certain emanations inform them of the imminence of an event which is going to provide them with an abundance of food for their grubs; and, heavy with eggs, they already begin frantically laying in the nostrils, in the mouth, and in the corners of the eyes.

Life has scarcely ended before more flies arrive on the scene. As soon as the pitiful breath of corruption becomes noticeable, still more arrive: the blue fly, the green fly, whose scientific name is *Lucilia Caesar*, the big fly with the black and white striped thorax known as the 'great sarcophagian'. The first generation of these flies which come hurrying along at the horrible signal can itself form seven or eight generations inside the corpse which go on living and piling up for between three and six months. 'Every day,' says Mégnin, 'the grubs of the blue fly increase two hundredfold in weight . . .' The skin of the corpse is then a yellow shading slightly into pink, the belly is light green, the back dark green. Or at least these would be the colours, if all this were not happening in the dark.

Then the decomposition changes in character. It is the turn of the butyric fermentation, which produces fatty acids commonly known as corpse fat. It is the season of the dermestes—carnivorous insects which produce long-haired grubs—and of the moths called aglossas. The grubs of the dermestes and the caterpillars of the aglossas are remarkable in that they can live in the fats 'which form like lard at the bottom of coffins'; some of these fats will later crystallize and shine like sequins in the final dust.

Now comes the fourth wave. It accompanies the caseic fermentation, and it consists of flies called pyophilas, which give cheese its maggots—maggots which can be recognized by their characteristic leaps—and beetles called corynetes.

The ammoniacal fermentation, the black liquefaction of the flesh, brings on a fifth invasion, this time of flies—the loncheas, the ophyras and the phoras—in such large numbers that on corpses exhumed during this period, the blackish remains of their chrysalises, according to one pathologist, 'look like bread crumbs on knuckles of ham,' and these clouds of flies escape from the coffin if it is raised and opened during this phase. The black deliquescent decomposition is also preferred by certain beetles; the silphas and the nine species of necrophores.

By now putrefaction has practically completed its work. The following period is that of the desiccation and mummification of the corpse under its shroud and its clothes stiffened by the gelatinous liquids of the previous period. All the soft matter that remains, in the form of organic, farinaceous and friable paste, and of ammoniacal soaps, is eaten by another species of creature: round and crooked acarians, scarcely visible to the naked eye. Every two weeks, their number increases tenfold: to begin with, there are twenty of them; after two and a half months, there are two million.

The acarians are followed by a seventh immigration. The newcomers are a species of moth, the aglossas, which had already appeared during the discharge of the fatty acids and had then disappeared. These gnaw, saw and nibble the parchment-like tissues such as the ligaments and tendons, which have become hard and resinous in appearance, as well as the body hairs, the hair of the head, and the graveclothes. The body is now a golden bronze colour, and gives off a strong smell of wax.

Finally, three years after death, the last cloud of workers arrives. What do these find to devour? Everything that is left, everything, down to the remains of the insects which in their larval state have followed one another inside the corpse. The final effacer is a tiny black beetle whose scientific name is *tenebrio obscurus*.

After this last visitor, nothing whatever is left except, in spite of *tenebrio obscurus*, a few remains of remains around the whitened bones, and a small compact mass at the bottom of the brain-pan. This sort of granular brown mould, this powder on the human stone, which might be taken to be the last residue of the flesh, is not even that. It is the accumulation of the shells, the pupae, the chrysalises and the dejecta of the later generations of devouring insects.

Three years have elapsed. It is all over. The creature which adored and was adored has in three years completely returned to the mineral kingdom. The stench has disappeared; it was the last sign of life: it vanishes, alas, and even the mourning is over.

And every inhabitant of the globe will have undergone this process in a few years. Even while I have been thinking, a quarter of an hour perhaps, a thousand human beings have died on earth.

Their bodies, agglomerations of cells; their cells, agglomerations of atoms (indivisible fragments of matter) have been consigned to other combinations. The cell! This organic unity varies in size between one thousandth and one ten thousandth of a millimetre. The atom! This is an unknown, conjectural element.

If we assume it to be of a size within the bounds of probability, taking as a basis the infinite smallness of anatomical elements, we find that a sphere of matter with the diameter of a pinhead would contain a quantity of atoms represented by an eight followed by twenty-one noughts, and that, to count all the atoms in a pinhead, at the rate of one per second per person, the whole of mankind, working without respite, would take two hundred thousand years.

It is out of this dust that the globe is made.

And the globe itself is nothing in the universe.

. . . On a sheet of paper, a tiny dot which is scarcely visible; round it, a circle which takes up the whole width of the sheet. The dot is the earth; the circle represents the sun; this is the ratio

between them. On another sheet, a dot made with the very tip
of the nib: this is the sun, which was so large on the previous
sheet. A sphere is represented by a circle which stretches from
one side of the paper to the other: this is a star called Canopus.
The sun is as tiny in relation to Canopus as the earth was in
relation to the sun. And Betelgeuse, that bright celestial point
so much beloved of our ancestors, has a diameter as vast as the
distance from the earth to the sun. This greyness on this piece
of paper is not grey colouring, but innumerable tiny dots close
together. Each dot is a star, like the sun of Canopus, or even
larger . . . This is a fragment of the chart of the heavens: an
infinitesimal fragment, since the number of stars which have
been observed is estimated at a hundred million, and on this
sheet of paper there are about three thousand. We can observe
only a hundred million stars because our optical instruments
cannot extend our field of vision beyond stars of the twenty-first
magnitude, and allow us to see only seventeen thousand times
more stars than would be seen by the naked eye; but who would
dare to assert that the most distant stars discernible by us mark
the limits of the universe? And the size of these stars, however
enormous it may be, is nothing in comparison with the expanse
of empty space that separates them. The nearest star to us after
the sun, the star Alpha in the constellation Centaurus, is twenty-
five billion miles away. Arcturus, which is two hundred milliard
miles away, moves through space at the speed of eighteen hundred million miles a year—yet in the three thousand years men
have observed it and marked its place on astronomical charts, it
does not seem to have moved. The star numbered 1830 in
Groombridge's catalogue is five hundred billion miles from us
. . .

Because of its fantastic speed, light enormously reduces these
figures for us and makes us more conscious of their immensity
. . . Light travels through space at the speed of two hundred

thousand miles per second. It takes just over eight minutes to
reach us from the sun, so that the picture we have of the sun is
as it was eight minutes before we looked at it. It takes four years
and four months for light to reach us from the nearest star, and
thirty-six years for it to reach us from the North Star . . . It takes
several centuries to reach us from certain other stars which we
consequently see as they were several centuries ago. And if those
stars look at us, they must see us at the same dizzy interval of
time . . .

That constellation which crowns the living and dying city
with a diadem so vast that it is saddening, remains a mystery to
us. At the very most, we suspect that each of its points has some
analogy with the burning sun, with that ball of fire bristling with
flames as large as the distance from the earth to the moon. If the
eyes on one of those stars are more piercing than our own, what
do they see down here, at this moment when I am writing? . . .
Among the huge formations of the earth, still twisting and shuddering from some vast geological upheaval, they see a solitary
being pull itself up from the ground to which all four of its limbs
are attracted, and turn upwards a face which is still bestial and
frightened of the dark . . . And between yet another star and
ourselves the exchange of light has not yet taken place since it
came into existence, and when at last its image reaches us, the
star itself may have been destroyed for ages past.

These eternities make me think of Time. For how long now
has the earth existed? Since the gaseous mass of this world detached itself from the equator of the solar nebula, how many
billions of centuries have passed? No one knows. But we think
that for the second phase—by far the shorter of the two—of its
transformation, that is, in order to pass from a liquid to a solid
state, three hundred and fifty million years had to elapse.

If the atom is the most minute element of matter, this is the
most immense: the stellar universe. Not the real or even the

visible totality of the firmament, for both are incommensurable, but that part which science has measured. Scientific investigation is limited to a radius of five hundred billion miles from the earth. The world beyond that radius, which includes only the nearest stars, does not offer us, in relation to the movement of the earth, a visible displacement which would enable us to estimate their distance from us, and we have no other indications as to the possible dimensions of sidereal space. That portion, then, of our universe which is subject to mathematical calculation is represented by a sphere with a radius of five hundred billion miles. The numbers which express this sphere are the greatest that can be applied to reality. They give a volume of over two thousand sexdecillion cubic yards. As, on the other hand, the number of atoms in a cubic yard is of the order of one decillion (if we refer back to the hypothetical dimensions we gave the atom) the ratio between the greatest and the most minute of objects is a number such that science has no term to express it. No one has ever used it: possibly I am the first man to do so in the immense desire for precision which is tormenting me tonight. This virgin number which formulates the quantity of atoms the universe contains, consists of a two followed by eight-seven other figures. Nothing can give any idea of the immensity of this number, which expresses the whole of Nature from its very foundations to its farthest attainable frontiers.

And yet this number, which looks so monstrous, must be deformed even more and multiplied by fifty trillions into a number containing one hundred and two figures, if we are to admit Newcomb's theory which, based on the movements and speeds of the stars according to the immutable laws of gravitation, limits the whole of our stellar system to a spatial forty quintillion miles in diameter, harmoniously occupied by 125 million stars.

What can anyone do against all that?

What can I do, I, sitting here, dazzled by the papers I am

reading beneath this lamp which casts an octagonal shadow touching my inkstand, and whose diffused light scarcely reveals the ceiling or the window, gleaming black behind its thin curtains, and leaves the walls of the room almost in darkness?

I stand up. I wander about my room. What am I? What am I? Oh, I must, I must find an answer to this question, because another question hangs from it like a threat: What is to become of me?

Standing in front of the large mirror over the mantelpiece, I gaze at my reflection, seeking in myself for something with which to counter my insignificance. If I can find nothing, I am done for . . . Am I the triviality I seem to be, immobilized and stifled in this room, as if in a coffin too big for me?

Instinctively, a soothing intuition, as simple as I am myself, banishes the terror which assails me, and I tell myself that it isn't possible, that there is an immense, universal misunderstanding.

◐

What was it that dictated what I have just thought? What impulse was I obeying?

A faith which common sense, religion and science have accumulated in me . . .

That commonsense is the voice of the senses, and that loud, insistent voice reiterates that things are as we see them. But in my heart I know perfectly well that that isn't true. And the first thing we must do is to rid ourselves of that coarse husk of our everyday life.

The contradictions inherent in a complacent acceptance of appearances, the innumerable errors of our senses, the capricious creations of dreams and madness, warn us against heeding this pitiful advice. Common sense is an honest animal but a blind one. It cannot recognize truth, which hides from the first glance, and which, to use the magnificent phrase of the ancient sage, 'lives in a well.'

Science . . . What is science? Pure, it is reason arranged by itself; applied, it is an arrangement of appearances. Scientific 'truth' is an almost total negation of common sense. There is scarcely a single aspect of the world of appearances which is not contradicted by the corresponding scientific affirmation. Science tells us that sound and light are vibrations, that matter is composed of forces . . . It imposes belief in an abstract materialism. It replaces crude appearances by formulae, or else it admits them without question. It gives rise to the same contradictions, but on a more complex and difficult level, as does superficial realism. Even in the stronghold of its own worlds of experiment and logic, it has to use fictional data and suppositions. Whether it is applied to consideration of the earth as great or small, it always stops short. On the one hand, it is arrested by the problem of the divisibility of space, and on the other, it is halted by a choice of two absurdities: 'Space is infinite' and 'Space ends somewhere.' It does not see truth any more than does common sense; in any case that is not its function, since its only object is the abstract or practical systemization of elements whose inner significance it never considers.

Religion . . . It rightly asserts that common sense lies and science is non-committal; and it adds that we should be certain of nothing without the assurance of God. That was how religion stopped Pascal, by interposing its false bottom between him and the truth. God is merely a ready-made reply to mystery and hope, and there is no other reason for the reality of God but our longing for it.

Does this boundless world, therefore, which I have just seen rise up against me, rest on nothing? And if so, what is certain, what is sure?

◑

To help myself, I once again evoke the living creatures in whom I believe, those persons whose faces and eyes I have seen light up in the next room.

I see again a succession of faces, in the *de profundis* of the dusk, shining forth like supreme victories. One contained the past; another, its attention entirely concentrated on the window, was taking on the complexion of the sky; another, in the damp, misty darkness, was thinking of the sun as a sun; another, pensive and melancholy, was full of the death which would soon devour it; and all were surrounded by a solitude which began in this room, but was endlessly prolonged.

And I who am like them, I who contain within my thoughts the implacable past and the dreamt-of-future and the greatness of others; I who regret, desire and meditate, with my incurably questioning face—am I to be turned to dust by the dream of stars which I have just had? Is it conceivable that I am nothing, when at other moments it seems to me that I am everything?

And now I begin to understand . . . I ignored the function of thought in my evocation of the order of things. I regarded it as enclosed within the body, never going any further, adding nothing to the universe. But is the soul nothing in us but a breath like the breath of life, an organic function; and are we as insignificant alive as dead?

No! And this is where I put my finger on the misconception.

Thought is the source of everything. It is with thought that we must always begin . . . Truth has been turned upside down.

And now I begin to see signs of madness in my meditation a little while ago. That meditation was like myself: it proved the greatness of the mind which thought it, and yet it stated that the thinking creature was nothing. It annihilated me, who had created it.

. . . But am I not the victim of an illusion? I hear myself object that what is in me is the image, the reflection, the idea of the universe. Thought is only the phantasm of the world lent to each of us. The universe exists objectively outside me, independently of me, on so huge a scale that it reduces me to nothingness as if I were dead already. And if I am indeed non-existent, or if I shut my eyes, it makes no difference: the universe will still exist.

A sudden anguish, the first pain of a wound, grips my heart . . . Then a cry mounts within me, lucid, conscious and unforgettable, like a sublime chord:

'No!'

No. That is not true. I do not know whether the universe has any reality apart from me. What I do know is that its reality occurs only through the instrumentality of my thought, and that in the first place it exists only through the concept I have of it. It is I who have brought the stars and the centuries into being, I who have evolved the firmament in my head. I cannot emerge from my mind. I have no right to do so, without falling into error or falsehood. I have no power to do so, either. Try as I may to struggle as if to escape from myself, I cannot invest the world with any reality other than that of my imagination. I believe in myself and I am alone, since I cannot emerge from myself. How could I imagine, except in madness, that I can emerge from myself? How could I imagine, except in madness, that I am not alone? What could possibly convince me that beyond the impassable frontiers of thought the universe has an existence separate from my own?

I turn to metaphysics, which is not a science: it lies outside the scientific domain, and is closer to art, seeking like art for absolute truth—for if a picture is powerful and a poem is beautiful, that is thanks to truth. I read through books. I consult savants and thinkers. I gather together the whole arsenal of certainties that has been collected by the human mind, I listen to the great voice of him who sifted every faith and every system through the screen of his awesome mind, and I read this very truth which was imposing itself upon me: It is impossible to deny our concept of the world, but it cannot be proved to exist outside the concept we have of it.

And now that I have this affirmation strictly and securely confined in words, now that I possess this sublime treasure, I can never again detach myself from its miraculous simplification.

No, there is no certainty that that truth which begins in us, continues elsewhere; and when, having uttered the phrase which no one after him has even considered denying—'I think, therefore I am'—the philosopher tried, step by step, to argue the existence of something real outside the thinking creature, he moved further and further away from certainty. Of all the philosophy of the past, nothing remains but this clear statement which sets within each one of us the principle of existence: of all human research, nothing remains but this immense discovery which I had already read as in a book in the difference and the solitude of each face. The universe, as it seems to appear to us, proves only ourselves, who believe we see it. The external universe, by which I mean the terrestrial globe with its eleven types of movement in space, its horizons and the ebb and flow of the sea, its quarter of a billion cubic miles, its one hundred and twenty thousand vegetable species, its three hundred thousand animal species, and all the solar and sidereal systems with their history of transformations, their origins and their milky ways—all this is a mirage and an hallucination.

And in spite of the voices which, even from our inner depths, cry out against what I have just dared to think, as a mob cries out against beauty; in spite of the sage who, while admitting that the universe is an hallucination, adds without proof that it is 'a true hallucination'—I maintain that the infinity and the eternity of the universe are two false gods. It is I who have endowed the universe with these exorbitant qualities, which exist in me (I must have endowed it with them since, even if it possessed them, I could not prove the presence of what cannot be proved, and would have to contribute them from my own resources, to complete the limited concept I have of it).

Nothing can prevail against the absolute statement that I exist and cannot emerge from myself, and that all things—in space, time or reason—are only ways of imagining reality, and so to speak vague powers which I possess.

It was with a kind of shudder that I found in the austere book this rendering of the human cries which have reached my ears. The human heart revealed itself in all its anguish in the cold, deliberate phrases of the German writer. Perhaps a certain gravity is needed to free oneself from the bonds of appearance, and to comprehend the grandiose formulas of truth thus purified. But I maintain that these words are the most magnificent ever addressed to mankind, and that they make the book of the Koenigsberg philosopher the work which comes closest to being a real Bible. The words of Jesus Christ, designed to govern society on noble lines, appear superficial and utilitarian in comparison.

It is a matter of solemn and capital importance that the essential words should be wrung from the heart of silence, that reason should be set where it belongs, that truth should be restored. This is not a question of a futile discussion of formulas, but of a frightening personal problem which obsesses me, a matter of life and death to me, a supreme judgement in which I am involved and from which there is no appeal.

◐

Everything is in me, and there are no judges, and there are no limits, and there are no bounds to me. The *de profundis*, the striving not to die, the desire that declines as its cry rises, these

things have not ceased. It is in unrestricted liberty that the incessant mechanism of the human heart operates (always something new, always). It is such an unreserved effusion that even
death is effaced by it. For how could I imagine my own death
except by emerging from myself and considering myself as if I
were not I, but another?

We do not die . . . Each being is alone in the world. It seems
absurd and contradictory, to utter such a phrase. And yet that is
the truth . . . But there are several beings like myself . . . No,
it isn't possible to say that . . . To say that, we should have to
stand apart from truth, in a sort of abstraction. There is only one
thing we can say: *I am alone.*

And that is the reason why we do not die.

At this time of the evening, bent forward in the dusk, the man
had said: 'After my death, life will go on. Every object in the
world will peacefully remain in its accustomed place, while
every trace of my passage through life will gradually disappear,
and the void I made close up.'

He was mistaken. He was mistaken in speaking thus. He took
all the truth with him. Yet we saw him die. He is dead for us,
but not for himself. I feel that there is a truth there which is
terribly difficult to understand, a fearful contradiction, but I
hold it in my grasp and am groping for the halting words that
will express it. Something like: 'Each being is the whole truth
. . .' I come back to what I said just now: We do not die because
we are alone; it is the others who die. And this phrase which
trembles on my lips, at once sinister and radiant, proclaims that
death is a false god.

But what of the rest? Even supposing that I had the wisdom
and the power to rid myself of the obsession with my own death,
there would still remain the death of others and the death of so
much feeling and sweetness. It is not the manner of conceiving
truth that will alter suffering, for suffering is like joy, an absolute.

And yet . . . our infinite misery is undistinguishable from pride and even happiness—proud, icy happiness. Is it with pride or joy that I begin to smile in the first glimmer of dawn, beside the fading lamp, as I gradually come to realize that I am universally alone? . . .

FIFTEEN

This is the first time I have seen her in mourning, and in these dark clothes her youth is more resplendent than ever.

Their departure is at hand. She looks around her to make sure she has forgotten nothing in the room which has been prepared again for others, a room which already seems characterless and deserted.

The door opens, and as the young woman, interrupted in what she is doing, raises her head, a man appears in the sunny opening.

'Michel! Michel! Michel!' she cries.

She stretches out her arms, and, pausing there with all her attention fixed on him, remains for a few seconds as motionless as the light.

Then, despite the place she is in, the purity of her soul, and the modesty of her whole existence, her virgin legs tremble and she is on the point of falling.

He throws his hat on the bed with a sweeping romantic gesture. He fills the room with his presence, his solidity. His footsteps make the boards creak. He is already beside her, holding her. Tall as she is, he dominates her by nearly a head. His strong features are stern and handsome; his face, crowned by thick black hair, is fresh and clean-cut and, as it were, new-looking.

A jet-black moustache, drooping slightly, shades the bright red mouth, as glorious as a wound. He places his hands on the young woman's shoulders and looks at her, preparing and opening his famished embrace.

◐

They clasp each other, swaying to and fro. In the same breath they utter the same words: 'At last!' This is all they say, but for a few moments they repeat these words in an undertone; they sing them. Their eyes exchange the same sweet cry, their breasts communicate it to each other. It is as if they were binding and penetrating each other with it. At last their long separation is over, and their love has triumphed; at last the two of them are together . . . And I see her tremble from head to foot; I see how her whole body welcomes him, while her eyes open and close again on him.

With an immense effort they try to talk to each other, since words must be spoken. The scraps of phrases they exchange keep them standing for a moment.

'The waiting, the hoping!' he stammers distractedly. 'I thought of you all the time; I saw you before me all the time.'

He adds more softly, more ardently:

'Sometimes, in the middle of a commonplace conversation, somebody would suddenly mention your name, and it would go straight to my heart.'

He is breathing hard, and at times his muted voice bursts out. He does not seem able to speak quietly.

'How often I used to sit with my face in my hands, on the brick balustrade of the terrace overlooking the straits! I didn't even know in what part of the world you were, and yet, far as I was from you, I could not help seeing you.'

'Often, on hot nights, I saw at the open window because of you,' she says, bowing her head . . . 'Sometimes the air was suffocating in its sweetness—like two months ago at the Villa des Roses. I had tears in my eyes.'

'You wept?'

'Yes,' she says softly, 'I wept for joy.'

●

Their mouths meet, their two small scarlet mouths, of exactly the same colour. They are almost indistinguishable, lost in the creative silence of the kiss, which unites them inwardly and turns them into a single dark river of flesh.

Then he draws back a little to see her better. He puts an arm round her waist, and presses her tightly to his side, his face turned towards her. Then he puts his free hand on her belly. I can see the shape of her legs and her belly; I can see the whole of her in the brutal but superb gesture with which he sculpts her.

His words, spoken emphatically, fall more heavily upon her.

'Out there, among the countless gardens by the sea, I wanted to dig my fingers into the dark earth. As I roamed about, I tried to imagine your body, and I sought for the perfume of your flesh. And I stretched my arms upwards to the sky, to come as close as possible to your sun.'

'I knew that you were waiting for me and that you loved me,' she says, in a sweeter voice but with just as deep emotion . . . 'In your absence, I was always conscious of your presence. And often, when a ray of sunlight entered my room at dawn and touched me, I imagined that I was being sacrificed to your love, and I bared my breast to the sun.'

Then she says:

'Sometimes, thinking about you at night in my room, I would admire my body . . . '

Trembling, he smiles.

He keeps on recounting the same obsession, scarcely changing his words, as if they were all he knew. He has a childish soul

and a limited intelligence behind the perfect sculpturing of his
brow and his huge black eyes, in which I can distinctly see the
woman's face, a few inches away, floating like a white swan.

She listens devoutly to him, her mouth half open, her head
thrown slightly back. If he were not holding her, she would fall
on her knees before this god as beautiful as herself. Her eyelids
are already dark as if bruised by his powerful presence.

'The thought of you saddened my pleasures; but it consoled
my sadness.'

I cannot tell which of them murmured these words. They
embrace passionately, swaying like two tall flames.

His face is burning.

'I want you . . . Ah! During my nights of sleeplessness and
desire, lying with my arms stretched out before your image, I
suffered a crucifixion of loneliness.

'Be mine, Anna!'

She longs to give herself to him. She is radiant with consent.
Yet her faltering gaze contemplates the room.

'Let us respect this room,' murmurs her voice.

Then she feels ashamed of her refusal, and stammers straight
away:

'Forgive me.'

Her hair and her dress, unfastened, ripple and fall about her.

The man, halted in the blind impulse of his desire, looks
round the room. A frown of wild suspicion furrows his brow,
and for a moment the superstition of his race appears in his eyes.

'Wasn't it here . . . the death?'

'No,' she says, leaning against him.

This is the first time that the subject of the dead man has been
touched upon in the simplicity of their reunion. The lover, carried away by passion, has so far spoken only of himself.

Not only does she surrender, but she tries to match her movements with his, to do what he wishes, swaying and falling with

him, attentive to his male desire. But all that she can do is press herself against him and draw him to her, and this silent scene is more pathetic than the poor words they offer each other.

Suddenly she sees him half naked, his body altered in form; her face flushes so red that for a moment I think it is covered with blood, but her eyes smile with terrified hope and acceptance. She adores him, she admires him completely, she wants him. Her hands clutch the man's arms. All the dark, hidden temptation in her leaves her and rises to the light. She admits what the virginal silence concealed; she shows her brutal love.

Then she turns pale, and for a moment she remains as motionless as if she were dead. I can feel that she is a prey to a superior force which is alternatively freezing and burning her . . . Her face, one of the most beautiful ornaments of the world, so radiant that it seems to offer itself to the gaze, is convulsed and contorted; a grimace hides her features; the slow, rounded harmony of her gestures is broken and lost.

He carries the tall, graceful girl to the bed . . . I see her legs parting to reveal the fragile, tender nudity of her sex.

He covers her and attaches himself to her, groaning softly, trying to wound her, while she waits, her whole body offered to him.

He wants to rend her and presses down on her, his face shining with a sombre fury beside her pale face with the closed, bluish eyes, and the lips parted to reveal the teeth as if to show the horrors of the skull. They are like two damned souls occupied in suffering horribly, in a panting silence from which a cry is about to rise.

She groans: 'I love you' in a low voice, like a hymn of thanksgiving; and while he cannot see it, I and I alone see her pure white hand guide the man towards the bleeding centre of her body.

At last the cry springs forth from this labour of violation, from this murder of the passive resistance of a closed, virginal woman.

'I love you!' he screams with a triumphant, frenzied joy.

And she screams: 'I love you!' so loudly that the walls tremble slightly.

They plunge into each other, and the man hurries towards his pleasure. They rise and fall like waves; I can see their organs swollen with blood. They are heedless of the world around them, heedless of modesty, virtue, the poignant memory of the dead man, crushing everything beneath them, covering everything.

I look upon the monstrous, multiple creature they form together. It is as if they were trying to humiliate, to sacrifice everything that was beautiful in them. Their mouths twist as they offer themselves to be bitten; their foreheads are marked with the dark lines of frenzy and desperate effort. One of the magnificent legs is stretched out beyond the bed, the foot is twisted, the stocking has slipped down over the lovely flesh of golden marble, the thigh is stained with froth and blood. The young woman looks like a statue which has been knocked off its pedestal and mutilated. And the man's profile, with its frantic eye, looks like that of a criminal lunatic thirsting for blood.

They are as close together as it is possible to be: they are holding each other by both hands, by the mouth and by the belly, pressing their faces together so that they can no longer see, blinding each other with their eyes too close together; then, turning their necks, they avert their gaze at the moment they make the fullest use of each other.

By chance they attain happiness at the same time, slowed down by the longer harmonies of ecstasy. The skin all round the woman's mouth is moist and sparkling, as if their kisses were flowing and shining out from it.

'Ah, I love you, I love you!' she sings, she coos, she gasps.
Then there follow inarticulate noises, which come from her as
if in bursts of laughter. She says: 'Darling, darling, my precious
darling!' In a voice that is broken as with tears, she stammers:
'Your flesh, your flesh!' and a string of phrases so incoherent that
I dare not even recall them.

●

And then, as always happens, as the others did and they themselves will often do in the unknown future, they rise awkwardly
to their feet, saying: 'What have we done?' They do not know
what they have done. Their half-closed eyes turn from each
other towards themselves, as if they were still in possession of
their bodies. The sweat runs down like tears, leaving furrows on
their skin.

I can no longer recognize her. She seems completely
changed. Her face looks withered, ravaged. They do not know
how to talk of love any more, yet they look each other full in the
face at the same moment, with pride and servility, because they
are two. The woman seems more affected than the man, despite
their equality; she has been marked for life, and what she has
done is greater than what he has done. She holds firm the guest
of her flesh, while the mist of their breath and their warmth
envelops them.

●

Love! On this occasion no ambiguous stimulus was needed to
urge these creatures into each other's arms. There were no veils,
no darkness, no guilty subtleties. Nothing but two bodies, young
and beautiful, like two magnificent pale animals, coming together with the instinctive cries and gestures of all eternity.

If they violated memories and virtues, it was because of the very force of their love, and their ardour purified everything like a funeral pyre. They were innocent in the midst of their crime and ugliness. And these two have no regret or remorse; they are still triumphant. They do not know what they have done: they imagine that they have come together.

●

They are sitting on the edge of the bed. In spite of myself, I draw back my head in anguish at seeing them so close and terrifying. I am afraid of the huge, all-powerful creature which would crush me if it knew that we were face to face.

His features preoccupied with what has been done, and his open shirt revealing the marble skin of his great chest, he takes in his own dark hand the soft hand which is now calm and asleep, and says:

'Now you are mine for ever. Through you I have learnt what divine ecstasy is. My heart is yours and yours is mine. You are my wife for ever.'

She says: 'You are everything in the world to me.'

And they press more closely against each other, filled with a growing, demanding adoration.

And just as they did not know what they were doing, they do not know what they are saying, with their mouths moistened by each other, their fixed, dazzled eyes which serve only for caresses, their heads full of words of love.

They are setting off on the road of life like a legendary couple, radiant and inspired: the knight with no darkness about him except in the black marble of his hair, and wearing wings of iron or a wild beast's mane on his brow; and the priestess daughter of the pagan gods, an angel of Nature.

They will shine in the sun; blinded by its light, they will see nothing around them; and they will know no violence other than that of their two bodies, in the superb anger of their passion, or that of their jealous hearts, for two lovers are much more enemies than friends. And they will know no suffering other than the fierce tension of desire, as night oppresses their bodies with a heat as compelling as that of the bed.

It seems to me as if, through changes of setting and period, I can follow them with my eyes through a life which is nothing for them but plains, mountains and forests; I watch them, veiled by light, protected for a time from the fearful spells of memory and thought, armed against the perils of darkness and the countless snares of the great hearts which, in spite of everything, they possess.

I can read this prelude to their destiny in this first embrace of theirs, every detail of which I have respected in my lofty contemplation: this embrace which I have seen in its grandeur and its triviality, and which I have done well to see thus.

◑

There is a feminine form at the far end of the dusky room. Another woman? I have the impression that it is still the same one . . .

In the half-light she is undressed, pale and white, with bloodstained bandages beside her. Her back bent, her head bowed, she is bleeding . . . Sadly attentive to her weakness, she looks at herself bleeding like an urn being emptied.

I have never felt so conscious of the sacred poverty of human beings. This is not a malady but a wound, a sacrifice. It is no more a malady than her heart. It has clothed her in scarlet like an empress.

. . . For the first time since I have been here, a feeling of piety prompts me to avert my eyes.

The obscure reign of the believer has its rewards: we admire everything we take the trouble to observe. For each one of us, our mother is simply a woman we understand better than the rest.

●

I look no longer. I sit down and lean my elbows on the table. I think of myself. What point have I reached? I am quite alone. I have lost my job. Soon I shall have no money left. What am I going to do in life? I don't know. I shall look around: something is sure to turn up.

And calmly, peacefully, I hope.

. . . There must be no more sadness, no more anguish or fever . . . I must go far, far from all these terrible, solemn things which are so painful to behold, to spend the rest of my life in peace and tranquillity.

Somewhere I shall lead a regular, useful existence . . . and make a steady living.

And you, you will be there, my sister, my child, my wife . . .

You will be poor, the better to resemble all other women. So that we can live, I shall work hard all day, and I shall serve you in that fashion. You will toil affectionately for us in the room which, during my absence, you will have only the pure and simple company of your needlework . . . You will display a neatness which forgets nothing, a patience as vast as life itself, and a motherhood as solid as the earth.

I shall come home and open the door in the darkness. I shall hear you coming from the next room, bringing the lamp; a dawning light will herald your approach. You will hold my attention by telling me all that you have done during my absence, quietly and with no other object than to give me the words and the life that are in you. You will tell me your childhood memories. I shall not understand them completely, for naturally you will only be able to give me a few inadequate details; I shall not understand them, I cannot possibly understand them, but I shall love that sweet foreign tongue in which you will murmur them.

We will talk together of our future child, and you will bow your milk-white brow and neck as you picture him, while we listen in imagination to the cradle rocking with a sound of wings. And when we are tired, and even when we are old, we shall dream fresh dreams of our child's early years.

After that dream, we shall not think far ahead, but we shall think tender thoughts. In the evening, we shall think of the night. You will be full of contentment; your inner life will be joyous and full of light, not from what you have seen, but from what is in your heart; light will shine from you as from a blind man.

We will sit up late, facing each other. But little by little, as the night draws on, our words will become fewer and vaguer. Sleep will pluck off the petals of your soul. You will rest your head on the table and fall asleep; and you will feel my gaze upon you as I watch over you . . .

Tenderness is greater than love. I have no admiration for carnal love when it is naked and alone; I have no admiration for its frenzied, selfish paroxysm, so brutal in its brevity. And yet, without love, the attachment between two human beings is always fragile. Love must be added to affection, for affection needs what love alone can bring to a union, in the way of exclusiveness, intimacy and simplicity.

SIXTEEN

I went out into the streets like an exile, I, the ordinary man, I who am so like, I who am too like all the rest. I walked the streets and crossed the squares, my eyes fixed on something I could not grasp. I appeared to be walking, but it seemed to me as if I were falling from one dream into another, from one desire into another . . . A door standing ajar, an open window, other windows glowing softly with an orange light in the façades turned blue by the evening, filled me with anguish . . .

Someone brushed past me: a woman who said nothing to me of all that she could have said to me . . . I thought of the tragedy of the two of us. She went into a house; she disappeared; she died.

. . . With my senses dazed by another perfume which had vanished into the air, I stood there, a prey to countless thoughts, stifling under the cloak of the evening . . . From the closed window of a ground-floor room, by which I chanced to have stopped, there came the sound of music. I recognized, as I would have recognized distinct human words, the beauty of a sonata, with its profound rhythms, and for a moment I stood listening to what the piano was confiding to those who were in the room.

Then I sat down on a bench. On the other side of the avenue, lit up by the setting sun, I saw another bench on which two men had just sat down. I could see them clearly. Both seemed overwhelmed by the same fate, and a tender bond united them: it was obvious that they were fond of each other. One talked, the other listened.

I pictured some hidden tragedy rising to the light of day . . . Throughout their youth, they had loved each other dearly; their thoughts had been the same and shared completely. One had married: the one who was speaking and who seemed to be nurturing their common sadness. The other had maintained friendly relations with the young couple; he may have felt a vague desire for the wife, but he had respected her happiness and her peace of mind. And now his friend was telling him that his wife no longer loved him, although he still loved her with all his heart. She held aloof from him, turned away from him, and smiled and laughed only when they were not alone. He admitted his anguish, the hurt to his love, to his rights. His rights! He had imagined that he had rights over her, and he had lived in this unspoken belief; but then he had looked within himself and had realized that he had none . . . And now the friend pondered on some special remark she had made to him, on some smile she had given him. Although he was good and kind, and still entirely pure, a tender, warm and irresistible hope began to insinuate itself into him; little by little, as he heard the despairing confidences, he raised his head and smiled in thought at the woman . . . And nothing could prevent this evening, which had turned to grey and enveloped the two men, from being at one and the same time an end and a beginning.

A couple, a man and a woman—the poor creatures are nearly always in pairs—came up, passed by and walked on. The emptiness that separated them was plain: in the tragedy of life, separation is the one thing which is visible. Once they had been happy, and they were happy no longer. They were already almost old; he did not care for her, and yet he knew that the moment was approaching when he would lose her . . . What were they saying? In a moment of abandon, trusting in their present

peace, he was confessing an ancient fault, a deception scru-
pulously, religiously concealed until now . . .

Alas, his words were digging a pit of irreparable distress; the
past was coming to life again; the vanished days which had
seemed so happy were turning to sadness; and their whole life
was plunged into mourning.

These passers-by were followed by two others, this time very
young, and once again I imagined their colloquy. Their lives
were beginning: they were going to love each other . . . Their
hearts were so shy about recognizing each other! 'Do you want
me to make that journey? Do you want me to do this and that?'
She replied: 'No.' A feeling of inexpressible modesty gave to this
first avowal, so humbly solicited, the form of a disavowal . . .
But already, secretly, boldly, their thoughts were rejoicing in the
love imprisoned in their clothes.

And others, and still others . . . In this couple, she was silent,
he was speaking; he was finding it painful and difficult to master
his emotions. He begged her to tell him what she was thinking.
She replied. He listened, and then, as if nothing had been said,
implored her again, more fervently. There he was, stumbling
along uncertainly between day and night; she had only to say a
single word, provided he believed it. In the immense city he
appeared to be clinging desperately to this one body.

A few moments later I was separated from these two thinking
lovers, those two lovers who watched each other and persecuted
each other.

On every hand man and woman rise up one against the other:
the man who loves a hundred times, and the woman with so
much power to love and so much to forget.

I set off again, coming and going in the midst of naked reality.
I am not a seeker after the strange or the exceptional. Desiring,
calling, crying out, I recognize myself everywhere. With everybody I reconstruct the truth spelt out in the room next to mine,

the truth which states: 'I am alone, and I long for what I lack and for what I no longer have.' That is the desire by which we life, and from which we die.

I passed by some little shops. I heard shouts and screams of: 'Yes! No!' I stopped, astonished by the violence of these cries. And in a cage I made out a little agitated shadow. It was a parrot, and the cries I could hear were but a meaningless noise, the sound emitted by a thing.

But because that sound was outside humanity, although it took a human form, it reminded me of the importance of the human cry. Never had I thought so seriously of all the affirmation or negation which could issue from the mouth of a thinking being: the giving or the refusal of the human creature whose dark heart was always before my humble eyes during the day, to lead me and guide me, and whose face appeared to me in the dark.

But there was nothing for me. Now I was weary from having desired too much; I felt suddenly old. I would never recover from the disease implanted in my chest. The dream of tranquillity which I had dreamt a little earlier had appealed to me and tempted me only because it would never be fulfilled. And even if it were, I would dream another dream, for my heart too was a dream.

◐

Now I sought to hear words. Those people who lived my truth, what did they say when they spoke of their own accord? Did the echo of my thoughts issue from their mouths, or error, or falsehood?

Night had fallen. I sought for words similar to my own, words to support me and sustain me. And it seemed to me that I was groping forward, as if I expected someone to come round a corner and tell me everything.

I decided not to go back to my room this evening. Tonight I

did not want to leave the human throng. I looked for some living place.

I went into a large restaurant in order to surround myself with voices. Hardly had I passed the huge glittering door, which a uniformed doorkeeper kept opening and shutting, when I was overwhelmed by countless colours, perfumes, sounds. It seemed to me as if the elegant diners—the men a black-and-white drawing in their tail coats, the women a medley of bright colours— were performing some sort of fastidious rite in this luxurious, red-carpeted conservatory. There were lights everywhere, in silver festoons, in golden globes, and in soft orange shades like little dawns in the midst of each group of diners.

There were very few places free. I sat down in a corner, next to a table already occupied by three diners. I was dazed by the hissing lamps, and my soul, so patiently inured and initiated in the immense happenings of night, was like an owl torn from the great black sky and tossed derisively into the midst of a fireworks display.

I was going to try to warm myself at this vast light . . . After ordering my meal, in a voice which I had to steady first, I tried to examine the faces of the other diners. But it was difficult to see clearly those around me. The mirrors multiplied them as well as the walls: I saw the same brightly-lit row, both full-face and profile. Couples and groups kept going out, surrounded by officious waiters holding at arm's length cloaks or fragile coats which seemed as complex as their owners. New arrivals came in. I noticed that the women, at first sight, were adorably pretty, and that they all looked alike, with their powdered faces and their mouths like cupid's bows; but as they came nearer, one or more defects appeared, and robbed them of that ideal prestige with which the first glance had endowed them. Most of the men, in conformity with the fashion of the time, were clean-shaven, and wore hats with flat brims and overcoats with sloping shoulders.

While my eye mechanically followed the white-gloved hand

that helped me to soup from the silver-plated tureen, I listened
to the buzz of the conversations going on around me.

I could hear only what my three neighbours were saying.
They were talking about people whom they knew in the room,
and then about several friends, in a tone whose constant irony
and persiflage surprised me.

There was nothing remarkable about what they were saying;
this evening would be wasted like the others.

A few moments later, the head waiter, while lifting some fil-
lets of sole, which were swimming in a thick pink sauce, from
an oblong metal dish, in order to place them on my plate,
pointed out one of the diners to me, with a nod and a sly wink:

'That's Monsieur Villiers, the famous writer,' he whispered
proudly.

And so it was: he looked quite like his portraits, and his recent
glory sat graciously upon him.

I envied this man, who knew how to write, how to express his
thoughts. With a certain admiration, I looked at his distinguished, worldly silhouette, the charming modern outline of his
profile, flowing into the delicate silkiness of his moustache, the
perfect curve of his shoulders, and the butterfly wing of his white
tie.

I was raising my glass to my lips—a glass so fragile that the
wind outside would have snapped its stem—when suddenly I
stopped and felt all my blood rush to my heart. This is what I
had heard:

'And what is your next novel about?'

'It will be about truth,' replied Pierre Villiers.

'Eh?' said the friend.

'A succession of people shown as they really are.'

'What is the subject?' they asked.

Others were listening. Two young men dining near them had
stopped talking, and though sitting idly were evidently listening

hard. In a sumptuous scarlet corner, a man in a dinner jacket was smoking a large cigar, with tired eyes and drawn features, his whole life concentrated on the odorous emanations of the tobacco, while his companion, her bare elbows on the table, surrounded with perfume and sparkling with jewels, laden with the burdensome artificial royalty of luxury, turned towards the speaker a face which was all nature and moonlight.

'This,' said Pierre Villiers, 'is the subject which permits me to be amusing and true-to-life at one and the same time: a man pierces a hole in the wall of a hotel room and watches what happens in the next room.'

◖

At that moment I must have looked at the speakers with a distracted, pitiable expression . . . Then I hurriedly bowed my head, with the ingenuous movement of a child afraid of being seen . . .

They had spoken about me, and I felt as if some strange plot were being woven around me. Then, all of a sudden, this impression, in which all my common sense had totally deserted me, disappeared. Obviously it was a coincidence. But there remained a vague apprehension that they would notice that I *knew*, that they would recognize me.

They went on talking about the idea which had been put forward. Insensible to everything else, and straining to hear and not seem to be listening, I hung on to their conversation like a parasite.

One of the novelist's friends begged him to give them more details of his work. He consented . . . He was going to tell them all about it in front of me!

◖

He described the book he had written. Using words, gestures and mimicry admirably, with witty, lively elegance and an infectious laugh, he evoked for his listeners a series of scenes which were unexpected, brilliant and astonishing. Helped by his original subject, which gave so much contrast and intensity to every scene, he recounted absurd and amusing incidents, piled on picturesque and piquant details, and proper names both typical and witty, interspersing them with ingenious situations, and produced irresistible effects, all in the latest fashion. Everyone said: 'Ah!' and 'Oh!' and opened their eyes wide in admiration.

'Bravo! Sure to have a tremendous success. It's a fantastically amusing subject.'

'All those fellows passing in front of the traveller are funny, even the one who commits suicide. Nothing has been left out. All humanity's there!'

But I for my part had not recognized a thing in all that he had said.

Astonishment and a sort of shame overwhelmed me, as I listened to this man seeking what amusement could be derived from the sombre adventure which had been tormenting me for a month.

I recalled that noble voice, now silenced, which had declared so forcefully and firmly that the writers of today imitated caricaturists. I, who had penetrated into the very heart of mankind and returned, found nothing human in this dancing caricature. It was so superficial that it was false.

And in front of me the implacable witness was saying:

'Man stripped of his externals: that is what I wish to show. Others stand for imagination; I stand for the truth.'

'The book even has philosophic implications.'

'Possibly. In any case, I wasn't looking for them. I'm a writer, thank heavens, not a thinker.'

And he continued to travesty truth, while I could do nothing
to stop him—truth, that profound thing whose voice was in my
ears, its shadow in my eyes, and its taste in my mouth.

◐

Am I so utterly forsaken? . . . Will no one give me alms?

I went out through the large swinging mirrors of the doors. I
entered a theatre presenting a play whose appearance was hailed
a week ago as an important event. An echo of its success had
lingered in my memory. The title, *The Rights of the Heart*,
tempted and invited me.

I bought a ticket and found myself sitting in the middle of the
great auditorium, buffeted by the warmth of the crowd under
the bright lights.

The curtain rose, sending a gust of cool air over the audience,
and each of us was filled with a sort of hope, as we waited for
the creatures about to live in front of us.

I looked at the stage exactly as I looked at the room. I listened,
I recorded word after word, I spelt out . . .

The young sculptor Jean Darcy, just back from Rome with
his dreams of marble, was at a reception in the house of the
banker Loewis. A brilliant gathering crowded the gilded
drawing-rooms. Members of the Institute, wearing the riband
of a Commander of the Legion of Honour, rubbed shoulders
with immensely rich men about town; all the celebrities of Art,
Letters, Law, Politics and Finance were vying with each other
for the crown of backbiting and the smiles of pretty women.

The conversation of the guests was concentrated in a little
group where the voices were slightly lowered: they were talking
about their host.

'You know he is being given a title: "Count Loewis!"'

'He has rendered considerable services to the Pope in these

difficult and troubled times; His Holiness is greatly attached to him.'

'It seems,' said an ingenuous young lady, 'that in Italian he calls him simply "Papa".'

'A new escutcheon! He obviously felt the need for it!'

'Oh, this one won't smell, and for a very good reason.'

'And what motto is it to bear? I suggest: "He who loses himself, wins in the end."'

'And I, "God saves those who save their skin."'

'And I,' said a man, with a Levantine profile, 'propose "*Nihil circonscire sibi.*"'

A society woman, nodding in the direction of the last speaker, whispered to her neighbour, behind her fan: 'He sees the mote in his neighbour's eye and overlooks the beam in his own.'

'Joking apart, you know, in strict confidence, that the future Count is starting a newspaper?'

'No, I didn't know that.'

'Nor did I. It's curious how few people know about it, considering that it's a matter of strict confidence.'

'A paper with a big news service. But really a business undertaking, floating companies and so on . . .'

'Don't miss tomorrow's thrilling bankruptcy . . .'

'Oh, the stories one could tell about the master of the house if one were spiteful. Not to mention the mistress . . . of the master of the house.'

'She's a new one; she won't leave his side, and follows him everywhere.'

'Apparently she's longing to see Belgium.'

'They say he leads a life of debauchery.'

'Only on the surface, to his great sorrow; the spirit is willing, but the flesh is rather weak. He has a strong head and stomach, but that's all. You know his nickname? The Satyred . . .'

'And his wife doesn't complain?'

'Oh, you know, she doesn't mind: she has undergone a little operation, so that now . . . well . . . it's the very end.'

'It seems her dowry was fifty million francs; but he must have had some money of his own.'

'You do him an injustice. It's true that when he was twenty, he did inherit ten million from his . . .'

'From the only man who was indisputably not his father?'

'The same. Well, everything had gone, but luckily for him, he knew how to please.'

'Every rose has its thorn, though, and it seems he has been cruelly punished for flitting from one woman to another.'

'Yes . . . But what would you? No woman has ever been able to keep an infection to herself.'

'Anyhow, the fact remains that apart from that, he was justified in saying to the Marquis of Canossa: "I have always been lucky with women." To which the Marquis simply replied: "Except with your mother."'

'Ah, his mother! She was a character, that woman. When she died, they were pretty badly off, so at her funeral they put out a lot of tables covered with exercise books in which the mourners could sign their names.

'That covered up the paucity of the furniture, which had all been sold. But in any case there were only three signatures.'

'Poor old woman! Luckily she was spared that last ordeal.'

'Yes, I remember there wasn't much of a crowd. The only people there were forced to go, like me. It was no joke, I can tell you! Luckily, I had a bad foot, and that took my mind off it all.'

'Well, anyhow, she's dead, and up there in heaven . . .'

'So much the better; she at least can hear us.'

'He went in for politics ten years ago. After a series of utter failures, he said to those who had supported him and were beginning to show their teeth: "What are you complaining about?

I haven't been able to do anything for your ideas, but at least I've given you a leader." '

'It was he too who said—and no one has ever been able to discover whether it was out of ignorance of the language or too great a knowledge of himself: "Like so many others, I too shall be able to boast that I have added my little stumbling-block to the social edifice." '

'What was that story about Miss Lemmon, with whom he was on such intimate terms?'

'I thought she was the last word in piety. People say she's a lay nun.'

'Yes, of a very special order.'

'A praying mantis, eh? But what's the story?'

'She was deceiving him; in the end he caught her with Renaudes, and the scales fell from his eyes.'

'Well, that makes a few less anyhow.'

'He wanted to retire in good order, as he doesn't like scenes; but suddenly matters took a turn for the worse with a quarrel in public and a kick in the rear. He was very annoyed that so much fuss should be made about a wretched little kick, which to him seemed scarcely worth mentioning. When his rival's seconds called to see him, he exclaimed: "But what's wrong with all these people, bothering me about something that boots so little?" '

'It wouldn't be so bad if at least he gave you some decent food! What a dinner! Did you notice the peas?'

'Yes, the dye was running . . . And the size of them! They ought to have served just one with every portion. As for the coffee, it was so weak I couldn't summon up enough strength to protest.'

'Percolated water . . .'

'No, no, it wasn't as bad as all that. On the contrary, this dinner has reconciled me with him: the sauce helps you to swallow the host.'

'As for me, I thought it was an excellent dinner: I could begin all over again quite easily!'

'He orders his meals from second-rate caterers who are quite out of fashion. I won't mention any names; if I knew them people would think I was an ignoramus.'

'It seems that the other day it said on the Menu: "Hors-d'oeuvre *ad lib*," and his son, young Paul, said: "oh no, this is going too far, Papa!"'

'He's another character. He writes verses. He's a poet. A modern poet, too, aggressive and pushing: a pen-pusher.'

'Have you heard his nickname? He's so original that they call him Francis Copied.'

'He finances little feminist reviews for twenty-year-old virgins and forty-year-old semi-virgins.'

'They say he's living with that skinny madame X——.'

'What, the one who's acting in the *Cid* with the lugubrious Z——?'

'Yes, the weeping willow with the willowy weeper. Well, it seems that he's bored with her.'

'Because she's a society woman?'

'No, chiefly because she's a woman.'

'Ah, yes, it appears that there's no doubt that he has some peculiar tastes . . . I don't dare to talk about them in the presence of ladies . . . Because they wouldn't be interested.'

'You know he writes for the stage? He has written a one-act play for the Théâtre des Italiens.'

'Him, an act? An act against nature, yes . . .'

'Let us be fair: his tastes are not so limited when it's a question of his interest.'

'Oh, yes, he's a clever fellow; he knows when to do an about-turn.'

'Now I know why his mother called him a weather-cock the other day.'

'What's he going to do on his father's paper?'

'He'll be at the business end.'

'Don't be spiteful! He never says anything against anybody.'

'No, especially when they have their back turned.'

'Anyhow, he's an ill-mannered boor; the other day, at my house, he said the ceiling was too low.'

'He must have thought he was still under the table.'

'The ceiling too low, in my house!'

'Whereas we all know, dear Madame, that there are street-lamps in your ante-room.'

'But really our host's entire family is the last word in vulgarity; I am too good a friend of theirs not to have noticed that long ago.'

'It's the niece who really takes the biscuit.'

'Yes—she's so made up you never know if you're looking at her or her portrait.'

'She lives on her own doesn't she?'

'In a manner of speaking. The other day (she must have been feeling particularly soft-hearted) she said to that nasty little woman journalist who looks like a cook and whom they call the Victory of Camelface that she found talking to men an enriching experience. "Nobody in Paris doubts that," replied the little bitch.'

'She has dreams of purity, but dreaming won't make you a semi-virgin again.'

'They say—and I tell you this in absolute confidence—that for some time now she has been living with an old gentleman. Well, people *hope* that he is her father . . .'

For the first time a slight murmur ran round the theatre at the words 'people hope', but it was obvious that this protest was purely a matter of form and that the audience was really amused . . . And the rest of the act was greeted with lively and increasing pleasure, as the obscene witticisms spread out and touched the men in their tailcoats and the women in their low-cut gowns.

After the first act, which outlined the love of Jean Darcy for the beautiful and understanding Jeanne de Floranges (a part played by a great actress), one could tell from the febrile atmosphere in the corridors that the play was a great success.

'What witticisms!' people kept exclaiming rapturously. 'Nothing but witticisms.'

The second act was just like the first. Although there was plenty of action and variety, it was constructed in the same way, with slight and artificial combinations of incident and dialogue which strove for effect. Sometimes the effect was brutal and poignant, because of the violent impression made on our sensibility by the sight of the emotions of a creature similar to ourselves, moving about a few steps away. But the hollowness of the method showed through everywhere. Yes, it was 'nothing but witticisms', fading away into thin air. Yes, these people were 'playing', were offering a poor imitation of some deep truth, in order to reveal it to us. But they did not take me in.

The second act came to an end. The third began. Jeanne de Floranges wondered if she had the right to link her destiny to that of the young artist who loved her as deeply as she loved him, but who was very poor, and, if he married her, would be forced by inescapable material necessity to sacrifice his genius and his future fame. The heroine, noble woman that she was, after a struggle with her conscience complicated by an episode involving jealousy, decided that she did not have that right, and by allowing Jean Darcy to believe that the worldly Jacques de Linières was her lover, separated him from her for ever. Jean would despise the woman he had regarded as his guardian angel and inspiration, but he would get over it. He would marry Rachel

Loewis, who, despite the wealthy and corrupt environment in which she had grown up, was a pure young girl and secretly loved the artist. He would fulfil his destiny. The rights of the heart were vanquished by the rights of the future.

In the auditorium, pandemonium broke loose. After the last act, in which the case for self-sacrifice was argued and then accepted, and the heroic act of treachery was flung in the faces of the lover and the audience, in a sudden, breath taking *volte-face*, everyone went wild as the curtain came down, shouting, bruising their hands with clapping, kicking the wooden panelling of the boxes, banging their sticks on the floor, stamping and cheering.

. . . The audience drifted out of the theatre, and what little seriousness there was behind the success melted away among the groups of fur-coated ladies and gentlemen pushing their way slowly to the exit.

'These plays are always the same. In the end, you can't remember a thing about them.'

'Well, what of it? So much the better, I say. I go to the theatre to relax, not to fill my head with problems.'

'I don't know if it will last a hundred performances . . . Anyhow, we've seen it a hundred times already.'

I heard someone say the name of a gentleman who had just spoken. It was Monsieur Pierre Corbière, the dramatist whose play *Zig Zag* was being presented at a big theatre nearby: three acts sparkling, so people said, with allusions to living personalities.

The writer was recognized: hats were raised in a circle round him, as if the wind of his passing had blown them off; and favoured hands stretched out for the honour of touching his. He strode on, adulated and triumphant. He was like his colleague: he had won wealth and fame by using his facile cleverness, his glib command of parisianisms, his flair for topicality, to flatter and fawn upon the rich theatre-going public. I hated and despised him.

●

Now I was walking under the sky, those vast plains of heaven into which so many empty words are cast.

All that I had just seen would soon moulder away. It was all too fashionable not to be out of fashion tomorrow. Where were they now, the brilliant authors of recent years? Their names survived, but no one knew why.

My contact with the truth had taught me to recognize error and injustice, and forced me to loathe these frivolous passing distractions because they aped the work of art. True, their success was not important. The enthusiasm displayed at a splendid first night was generally just an insignificant event, and all these plays—titles, subjects and actors included—were soon dead and buried one on top of the other. But meanwhile, for a few evenings, they held the attention; they enjoyed and thrived on an undeniable triumph. I would have liked them to be strangled at birth.

●

The room was flooded with the light of the moon which was penetrating the window as if it were space. In the magnificent setting there was a vague white group: two silent creatures with marble faces.

The fire was out. Exhausted, the clock had fallen silent and was listening with its heart.

The figure of the man dominated the group. The woman was at his feet; they were doing nothing, tenderly. They were looking at the moon, like monuments.

He spoke. I recognized the voice, which suddenly lit up his shadowy face for me: it was the lover and the unknown poet I had seen twice before.

He was telling his companion how that evening, going home, he had met a beggar-woman with her child in her arms.

She was moving forward, half pushed, half swept along, by the homegoing crowd, for in certain busy streets, the current flows all one way at night. Thrown up under a porch, next to a corner-stone like a reef, she had stopped there and was huddling against it.

'I went up to her,' he said, 'and I saw that she was smiling.'

◐

'What was she smiling at? At life, because of her child. In the besieged refuge of that doorway in which she was nestling, looking out at the setting sun, she was thinking how the child would grow up in the years to come. However terrible those years might be, they would be around him, for him, in him. They would be part of every breath he drew, every step he took, every glance he gave . . .

'Yes, that was the reason for the profound smile of that creator, who bore her burden, raised her head and gazed into the light, not even lowering her eyes to the shadowy figure of the child or lending an ear to its crazy babbling . . .

'I have been working on that idea.'

For a moment he remained motionless; then, softly and without pausing, in that other-worldly voice which we assume when we are reciting, when we obey what we are saying and can no longer control it, he went on:

'The woman, swallowed up by the shadows, smiles at the gathering dusk, as if it were a tide vaguely ebbing from deep inside her rags, torn and shapeless like a river's banks . . . Silent

under the silent waves, flotsam from every spiritual shipwreck,
she shines with a starry light as if all were praying to her. Un-
thinkingly, with the child in her arms, she has found her way
to this cornerstone; she must have a divine heart to be so weary.
She is quite defenceless, but she is the first to smile. She loves
the sky, the light which the obscure child will love, the chilly
dawn, the oppressive noonday sun, the dreamy evening; he will
grow up, a saviour in his way, so that all these things may live
again. He who is in darkness now, trembling at the foot of the
path she has climbed, will begin life anew, the only paradise we
have, the supreme gift of Nature. To beauty he will give beauty;
with his song and the murmur of his voice, he will remake eternity. And holding the new-born child more closely as the setting
sun gilds her rags, she looks down with glowing eyes at all the
sunshine she has created . . . Her arms quivering like wings,
she is dreaming with fond words; the passers-by would be dazzled
if they turned to look at her; and the sunset bathes her head and
neck in a rosy glow: she is like a huge rose opening, leaning
towards everything . . .'

My attention caught the rhymes as tenderness finds tenderness in the dark. I felt the rhythm of his words gripping me,
dominating me. It had already stirred me the other evening,
when in an effort to console her he had drawn from his memory
fragments of his poem, carefully wrought words which glittered
suddenly like diamonds in the dark; but now I had a feeling that
this poem was more important.

He swayed a little, utterly possessed by the invincible music,
obeying it as unquestioningly as the regular beat of his heart;
and I felt the life of his sweet words beginning to throb within
me. He seemed to be searching, remembering, believing, to an
infinite degree. He was in another world, where everything seen
is true, and everything said is unforgettable.

She remained at his knees, her eyes were lifted up to him; she was all attention, being filled with his poetry like a precious urn.

◉

'But her smile,' he went on, 'was not only admiration for the future. There was also something tragic in it which moved me deeply and which I understood . . . She adored life, but she hated men and feared them, again on account of the child. She was already fighting for him with the living, to whom he scarcely belonged as yet. And with her smile she flung down a challenge to them. She seemed to be saying to them: "He will live in spite of you, he will prevail against you, and he will make servants out of you; he will conquer you in order to be your master or to win your love, and with his tiny breath, he whom I hold in my maternal embrace defies you." She was awe-inspiring. I had seen her at first as an angel of goodness. Now, although she had not changed, I saw her as an angel of pitiless rancour: "I see a sort of hatred for those who will curse him convulse her face, resplendent with superhuman motherhood; I see her bleeding heart which contains one other heart, which foresees good and evil, which hates men and counts them like the angel of destruction. At the mercy of the great tide, the mother with her terrifying talons rises up and smiles with her ravaged lips."'

Aimée was looking at her lover in the moonlight. Their glances seemed to me to mingle with his words . . . He went on:

'I end with the grandeur of the human tragedy, as in everything I write, and which I go on repeating with the monotony of those who believe themselves to be right . . . "Oh, all that is left to us, with no God, no refuge, no rags to cover us, is the revolt of our smile; the revolt of our joy in the evening, the grim bleeding of the day, as we stand on this world of the dead . . . We are divinely alone, and the heavens have fallen upon us."'

The heavens have fallen upon us! What a phrase he had just pronounced!

That phrase, still echoing in the silence, was the noblest cry life had ever uttered, the cry of deliverance which my ears had been blindly seeking for until now. I had sensed it growing more distinct whenever I had seen a sort of glory inevitably ennobling the pathetic shades of the living; whenever I had seen the human mind turning back to the world . . . But I needed to hear it said before grandeur and misery could finally be united, to make the keystone of the heavenly vault!

Those heavens, by which I mean the blue expanse which our gaze embraces, and the blue expanse beyond, which only the thought can see: the heaven of purity and plenitude, and the infinity of supplicants; the heaven of truth and religion—all that is in us and has fallen upon us. And God himself, who is all those different heavens at once, has fallen upon us like thunder, and his infinity is ours.

We have the divinity of our immense misery; and our solitude, with its burden of thought, tears and smiles, is inevitably divine by virtue of its universality . . . Whatever our anguish and effort in the dark, and the futile toil of our incessant heart, and our ignorance and destitution, and the hurts which are other people, we must consider ourselves with a sort of devout respect. It is this feeling which gilds our brows, uplifts our hearts, embellishes our pride, and will console us in spite of everything, when we have accustomed ourselves, in all our petty occupations, to take the place once held by God. Truth itself bestows an adequate gratification, both practical and so to speak mystical, on that supplicant from whom heaven springs.

●

. . . He was talking quietly, in a desultory fashion, about his poetry, but the words he was pouring out to the listening woman were less and less significant and were so to speak gradually shrinking.

She sat at his feet, but her face was raised: he was above her, but bent towards her. A ring shone on one of their hands. I saw the oval of the woman's face, the curve of the man's brow and, beyond them, darkness stretching into infinity.

Having demonstrated that we were divine, he was saying that only our most basic elements were common to us all. Character and temperament, under the influence of countless circumstances, were, he said, as many and diverse as facial features; but fundamentally there were immense crude resemblances, like the pallor of skulls. Thus every work of art which compared two human beings, saying that one face was like another, was either a heresy or else a profound truth.

'That is why,' said the man, 'the true poem of humanity is not made of local colour or social documentation, or plays on words, or ingenious plots. It grips you with a religious chill. It consists of the painfully monotonous and perpetually heart-rending essence of the human race, around whom darkness and solitude efface the place in which they are and the time in which they live.'

Then he spoke about poetry and said that what gave a poem its value was simply its movement, in other words the way in which each stanza began, in which the beginning of each phrase revealed some truth; and that what was difficult was the need to have an overall impression of the work, to serve as a guide, before the poem was begun. Also that it was obvious from the elaboration of any poem, however short, that creation implied beginning at the end. Then he spoke of words themselves: vague things, but striking when set in order, although at the moment they were taken out of circulation they were crude and obscure. He made this admission:

'I have such a respect for the absolute truth that there are times when I dare not call things by their name . . .'

She was listening to him. She said: 'Yes,' very softly, then fell silent again. Everything seemed to have been carried away by a sort of gentle whirlwind.

'Aimée . . .' he said in an undertone.

She did not move; she had fallen asleep, with her head on her lover's knees. He thought himself alone. He looked at her and smiled. An expression of pity and kindness passed over his face. His hands stretched half out towards the sleeping figure, with the tenderness of strength. I saw before me the glorious pride of charity and condescension as I looked at this man whom a woman prostrated before him had turned into a god.

SEVENTEEN

I have given notice, I am leaving tomorrow, in the evening, with my vast store of memories. Whatever events, whatever tragedies the future holds for me, my thoughts can never be more weighty or more grave, even when I have lived life to the full.

The last day. I stretch upwards to look. But my body is an agony of pain. I can no longer stand upright: I stagger and fall back on my bed, repulsed by the wall. I try again. My eyes close and fill with painful tears. I wanted to be crucified against the wall, but I cannot. My body becomes heavier and heavier, and hurts more and more; my flesh turns against me, and the pain spreads, attacking my back, my face, putting out my eyes, turning my stomach.

I hear someone talking through the bricks of the wall. The next room vibrates with a distant sound, a misty sound which scarcely penetrates the wall.

I shall never again be able to listen; I shall never again be able to look into the room. From now on, I shall never again be able to see or hear anything distinctly; and I who have not wept since childhood, weep like a child because of all that I shall never have. I weep for the beauty and grandeur I have lost. I love everything I might have embraced.

Down the days and the years, all the prisoners of rooms will go on passing through this room, with their fragments of infinity. And in that hour when colour fades from everything, they will sit near the light where they will look as if they were crowned with haloes; they will lean and drag themselves towards the void of the window. They will wait for each other with eager mouths; they will exchange a first or last futile glance. They will open their arms; they will give themselves up to their groping embraces. They will love life and be afraid of disappearing. They will seek on earth for a perfect union between two hearts; and in heaven for eternity among their mirages, and a God in the clouds.

◗

The monotonous murmuring of voices trembles continuously through the wall. I can hear nothing but a noise; I am like all those who are shut up in a room.

I am lost, as I was when I first came here; that evening when I took possession of this room worn threadbare by the dead and the departed—before this great new light had been shed on my destiny.

And perhaps because of my fever, perhaps because of my extreme pain, I imagine that someone there is declaiming a great poem, that someone is speaking of Prometheus. He has stolen light from the gods, and in his entrails he feels his suffering, perpetually fresh, perpetually renewed, growing every evening, when the vulture flies to him as to its nest. And the voice declares that because of our desires we are all like Prometheus; but there is no vulture, and there are no gods.

There is no paradise other than what we ourselves take into the immense tombs of the churches. There is no hell other than our mad longing to live.

There is no mysterious fire. I have stolen truth. I have stolen the whole truth. I have seen sacred things, tragic things, pure things, and I was in the right; I have seen shameful things, and I was in the right. Because of what I have seen, I have entered into the Kingdom of Truth, if an expression used by the falsehood and blasphemy of religion can be applied to truth without polluting it.

◗

Who will write the Bible of human desire, the simple, awe-inspiring Bible of that which urges us on from life to life, the Bible of our begetting, of our course through life, of our original fall? Who will dare to say everything? Who will have the genius to see everything?

I believe in a noble form of poetry: in a work in which beauty will be fused with belief. The more I feel incapable of such a work, the more I believe it to be possible. That sombre splendour with which certain of my memories overwhelms me, shows me from afar that it is possible. I too have sometimes had moments of sublime genius. Sometimes my vision has been mingled with a shudder of awareness so mighty, so creative, that the whole room has trembled like a forest with it, and there have truly been moments when the silence cried aloud.

But all that, I have stolen. I did win it for myself, but took advantage of it, thanks to the shamelessness of truth, which bared itself to my gaze. At that point of time and space at which I happened to find myself, I had only to open my eyes and hold out my beggar's hands, to fashion something that was more than a dream and less than a creation.

What I saw will vanish, since I shall make nothing of it. I am like a mother, the fruit of whose body will perish, after having been.

What matter? I have been granted an annunciation of all that is most beautiful. Through me, without causing me to halt, the Word has passed: the Word which does not lie and which, spoken again, will give eternal satisfaction.

●

But I have done. I am lying stretched out, and since I can no longer see, my poor eyes have closed up like a healing wound, my poor eyes are forming a scar.

And I seek some consolation for myself. *Me*—the last cry like the first.

One course alone is left open to me: to remember and believe. To maintain with all my might, within my memory, the tragedy of this room, because of the vast and painful consolation which has sometimes resounded in the depths of the abyss.

I believe that confronting the human heart and the human mind, which are composed of imperishable longings, there is only the mirage of what they long for. I believe that around us there is only one word on all sides, one immense word which reveals our solitude and extinguishes our radiance: Nothing! I believe that that word does not point to our insignificance or our unhappiness, but on the contrary to our fulfilment and our divinity, since everything is in ourselves.